Ever Bright

The Bright Series, Volume 2

T. J. Fier

Published by T. J. Fier, 2024.

EVER BRIGHT

First edition. October 31, 2024.

Copyright © 2024 T. J. Fier.

ISBN: 979-8227940766

Written by T. J. Fier.

Also by T. J. Fier

The Bright Series
The Bright One
Ever Bright

Watch for more at https://linktr.ee/tjfier.

To Sue, I couldn't do this without you!

Chapter 1

Alexa Baxter stepped into the circle of smooth satin. She pulled the silky fabric over her hips and looped her arms through the prom dress's delicate straps. Catching her reflection in the dressing room mirror, she frowned.

"Mateo, I'm not—this is not—why did you make me put this on?" She reached back, fumbling for the zipper.

"For once in my life, I want to see you in pink." Mateo, Alexa's best friend in the whole world, stood on the other side of the dressing stall curtain. She brushed aside the barrier and found him furiously sending off a series of texts.

She swore he spent more time on his phone than in the present. "Who are you—"

"Oh, you know my gossip queens." Mateo shrugged. "They can't give this boy the afternoon off. Anyway, you promised. And it's the biggest night of your high school life. Don't you want to look fabulous?"

"I feel exposed." Alexa peered down the plunging neckline. "I can almost see my—well, you can guess." On the dressing room bench, her phone buzzed and displayed a missed text from her boyfriend and another from an unknown number. Probably spam.

"Alexa? Are you ready to show us?" Alexa's mother, Cynthia, called down the dressing room corridor.

Of course she wasn't ready. She hadn't been ready when Mateo shoved the dress into her arms. Nor had she been ready for the appointment her mother made at Riverview's exclusive dress boutique. Her phone buzzed again, reminding her of the unread texts. As she reached for the phone, the dress straps slipped, forcing her to catch the bodice before it fell to her waist.

"This is impossible." Alexa broke into a cold sweat. "What the hell am I—Mateo, can you, uh, help me with the zipper?"

"Of course. Why didn't you say something?" Mateo tossed aside the curtain and marched into her stall.

Alexa clutched the dress to her chest. "Um, hold on—"

"I've seen you nearly naked a thousand times, Lex." Mateo rolled his eyes, brushing aside his dark red bangs. "Stand up straight." He pulled her shoulders back and tugged up the zipper. "Let's fix those straps." He slid the narrow fabric bands into place, then surveyed her reflection with a wide grin. "I was right. Ballet-slipper pink is perfect for your complexion. You look like a freakin' goddess."

"But black is my signature color." Alexa pointed to the haphazard pile of discarded clothes.

"Sid will love this. Now let's go show Mom and Andrea." Mateo whipped open the curtain and grabbed her arm.

"Ugh, do I have to?" Alexa groaned. She remembered the phone in her hand and quickly read the message: *We know.*

Alexa stopped dead in her tracks. She read the text several more times as an unsettling sensation twisted her gut. Why would a stranger send her something so cryptic? They must have the wrong number. Right? After what happened last October, she knew anything was possible.

"Lex, what?" Mateo paused. "Don't back out on me now. You promised to try on whatever dresses I picked."

"Sorry, wrong number." She tossed her phone into the dressing stall. "Let's get this over with."

They walked past racks of cocktail and prom dresses sparkling and shining like exotic birds. Afternoon sunlight poured through the windows and refracted off the several crystal chandeliers. Alexa bowed her head, feeling horribly out of place. Her cheeks burned as Mateo marched her to a round dais flanked by three huge mirrors.

"Oh, Alexa." Cynthia sighed from a gray velvet settee beside the dais. She clutched perfectly manicured hands to her chest. "You're stunning."

Alexa's sister, Andrea, looked up from her phone. Her jaw dropped. "Wow. Mateo, you might have a future as a stylist."

"Excellent choice, Mateo." The boutique assistant, Brandi, beamed from her perch beside the wall of mirrors. "I don't know how you got her to put that on. She was adamant about black and black only." The attractive young woman waved a dismissive hand to the collection of dark dresses hanging on a rack beside her.

"Just a little emotional manipulation from one friend to the next." Mateo shrugged.

"So, this is from Faviana." Brandi tossed out the long, billowy skirt. "Obviously, we need to hem it up a little. You're so petite." She leaned over Alexa, tugging at the loose bodice and waistline. "We can easily take this in, so you don't have to worry about—eh—"

"Nip slips." Mateo scrutinized Alexa from head to toe. He raised the dress's hem. Alexa squeaked and yanked the skirt from his clutches. "Brandi, is it okay if I grab her some shoes? Those Converse aren't doing her any favors."

Brandi waved toward a rack of shiny stilettos. "Go for it."

The boutique assistant became flustered when Mateo first butted into Alexa's dress selection, tossing gowns of every color *but* black into Brandi's arms. Seeing the irritation on Brandi's and Alexa's faces, Mateo had wisely complimented Brandi's vintage Ferragamo pumps. In a matter of minutes, he and Brandi became fast friends and ganged up on Alexa.

"I'm practically naked." Alexa studied her flushed reflection, fingers running over the neckline and the open back. Could she wear such a dress in public?

"No, you're just wearing something that isn't black and boxy for once." Andrea raised her phone and took a picture.

"If you share that with anyone—"

"I won't." Andrea shrugged and sat back in her chair. Several emotions crossed her face. Was Andrea jealous?

"Honey, you look so pretty," Cynthia murmured, eyes glossy with tears.

"You really do," Brandi assured Alexa. "With a few alterations, that'll fit you like a glove."

Mateo returned with a pair of glittering silver stilettos in his grasp. "If you put these on, I will buy you double mocha lattes for a week."

"You already promised me a week if I tried every dress you picked." Alexa flinched. "I'll fall over if I put those on."

Mateo placed the shoes in front of her feet. "Fine. Two weeks. We've got three weeks until prom to practice."

"Sid hasn't even technically asked me to go yet," Alexa grumbled as Mateo and Brandi helped her step into the shoes and buckle the delicate straps. She teetered for a moment, but Mateo steadied her.

"Oh, honey, you know they've already rented the limo." Mateo pursed his lips.

"I heard Drew's girlfriend mention they had reservations for some hot restaurant in Minneapolis." Andrea's expression soured as she spoke. She hadn't been asked to prom by any of the soccer boys she incessantly flirted with during lunch.

Since Alexa and Sidhit Diyani became a couple, Alexa also sat with the soccer boys' and girls' teams at lunch. Sid was one of the varsity soccer captains, after all. While she never felt comfortable among the high school athletes' posturing and bravado, Andrea drank in every second.

"How did I get here?" Alexa murmured, her blue eyes bright and huge in the store's brilliant track lighting. She turned to Mateo. "I never thought I would go to prom. It's so—"

"A high school cliché, yes, I know." Mateo studied the two of them in the wall of mirrors. "You look amazing, Lex. You should consider wearing this. Sid will totally freak out when he sees you."

"You think so?" Alexa's heart picked up its pace, thumping so loud she was sure everyone could hear. Her blush had spread from her cheeks to her neck and chest.

Yes, Sid would totally freak when he saw her in something soft and pink versus the black she preferred to wear. "It's just so—"

"Gorgeous?" Mateo leaned in and took a picture of Alexa's reflection before she could protest. "So, you're getting it, right? I mean, you're going to prom with one of the hottest guys in school. You should look the part."

Spots danced before Alexa's eyes. Mateo was right, even if she didn't want to admit it. Compared to the other well-coiffed teenagers in her new and unexpected friend group, Alexa stood out like a sore thumb. Sid swore he liked her just the way she was and didn't want her to be anything but herself, no matter what.

"Yeah, Lex, you *have* to get that dress, or I'll never speak to you again," Andrea teased.

"Oh, I second that." Mateo smiled, but it didn't reach his eyes. He studied Alexa for a moment. A tight crease formed between his eyebrows. He parted his lips to say something, then shook his head and buried his nose in his phone.

Alexa's mother rose from her chair, resting a hand against Alexa's back. "It's up to you, honey, of course."

"We still have that last black A-line halter to try on?" Brandi pointed to the dress rack. "Or if you want to try on one of the previous choices?"

"Absolutely not." Mateo glanced up from his phone. "I told everyone I was helping you pick a dress, and I don't want to disappoint. I have a reputation to maintain. Be brave, Lex. Try something new."

"He's right," Andrea said. "No one will expect you to wear a pink dress. You know they still call you the Queen of Darkness behind your back."

"They still call me that?" Alexa's breath came in short gasps.

Sid's friends were confused and annoyed that quiet, shy Alexa managed to weasel into their exclusive clique. They viewed her as an interloper who hadn't earned her place.

Mateo tossed a furious look in Andrea's direction. "Thanks, Andrea."

"Really?" Cynthia sighed. "Even after—well, sometimes I forget how cruel high school kids can be."

Cynthia didn't need to fill in the gaps. Alexa knew what her mother meant. Alexa nearly died six months ago, but in high school time, that was ancient history.

"Why didn't you tell me?" Alexa whispered to Mateo. As the newly crowned prince of Riverview gossip, Mateo would have heard everything. "What else do they say?"

"Ignore them." Mateo flipped his bangs out of his eyes. "They don't like how you and I went from the bottom of the social heap to the top. They wish we were still hiding in the art room during lunch."

Nothing had been the same for Alexa and Mateo since their week-long disappearance with Sid last fall, especially since neither Mateo nor Sid remembered what happened during their cross-country trek. Alexa, however, remembered everything. Every single moment, though she claimed the opposite. Because who in their right mind would believe three teenagers had run for their lives from

a monster chasing a unicorn in a Honda Civic? A unicorn
Alexa had promised to save.

A familiar ache quivered at the front of Alexa's brain.
No, she didn't want to think about that now, not in the
middle of picking out her prom dress. She needed to remain
in the here and now.

Sunlight glared off a passing car's windshield. A shock
of light flashed through the boutique. For a split second,
Alexa was blinded. She gasped as a series of images raced
through her mind: a unicorn shining brightly upon a hill, a
flash of lightning cutting across a dark sky, and the scream of
a creature ripped apart from the inside out.

Please, I do not want to go alone!

"No." Alexa clutched her head. The dull ache spasmed
into a full-fledged migraine.

Snap.

"Oh my God," Mateo gasped beside her.

Alexa dropped her hands to discover a crack snaking
across the mirror. Not again.

Andrea leaped from her seat. "Holy shit, what
happened?"

"Are you okay, Lex?" Mateo studied Alexa's face.

"Yeah, sure." The pain roaring through Alexa's brain
disappeared as quickly as it arrived. She glanced around the
room, worried about who else had seen the mirror
spontaneously crack. Her eyes landed near the boutique
entrance. Someone stood at the front door, hand raised in
greeting. Another glare of light burst behind them, blinding
Alexa once again.

"Alexa, what are you looking at?" Mateo tugged her arm.

"Nothing." Alexa covered her eyes. Had she seen someone at the door, or was her mind playing tricks on her again?

"Is it normal for your mirrors to crack like that?" Cynthia had switched from a concerned mother to a litigious attorney.

"I'm so sorry, everyone." Brandi approached the mirror, eyes wide. "How did that—hey, Alexa, let's get you back from the mirror."

Alexa turned back to the door as Brandi held out a hand to help her down from the dais. Whoever it was had left. Alexa shivered. For the past two weeks, she swore she caught shadowy figures following her everywhere. But whenever she turned to face them, they disappeared.

"Here, let me help." Mateo grabbed Alexa's other hand, eyes boring into her, asking a hundred unspoken questions. Alexa turned away.

"I'm going to change," Alexa said, her breath coming in gasps. "I'll take the dress. You're right. I should try something new."

Before anyone else could say a word, Alexa yanked the glittering stilettos from her feet and hurried back to the dressing room. The previous headache had been replaced by a mounting sense of panic and the inability to catch her breath. She tossed the changing room curtain closed, slumped against the wall, and fought the waves of anxiety pulsing through her body.

If only those who loved her knew the memories plaguing her day and night. She couldn't tell anyone the truth because the truth was beyond possible. Who would ever believe

Alexa had discovered a unicorn trapped in the park bathroom? A unicorn she tried to save from a monster, but in the end, allowed the same monster to destroy. That same monster had crawled into her head, possessed her, and told her things a girl from Earth should never know.

And that wasn't all. Both the unicorn and monster had left something behind. Not just trauma and shared memories. No, something Alexa didn't understand, something that allowed a panicked girl to break mirrors with her mind.

Chapter 2

"Lex, you okay?" Mateo whispered from the other side of the changing room curtain.

Alexa, fighting for breath, gasped. "Yeah."

"Your Mom is here with me. She's really worried about you."

The last thing Alexa needed was a swarm of people demanding explanations, suffocating her with kind words. If someone touched her, she would burst into tears and confess all the madness on endless rotation in her brain.

"Alexa, honey, can I come in there?" Cynthia's soft voice was high and tight with concern. "You don't have to get that dress if you don't want to. That black one with the tulle skirt was lovely too."

"This is not about a dress," Alexa spit out, her frustration strengthening her voice. She alone knew the true origins of her panic attacks. She had returned stronger and a little braver after the experience with Una yet broken at the same time. Everyone noticed the changes in her personality, the walls she erected, even against those closest to her.

"I wish you'd consider therapy, sweetie," Cynthia said.

Alexa glanced through the curtain's gap. One of Mateo's dark eyes stared back, his lips set in a familiar, frustrated line. Behind him, her mother clenched and unclenched her hands.

"Therapy won't help." Alexa twisted to reach the zipper at the back of the dress. Of course, therapy couldn't help when Alexa could never tell the truth about the horrors plaguing her day and night. No rational human being would believe her. At worst, they would put her away in some psych hospital and pump her full of drugs.

"I don't believe that's true." Cynthia's faint shadow paced on the other side of the curtain. "You're still dealing with some sort of trauma from—"

"Mom, no, please. I don't want to talk about it. See, I'm breathing again. I just need to get out of this goddamn—"

"Lex, I'm going to come in there and help you," Mateo announced and immediately walked in. The look on his face made Alexa squirm even more. "Cynthia, I got this. Just give us ten minutes."

Cynthia said, "Are you sure?"

"Totally." Mateo slowly unzipped the dress. "Lex just needs to get out of this thing, get a caramel macchiato, and she'll be back to her old self. Right, Lex?"

"Yep." Alexa bowed her head and stared at her feet.

"Okay." Cynthia hesitated, gripping the edge of the curtain.

Alexa knew her mother desperately wanted to help, wanted to know how to make her oldest daughter better, but had no clue how. "Thanks, Mateo."

Mateo helped Alexa out of the dress and hung it back on its lavender-scented hanger. Alexa put her typical uniform on: ripped black jeans and her favorite Rage Against the Machine t-shirt.

Mateo handed over her battered Converse sneakers and cleared his throat. "You have to stop doing this. Your mom is so worried. You're going to give her an ulcer."

"I know." Alexa ran a hand through her short hair. "Honestly, Mateo, I'm fine. I have my moments, but I get over them fast, don't I?"

"You're not fine." Mateo whirled around to face her. "I watch you pretend every day. You're pretty good at it most of the time, but I know you better than anyone else. And to be honest, it's tough for me to watch every performance, especially when you've never told me the truth about that week."

She knew which week he meant. She sighed, exhausted before the conversation even began. "I told you—"

"I know what you *told* me. You met a girl, Una, in Birkmose Park who was running from a dangerous ex-boyfriend. Burt, right? You said his name was Burt."

Alexa nodded. "Yeah, Burt."

"You promised to help Una and, apparently, Sid and I did too. For some reason, we drove all the way to Crater Lake to meet up with one of Una's friends, but the ex-boyfriend caught up with us, and then he and Una ran off together. But things get really nuts here: Sid and I remember nothing. Well, almost nothing."

"I'm not lying." Alexa couldn't meet his eyes.

"Sure, whatever, Lex." Mateo kicked her shoe, but Alexa stared at the floor. "Sometimes, I think I almost remember Una. She was kind of a bitch, wasn't she? So why can't I remember her face?"

Of course, he couldn't remember her face because Una wasn't a girl. Una was a Bright One, a beast that looked like a Great Dane-sized unicorn but happened to be one of the most dangerous creatures in all the multiverse. A multiverse no one on Earth knew existed.

"And I remember this other person. The ex-boyfriend, I think. I remember being in fear for my life and yours. I was worried you might die, and I'm not talking about when we were in the hospital in Oregon. I still feel it sometimes when I look at you."

Alexa met her best friend's gaze. "I'm not going to die. I'm right here."

"But you're *not* here, Lex. You haven't been here for a long time."

"I know, I know." She swiped her tears and grabbed Mateo's hand. "But there are things you're better off not knowing."

"That's not fair, Lex. Not fair to Sid or me. We deserve to know what happened. I deserve to know why my nightmares started when we got back. I haven't had a decent night's sleep in six months. Do you know how much concealer it takes to hide the shadows under my eyes?"

Alexa's chest tightened at the mention of Sid. "You're still having that same dream?"

Of the three of them, Sid was by far the most unscathed. Or, at least, he pretended to be. Occasionally, Alexa caught him staring off into the distance, darkness clouding his eyes. She never dared to ask him what he was thinking about.

"The one where I'm running as fast as I can from a giant storm cloud but can never get away? Yeah, every night. It feels so real. Clouds fill my mouth, my throat, choking me until I can't breathe."

Alexa shuddered. She knew the feeling. She had experienced something similar when the monster possessed her body. They had tried to destroy her from the inside out, but she managed to convince the monster—the Brume—that they were allies, not enemies. And then they used Alexa to kill Una.

"That sounds horrible," Alexa murmured, gathering her coat. She pushed aside the dressing room curtain.

Mateo grabbed her wrist. "Just tell me something. Anything, Lex, and I'll drop it for today. But you have to tell me something."

Alexa stared into the pleading eyes of her friend. Mateo was right. She had fed him a series of half-truths for so long that he deserved a moment of honesty. Maybe the questions would stop for a month or two until she could come up with another piece to give him.

"That strangling sensation you feel? I think it's because you saw it happen to me," Alexa said. "Burt tried to strangle me, but you saved me. You and Sid."

Mateo's eyes widened. "Oh, Lex. Why didn't you go to the cops when you remembered? Burt is still out there. He could be hurting other—"

"They—er—he's not."

"How do you know?"

"I just do. And that's another thing I can't tell you." Alexa hurried out of the dressing room before Mateo could ask more questions. She touched her throat, remembering the feeling of two giant hands closed around it, pressing against her windpipe, ready to crush her neck—a thousand voices speaking at once. *Stop lying to us.*

"Alexa?" Cynthia stood outside the dressing room, concern written all over her face. "You want to go? We can come back later when you're ready to make a decision."

Alexa straightened her shoulders, brushed away the tears staining her cheeks, and smiled. "No, I know what I want. I'll take the pink one."

Chapter 3

Alexa hated driving to school on sunny mornings. The glaring sun on the windshield reminded her of driving for her life across Wyoming, a furious unicorn in the back seat. Up until a month ago, she couldn't stand driving anywhere, even when her parents got her a new Honda Civic. However, her sister's lead foot and unbearable music choices eventually moved Alexa back into the driver's seat.

Alexa's taste in music had also changed. She could no longer listen to her beloved 90's grunge mix without a headache forming behind her eyes. The opening chords of any Nirvana song sent her heart racing. She refused to let go of Dave Grohl, so she switched to Foo Fighters. Weezer replaced Pearl Jam, and Beck took the place of Soundgarden. Radiohead was still safe, along with the late-90s Smashing Pumpkins, but Alice in Chains always brought tears to her eyes. She also found a love for Hole, Alanis Morisette, and Fiona Apple. A little feminine rage helped her get through each awkward day.

The bright, surfer jams of Sublime currently rocked her car, much to Andrea's chagrin.

"Someday, you'll listen to music from the twenty-first century," Andrea groaned, scanning her smartphone.

Alexa stopped at a red light, and the playlist switched to Bush. She adored the grinding opening chords to "Glycerin".

Gavin Rossdale's gentle but soulful voice lulled the low-level anxiety that came with driving. She closed her eyes for a moment, letting the throb of the electric guitar wash over her.

"Lex, hey!" Andrea barked from the passenger seat. "The light's green."

A car horn honked behind them. Alexa hit the gas, crossed the intersection and entered the high school parking lot.

"Sorry," Alexa said. "Lost in a daydream."

"You're always lost in a daydream."

"I am?" Alexa spotted Sid's silver Impreza and parked a few stalls down from it. A familiar flood of warmth spread through her chest and into her stomach. She hadn't seen Sid since Friday, which felt like years of separation. He and his family had gone to visit his aunt in Chicago. They had sent each other a constant stream of texts and pictures, but Alexa couldn't wait to be in his arms again.

"You know you are." Andrea checked her makeup in the mirror and ran her fingers through her hair. "Always on a different plane of existence beyond us mere mortals. Unlike Mom, I've decided it's your choice to be this way, and I'm not going to give you crap about it."

"What way?" Alexa's excitement weakened. Was she so obvious? Didn't Sid reach out to her once a day, gently tap her shoulder and say, "Where are you right now?"

"I used to think it was just this air of mystery you've managed to cultivate since October. Then I realized it wasn't an act. You're literally somewhere else half the time. Where do you go? No one knows. You're like a shadow. You've always been that way, but now it's so much more obvious."

"A shadow." Alexa stared out the window at the students flowing into the high school.

"No one cared before you started dating Sid. Now you're an object of analysis. I can't tell you how many people have asked me what's your deal."

"I'm just being me."

"And that's what drives them crazy." Andrea smirked and gathered her school bag. "That's why they call you stupid names like Queen of Darkness. They're jealous because they have no idea how to be like you."

"Why would they want to be me?" Alexa hurriedly opened her door and followed her sister.

Andrea tossed her long blonde hair over her shoulder and waved to a gaggle of sophomore girls on the JV volleyball team. The girls tittered in response, pleased by her attention. Alexa caught up to Andrea, noticing how those same girls studied her with a mixture of awe and confusion.

"See." Andrea jerked her head toward the sophomores. "You've broken all the rules of the high school hierarchy, and everyone wants to figure out how you did it."

"This is ridiculous," Andrea grumbled. "I'm just dating Sid. It's not that big a deal."

Andrea grabbed the door and held it open, glaring at her sister. "Don't be stupid, Alexa. It's a huge deal. Have some respect for your achievement."

"Achievement?" Alexa paused inside the front atrium, surveying the crowd for Sid's familiar mop of dark hair.

"And I say, lean in, girl." Andrea shrugged. "Enjoy your notoriety instead of being so self-conscious. You're the Queen of Darkness, so act like royalty."

"But that's just so—" Alexa spotted Sid's lanky but athletic figure at the edge of a group of glee choir kids humming through a piece of music. Her stomach flipped each time she saw him. And each time he saw her, his face broke into an incredible, sexy grin. Her breath caught in her throat, and she fought unexpected tears of relief.

Alexa still couldn't believe her luck. She had hidden her love for Sid since middle school, confident he would never know how she felt. But their harrowing adventure changed everything, even though his memories from six months ago were hazy at best.

Sid wrapped his arms around Alexa and lifted her from the floor as he whispered, "I missed you so much this weekend."

"I missed you too." Alexa melted into him, letting all her worries and fears disappear. The dark memories hovering in the back of her mind were easy to forget when the boy she loved held her tight.

"How are you?" Sid stood almost a foot taller than her.

She enjoyed letting her head fall back, gazing into his big, dark eyes. "A lot better now."

"I heard you went dress shopping." Sid waggled his eyebrows.

"Maybe." Alexa grasped his hands tight. How would he react when he saw her in a soft pink dress instead of her typical black?

"We had to drag her to the boutique," Andrea said. "She kept saying, 'Sid hasn't even asked me to prom.'"

"I didn't ask you?" Sid tipped Alexa's chin and gave her a feather-light kiss. "I thought I did. Didn't I?"

"Well, not directly." Alexa shrugged, her cheeks burning.

"Oh, my God, can we put a pause on the excessive PDA?" Mateo floated through the main doors with his typical posse of companions. The three beautiful but ruthless juniors, Madison, Emma, and Emily, twittered at his side, half of their attention focused on phones, half smirking in Alexa's direction. Mateo had dubbed them the "EME Team" once they picked him as their leader. Lately, Mateo had spent more time with them than her.

"Sorry." Alexa stuck close to Sid. If it were up to her, she would never let him go. Away from Sid, she was an unmoored boat, floating along a dark sea of memories she desperately wanted to forget. Beside him, she could get through anything. Occasionally, her dependence bothered her, but not that morning.

"You wouldn't believe the dress I found Lex yesterday," Mateo said with a sly smile. "I'd show you a picture, but that might be bad luck."

"I thought you deleted it?" Alexa trilled. She pictured herself standing in an oversized gown next to a broken mirror.

"Don't worry, I'm sworn to secrecy," Mateo said. "Anyway, you might not need it. It's not like Sid ever asked you to go, did he?"

"You're right." Sid cupped Alexa's cheek in his large, warm hand. "Looks like I need to fix that. Now seems like as good a time as any. What do you think?" Sid nodded to his friends collecting at the far side of the atrium. Alexa groaned inwardly. It was too early to face their insincere, calculating smiles.

A chorus of voices rose from behind them. Alexa turned from Sid to see the glee club members arranged in a loose semi-circle only feet away. The soft, bouncy rhythm of a familiar song rose from the singers' throats, a song she immediately recognized.

"I know how much you love Mazzy Star," Sid said as the crowd of students swelled around them. The glee club stepped closer, singing the opening lines of "Fade Into You."

Alexa glanced toward Mateo, who held up his phone, recording the moment. Sid's best friend, Drew, also raised his phone, his cold smirk almost ruining the moment for Alexa. Sid suddenly dropped to one knee as the glee club swelled into the chorus.

"Oh, no, Sid, you don't—" Alexa squeaked, her face red-hot as a hundred eyes turned in her direction.

"Alexa Baxter." Sid's dark eyes shone. "It's been an amazing six months since we first drove up to Birkmose Park. Do you remember?"

"Yes, of course—of course, I remember." Alexa's heart raced, thumping in her ears as the glee club continued to hum around them.

The day after Alexa had returned to Riverview, Sid had unexpectedly taken her back to where the whole crazy adventure had begun. The park where she had discovered a unicorn named Una was on the run from a monster who wanted to destroy it. Sid remembered nothing of the Bright

One or the Brume or the fact he and Alexa nearly died several times. What remained was a sense of familiarity between the two of them. He had found himself drawn to her in a way he couldn't explain but didn't question.

Alexa and Sid's relationship had started slowly. Painfully slow, in Mateo's opinion. First, one coffee date, then two, and a few more until Sid and Alexa's parents took them off "probation" and let them go on an actual date. After dinner and a movie, Sid took Alexa back to the top of Birkmose and shared their first kiss, a kiss Alexa never wanted to end.

After the kiss, they officially declared themselves boyfriend and girlfriend, much to the shock of Riverview High School. And now she was standing in the middle of a teenage dream, the boy she loved kneeling before her.

Sid said several more beautiful things, but Alexa could barely hear him. The whole school seemed to have turned out for Sid's "Prom-posal," holding up their phones to capture the moment. Alexa's knees knocked. She was horrified to be the center of attention, yet she was touched by Sid's public declaration.

"Alexa Baxter, I love you. Will you go to prom with me?" Sid bellowed, his voice echoing across the glass-filled atrium.

Alexa gasped. They hadn't said that key phrase to each other yet. Of course, Alexa was deeply, horribly, and irrevocably in love with him. But to have him say those words in front of the whole world? There weren't words to express her joy. She opened her mouth, but no words came out.

"Lex? Psst, Lex?" Mateo laughed. "Just nod your head. That's all you have to do."

Alexa did as she was told. As Sid embraced her and kissed her deeply, cheers burst from the surrounding crowd.

"Alright, alright, that's enough," an adult shouted from the back of the crowd. "Let's get to class, everyone. Show's over."

Students groaned, and the crowd dispersed. Mateo blew Alexa a kiss and hurried off with his mean girls in tow. Sid's friends backed away, knowing they could catch up with him later. One vice-principal cut through the crowd, waving students toward their classes.

"Here, wait." Sid dug into his back pocket and pulled out a black sachet tied with a sparkly bow. "I got this for you."

"You love me?" The words gushed out before she could stop them.

"Yeah." Sid blushed, placing the satin bag in her hands. "For a while. I just didn't know how to say it. I was worried...I don't know ..."

"That I didn't feel the same way?" Alexa giggled. "Seriously? Sid, I've loved you since I was twelve years old. Since the first time you sat next to me in Mrs. Jackson's Advanced English class."

Sid's cheeks reddened. "Really?"

"Okay, love birds, you need to go to class too." Vice-Principal Cole pointed down the hall.

"You got it, Mr. Cole." Sid beamed and gave Alexa one more quick kiss on the cheek. "I'll see you in second period. Hope you like it!" He gestured to his gift before loping down the hall.

Alexa untied the gift bag and found something glittering inside. She poured the necklace into her hand: a silver chain with a thumbnail-sized pendant. Sucking in a sharp breath, she turned the little figure over in her palm.

It was a silver unicorn.

A figure moved in her periphery. She looked up, ready to promise the vice-principal that she was on her way to class, but it was someone else standing at the front doors. The person disappeared once she turned her gaze in that direction.

"What the—"

"Alexa Baxter, did you not hear me the first time?" Vice-Principal Cole bellowed behind her.

"Sorry, I thought I saw someone at the doors." She turned back to the empty entrance.

"Visitors are my concern, not yours. Hurry up. You'll be tardy."

Alexa stammered a brief apology and automatically hurried in the direction of her first-period class. She was seeing things that weren't there again, just like she had at the dress shop. And what about that cryptic text message? Was her growing paranoia just another symptom of her distressed mind, or was she being followed?

She held the unicorn necklace tight as she raced to class, the figurine's miniature horn biting into her flesh.

Chapter 4

Alexa turned the unicorn pendant over and over in her hand as she made her way to American Civics class. Was the unicorn a sign? If so, a sign of what? Sid maintained he remembered next to nothing about what happened in October, yet he did something every so often that made her wonder. Unlike her and Mateo, he didn't worry about what might or might not have happened. Life was fantastic for Sid. She ought to follow his example. Why worry about monsters and lost unicorns when she was in love with the most perfect boy in the world? A boy who wanted everyone to know how much he loved her.

Her mood pivoted between utter joy—he loved her!—and despair. How could he love her when he didn't know the whole truth? She had kept so much from him, including what the otherworldly creature had left behind with her: her ability to break objects or send them flying when her emotions ran high. Or that one time when she woke in the middle of the night to find several books spinning in circles above her bed.

Sitting in the back of her classroom, Alexa tried to focus on the teacher's breakdown of the American judicial system. Ms. Ellefson was one of her favorite teachers at Riverview High, but she couldn't concentrate. Her mind flashed to the moment she last saw Una standing on the shallows of Crater Lake, refusing to back down despite its inevitable demise.

Una had cried out, "You showed me nothing but kindness. I will never forget it*,*" but only Alexa, shivering in the freezing lake, could hear that voice which plagued her both day and night.

And then the Brume annihilated the Bright One right in front of her.

"There are thirteen appellate courts that sit below the US Supreme Court." Ms. Ellefson paced in front of the class, pointing to different parts of the map on the projection screen.

Una didn't have a trial. A mercenary hired by the multiverse's primary governing body executed Una for being too dangerous to live. Alexa squirmed in her seat, staring at the scar on her left palm, a mark from when she touched Una's sharp horn. What was the name of the governing system again? Oh, yes, the Multiverse Governing Alliance, also known as the MGA.

"Our nation's ninety-four districts or trial courts are called U.S. District Courts." Ms. Ellefson switched to the next slide, displaying a more detailed map of the United States. "District courts resolve disputes by determining the facts and applying legal principles to decide who is right."

If the MGA found out the Brume hadn't wiped Alexa's memory, they would come for her too. If they hadn't already. Una was supposed to be no more than a fuzzy memory, like the impulse that had prompted Sid to buy her a silver necklace with a perfect little unicorn charm.

Alexa turned the miniature unicorn between her fingers, letting the tiny horn poke her fingertips. She was being paranoid. She was just a primitive little human, after all, and certainly not worth remembering. Right?

What would they do if or when they discovered the truth? What if they already knew? What about that text she received in the dressing room? *We know.* Who knows? And what do they know?

The end-of-class tone beeped. Alexa's thoughts returned to the present and she wondered where the last hour had gone. Andrea was right; Alexa could barely stay in the present half the time, her head a thousand miles from where it should be. She gathered her books and headed toward the door with the rest of the students.

"Alexa?" Ms. Ellefson's strong alto broke through Alexa's buzzing thoughts.

"Yes?" Alexa paused at the classroom door. She was supposed to meet Sid outside the cafeteria and walk to European History with him.

Ms. Ellefson gave her an uncertain smile, and Alexa knew they were about to speak about something uncomfortable. Ms. Ellefson must have noticed she had been barely paying attention.

"How are you doing today?"

Alexa shrugged. "It's been a day already."

"I heard about Sid's little display before school," her teacher said. "How romantic."

"Yeah. It was." Alexa's cheeks flared. She dropped her gaze to the tops of her Doc Martins.

"Is that why you couldn't focus?"

Alexa bobbed her head. "Sorry. There's just so much going on."

"That's right." Ms. Ellefson leaned against her desk, folding her hands into her lap. "Like what we talked about last week? Anyway, did you finally make a decision?"

"Decision?" Alexa played dumb, but she knew what Ms. Ellefson meant. Alexa admitted to her teacher last week—when caught daydreaming—that her college plans had changed. The University of Minnesota no longer felt like the right place for her if Sid was going to Harvard. Hence, she applied at the last minute to Boston University in November and was accepted.

"I know that Sid has early admittance to Harvard—"

"I'm not following him if that's what you think," Alexa said quickly.

"Boston University is an excellent school." Ms. Ellefson's voice was light, reassuring. "And if you want to study art, especially art history, you'll love being on the East Coast. Lots of museums and historical architecture. Have you told your parents?"

Alexa shook her head. "Not yet."

"But you'll tell them soon, right?"

"Yep, just searching for the right time."

"You don't think they'll be happy for you?"

"They'll think I'm being impulsive." Alexa eyed the door. She had avoided the conversation since January, and time was running out. Originally, her parents were disappointed she wanted to stay nearby and go to a school they believed was below her potential. Now she sensed they were relieved to have her stay close to home. If something went wrong, if she had another uncontrollable panic attack, they were only twenty to thirty minutes away. In Boston, Alexa would be on her own.

"Maybe. But you'll never know until you tell them."

"I'm sorry, Ms. Ellefson, but I have to get to the other side of the school." Alexa backed out of the classroom door, desperate to escape her teacher's scrutiny. "I'll, uh, see you tomorrow."

Before Ms. Ellefson could say another word, Alexa hurried into the hall, nearly colliding with a cluster of acne-ridden freshmen boys, then darted into the flow of student traffic. Her breath, as it often did, came in sharp bursts.

She knew how everyone would react when she finally shared the news. Her parents would pretend to be happy. And Mateo? For years they had planned to go to the U of M and study art together. But so much had changed between them after Una. Mateo went from curious to annoyed and, later, desperate to know what had happened. When she gave him only bits and pieces of truth scattered among lies, a rift had formed between them.

If Alexa went to the U of M with Mateo, he would fight to get the truth out of her. A truth she refused to share for his own sake. Then they would drift apart until he left her behind completely. If Alexa went to Boston University, she would be near Sid. She could stay with the only person who made her feel safe and loved and didn't ask too many questions.

Alexa had to follow Sid, if only to maintain her sanity. Maybe at some point, she could find a way to heal, forget, and move on. After another year or two, she might no longer find herself awake in the middle of the night, twisted in her bed sheets and weeping from the memory of Una's screams.

Sid met her at their usual spot between the two wings of campus. He strode over, grinning, then, noticing her distress, he looped his arm over her shoulder. "You look like you've failed a test."

"No, nothing that horrible." Alexa pressed a hand against the unicorn pedant, which hung over her thudding heart. "I didn't tell you, but I made the mistake last week of mentioning my plan to go to Boston College."

"Oh, I thought we were—"

"Yeah, we were going to keep it to ourselves until we told our parents. I know. I screwed up. I couldn't keep it bottled up inside and had to say something to someone, and Ms. Ellefson seemed like a neutral party."

"Hey." Sid leaned over, gazing down at Alexa. "So what? So she knows—no big deal. So you happen to be attending a school in the same city as mine. It makes sense. I love you. We love each other."

"Yeah, but you know what everyone is going to think?" Alexa shook her head, and checked the time on the wall. "Hey, we should go—"

"Who cares what everyone else thinks?" Sid grasped her hand and started in the direction of their next class. "I know I don't."

"We need to tell our parents."

"Totally. That's why I was about to invite you to dinner at my house tonight. Mom and Dad finally have a night off and wanted to have you over."

"Tonight?" Alexa's heart took off again, a wild horse pounding down the track. She had been to Sid's house plenty of times, but only when his sister and her nanny were around. She'd had a few interactions and polite conversations with Sid's parents, but a whole meal together?

"Yeah, let's tell them tonight. And then we'll tell your parents this weekend. They'll be happy when they find out you got into such a great school. So what if it happens to be near Harvard? I have no interest in living far away from you anytime soon. They'll understand. Sound good?"

Alexa held Sid's hand tight, ignoring the little spots floating on the edges of her vision. "We have to tell everyone eventually. After our parents, you know who comes next?"

"Mateo." Sid nodded, a grim set to his jaw.

Chapter 5

Alexa flipped through every item of black clothing hanging in her closet, unable to find the right shirt or pair of jeans to wear to dinner with Sid's family. Letting out a long groan, she tossed another band t-shirt on the floor behind her. In the background, playing on a wireless speaker, Weezer complained about social awkwardness and the unraveling of their sweater.

"This is impossible." She glanced over to the plastic unicorn, Stardancer, on her dresser, a figurine she had nearly thrown out after returning from her cross-country adventure. Lately, Alexa had begun speaking to Stardancer as if it was Una.

"What 90's alternative band t-shirt says, 'I'm not a loser, I'm just eccentric?'"

Stardancer stared back with empty, acrylic eyes.

"What would you know? You're not even from this planet."

Andrea cracked open the door to Alexa's bedroom. "Wow, Lex, you okay?"

Startled, Alexa yelped. The plastic unicorn quivered, its pink hair shivering against its white withers. Had Alexa made Stardancer move?

"I don't know." Alexa studied her favorite Alice in Chains vintage shirt for the third time before carefully returning it to the closet. "I have literally nothing to wear."

"You going somewhere this evening?" Andrea plopped onto Alexa's bed, grabbed a black sequined throw pillow from the floor, and pressed it to her chest. "With Sid?"

"I'm having dinner with his parents." She tugged out her least worn-out pair of black jeans from the closet. "I guess these'll have to do."

"That's ... exciting?"

"More like nerve-racking. I've never had a full sit-down meal with them before. They're usually performing life-saving surgeries or popping in and out while Sid and I watch a movie or something. Sid's parents are super brilliant, amazing people. I'm not sure they like me."

"Sounds like they barely know you, so why wouldn't they like you?"

Alexa sighed. "Well, I'm probably not what they expected their golden child would bring home."

"You don't know that." Andrea turned the pillow over in her lap, avoiding her sister's gaze.

"Varsity athlete and school valedictorian heading to Harvard falls for the weird artsy girl. Sounds like a cheesy teen rom-com."

"You're too hard on yourself, Lex. You never really cared what anyone thought about you before. Why now?"

"It's easy not to care when everyone ignores you." Alexa tugged a Smashing Pumpkins t-shirt from the closet. "This would look okay with my leather jacket, right?"

Andrea shrugged.

"So helpful." Alexa smirked and tossed her outfit onto the bed behind where Andrea sat. She fingered the unicorn necklace, realizing she still hadn't asked Sid what had prompted him to pick out such a gift.

"Sid loves you. That's all that matters, right?" Her sister tossed the pillow to Alexa, who easily caught it. "And you're charming enough ... sometimes."

"Ha, thanks for the vote of confidence." Alexa hugged the pillow. "It's just ... what if they hate me? I mean, I've kind of avoided them, to be honest. His parents have a ton of influence on his life. He admires them ... respects them. If they don't think I'm good enough—"

"You really need to keep working on that confidence. Do what they tell us to do in speech class. Stand up straight. Chin up. Smile and fake it till you make it."

"You want to go in my place?" Alexa laughed.

"Definitely not."

"I can't imagine life without him." The pillow sequins bit through Alexa's thin shirt. "I'm terrified of losing him somehow. Sometimes I think he's the only person who keeps me sane."

"Don't tell Mom that. She'll make you go to therapy for sure."

"I'm an adult. She can't make me do anything."

Her sister chuckled. "You know if she sets her mind to it, she'll make it happen." Andrea flipped back her hair and thought for a second. "Okay, so don't take this the wrong way, but do you ever worry about how much you need Sid? I've noticed you're kinda lost without him. Is that healthy?

I mean, what'll you do when you go to the U of M, and he goes off to Harvard?"

Alexa turned her gaze to Stardancer so her sister wouldn't see the lie in her eyes. "I'll figure it out."

"The two of you ... sometimes it seems like you're on your own planet when you're together." Andrea leaned forward and dropped her voice to a whisper. "Is it because you're, um, sleeping with each other? I've noticed sometimes that can make people obsessive—"

"Oh, my God, Andrea." Alexa hurled the pillow at her sister's head.

She batted it away. "But, like, you know what I mean, right? Have you and Sid—"

"That's personal." Alexa's cheeks flared red, a condition she seemed to be repeating over and over lately.

"Look, I get it. This is between you and Sid, and it's none of my business ..."

Alexa groaned and flopped onto the bed beside her sister. She couldn't help thinking back to when her parents were out of town, and Andrea stayed at a friend's house. She and Sid nearly did it that night, but both weren't quite ready. They agreed that if they wanted to take that next step, there shouldn't be a moment's hesitation. The memory burned hot in her mind, remembering how Sid looked when—

Thump.

"Whoa." Andrea sat up straight beside Alexa. "That was weird."

Alexa glanced over her shoulder toward her chest of drawers. Stardancer had somehow fallen into the middle of her bedroom floor.

Alexa also sat up, a curl of tension in her gut. "What happened?"

"I was looking at your closet when, I swear, that silly horse flew across the room. Like someone had literally tossed it. Hey, our house isn't haunted, is it?"

"I don't think that's possible," Alexa said, fighting the panic rising from her stomach to her chest and blossoming behind her eyes. Her foray into unintentional telekinesis appeared to be worsening and was clearly tied to intense emotional responses.

"So weird." Andrea slid off her bed and picked up the unicorn figure. "Didn't you, like, used to play with this thing all the time when you were little? I think Mom got rid of all my old toys. Why do you still have this? Aren't you a little old for unicorns?"

A door slammed below. "Hey girls, I'm home!"

Andrea handed Stardancer to Alexa. "Just wear what you usually wear, Lex. It's Sid who loves you, and I'm sure his parents will too."

With that, her sister hurried downstairs. Alexa turned Stardancer over in her hands, caressing the smooth plastic hair.

Since the first time a glass cracked a month ago, Alexa had ignored her new "ability." The drinking glass was easy enough to explain away, but fragile objects continued to break or fall around her. And now the incidents were increasing in frequency and intensity. What happened when she broke or threw something that couldn't be explained?

What if the use of her power somehow drew the attention of someone from the Alliance? Was such a thing possible? Alexa had odd moments of paranoia when she was out and about, especially when items broke or fell in public. She could never get over the feeling that someone or something had watched her. Maybe the Brume wouldn't be chasing a Bright One next time but her instead.

Alexa had to get whatever was wrong with her under control. Avoidance wasn't working. The unwanted power felt more like a disease slowly invading her brain.

She returned Stardancer to its place, and as she stared at the unicorn, she also tried to figure out what caused her telekinetic abilities to manifest.

Her thoughts returned to the anxiety surrounding her dinner with Sid's family. She was desperate for them to like her, but such a powerful desire often caused her to withdraw in social settings. Sometimes it was better not to say anything than say the wrong thing. What would his parents think when they found out she wasn't staying in the Midwest? How much would they freak out?

And, even worse, what if Sid didn't love her? What if his love was just the Brumes manipulating his memory? She was afraid to ask that one crucial question repeatedly circling her mind. Why did he love her? How had he gone from a person who barely acknowledged her existence to smiling every time she walked into the room?

Right on cue, Alexa's heart began to race, and her palms were sweating. Instead of shoving away her panic and insecurity, she grasped them tightly, letting herself feel all the awful, unwanted sensations, and then, as if her fear became manifest, she shoved it in Stardancer's direction.

The unicorn figurine quivered as if Alexa had gently blown upon the unicorn's its hair.

She panted, elated and horrified at the same time. Darkness clouded the edges of her vision. Tension gripped the back of her neck and, one more time, Alexa pushed all her emotions forward like an invisible hand through the air.

Stardancer whipped across the room, bounced off the bedroom window, and ricocheted into the bookcase near Alexa's bedroom door.

"Holy shit." Alexa said, sweat trickling down her brow. Her knees buckled, and she slumped onto the floor.

Her unwanted power was going to change everything.

Chapter 6

S id's family lived in a ridiculously large house overlooking
the St. Croix River. With two surgeons as the head of
the household—his mother an internationally known
cardiothoracic surgeon—the family could easily afford the
sprawling modern stone structure. In addition, Sid's parents
had recently discussed an upgrade since his grandmother was
planning to move in with them over the summer'.

Alexa never knew where to park when she pulled into
their looping concrete driveway. Someone had left one of
the three garage doors open, revealing Sid's father's recent
purchase: a Tesla Roadster. Like most sports cars in the
upper Midwest, the glossy electric vehicle wasn't used for
part of the year due to the snowy Wisconsin winters.
Practicality was hardly the point.

The house shone warm and bright like a lantern against
the fading sky. When Alexa locked her car, Sid appeared at
the front double doors. He had dressed for dinner, wearing
a crisp button-up and polished oxfords. His parents weren't
often home at the same time so having the entire family
together was a rare treat they liked to make an event.

"You look nice." Sid gave her his signature crooked smile
and held open the door, revealing the foyer beyond.

Alexa tugged at the sapphire blue knit shirt Andrea had
forced her to put on when she popped by Alexa's room

minutes before she was about to leave. "You won't regret it. It'll bring out your eyes."

"You wore it." Sid touched the unicorn necklace resting against her sternum. "Today was such a blur. I totally forgot to ask if you liked it."

"I love it." Alexa ran her fingers over the silver pendant. "What inspired you to get me this?"

"Remember that one day a while ago when I caught you drawing unicorns in AP Lit?"

Alexa remembered. He meant the morning after she had discovered Una. Alexa had barely slept the night before and couldn't stop drawing images of Una all over her notebook during class. Sid had noticed her sketches and, as a joke, she invited him over to meet the unicorn. She couldn't believe it when he showed up at her house.

Sid remembered the unicorn drawings and little else of that fateful day. Alexa had told Sid and Mateo the same lie. While Mateo knew her too well to believe her, Sid accepted the story. He wasn't interested in the truth. He had two worried but furious parents to deal with and a new, unexplainable fixation with Alexa. He occasionally questioned her explanations after she suffered a nasty panic attack. Much like her parents, he wished she would go to therapy.

Sid guided her into their extravagant foyer. A piled-stone water feature ran directly through the room. The trickling water soothed Alexa's nerves, while the various skylights and enormous indoor palms made her feel as if she had walked into an arboretum.

"You know, I sometimes have these super vivid dreams." Sid led Alexa through the foyer and up a couple of stone slabs toward the kitchen entrance.

Alexa could hear dishes clinking and she inhaled the warm, spicy smell of curry and cardamom.

Sid continued, "You, me, and Mateo are in your old Honda Civic. I'm in the back seat, and there's this unicorn sitting in my lap. It has these intense blue eyes, and sometimes it speaks, but I can't remember what it says."

Alexa nearly stumbled up the steps. "Really? A unicorn?"

"Must be my brain trying to remember what Una looked like." Sid shrugged. "I wish I could. I get the feeling she was a challenging, complicated person."

Alexa nodded, fingering the unicorn pendant. "From what I can remember, yeah. Super intense."

"Anyway, Mom's making shahi korma, my favorite. She used to cook it for Sunday dinner when she had the time. We get it maybe once a year or when Grandma stops by."

Alexa gripped Sid's hand tight and took a fortifying breath. She let him lead her forward and plastered the biggest smile she could muster upon her face.

"Lexa's here!" Sid's twelve-year-old sister, Naija, launched herself at Alexa. "I'm so glad you came."

Alexa held her tight. At least Naija liked her. When Alexa came over to watch movies in what they called the "cinema room," Sid's sister often curled up beside her, whispering a steady stream of commentary into her ear.

"And I'm so happy to be here," Alexa said, momentarily unable to let the girl go. She glanced at Sid's mother, Ira, and noticed for the hundredth time where Sid got his big, dark eyes. "Thank you so much for inviting me over. Dinner smells amazing."

Ira gave her a warm but tentative smile. "We're happy to have you. I heard Sidhit finally asked you to prom. A little last-minute, don't you think?"

"Did the choir sing 'Fade Into You'?" Naija bounced beside Alexa. "That was my idea. I know how much you like that song."

"They did. It was beautiful." Alexa poked the unicorn necklace. "Did you help him pick this out?"

Naija scrutinized the unicorn pedant, her eyebrows compressing before flying upward. "Oh, is that a unicorn? That's so pretty."

"It is, isn't it?"

"It's nice of you to join us this evening." Umar, Sid's father, pulled out a set of plates from a cabinet. "We've wanted to do this for quite a while now, but Ira and my schedules have been very demanding as of late."

"I understand," Alexa said as Naija tugged on her arm.

"I have something I want to show you in my room," Naija whispered loudly in Alexa's ear.

"Really? What is it?"

Naija wiggled in place. "You have to come see."

Alexa looked between Sid and his mother. "Is that okay?"

Ira said, "Dinner will be ready in ten minutes. Can you set your timer?"

Naija pulled out the latest iPhone from her back pocket, her bottom lip popping as she set the timer. "Got it. C'mon, Lexa, I have the coolest thing to show you."

Alexa followed the bouncing girl out of the kitchen, down a short hall, and up a set of stairs toward her room. One could appreciate a panoramic view of the river valley from the second-floor gallery. Alexa had arrived at the perfect time to catch the setting sun painting the trees in brilliant orange hues.

Naija's room was a cacophony of pastels, sparkle and, most of all, unicorns. Before Alexa stepped into the girl's room, she had no idea how many different types of unicorn-shaped items existed. The girl was besotted by everything unicorn, from the doe-eyed, rainbow-haired creature leaping across her duvet to the enormous plush toy overtaking a corner of her room.

The sight of so many unicorns, seeing bits of Una repeatedly in every mythical creature around her, caused Alexa to sweat. Luckily, most of the unicorns veered between pudgy cartoons and white horses with horns. None truly resembled Una.

"I got a new poster." Naija swept her arm toward the wall beside her bedroom door.

Alexa's knees almost buckled. Before her hung what could have been a replica of Una. The unicorn print, from the opalescent horn to the delicate cloven hooves, was a perfect match. The Bright One's blue eyes followed Alexa as she viewed the poster from the left and right. A memory blossomed: Una stepping out from the bathroom, bathed in the evening sun, a spot of light amongst the darkening tree line.

I must remove from this planet immediately. This is not where I need to be. I do not belong here.

Alexa shook her head to do away with the image. "Where did you get this?"

"I found it online." Naija beamed. "It's from an artist in China. I waited a whole two months for it to get here. You don't like it?"

Alexa managed to nod, her throat tight as she fought back the tears blurring her vision. She couldn't speak or look away from the unicorn's accusing gaze.

I need you. I cannot get off this damned planet without you.

Alexa had promised to save the Bright One and had failed.

"I like that it's different, like one of the deer in our woods." Naija pointed to the unicorn's muzzle. "Don't you love her eyes?"

Alexa remembered how Una curled in her lap on their journey, the streetlights dancing off its shimmering hide. The steady rise and fall of its chest as it slept peacefully beside her, trusting her to help it escape the monster—at least what it claimed to be a monster. However, the Brume wasn't technically a monster. Brumes were mercenaries taking care of a job—collecting Una.

"Lexa?" Naija's eyes rounded with worry. "Are you having one of your, uh, *episodes*?"

Alexa nodded, her throat already tight as she struggled to breathe.

"Do you want me to get Sid?"

Alexa nodded again, and Naija scurried out the door, calling for her brother.

Unfortunately, this wasn't the first time Naija had witnessed one of Alexa's panic attacks. The first time was when she, Sid, and Naija watched an action movie that was a little too violent. The villain in the film began choking the hero, and Alexa nearly blacked out on the spot. The villain's hands became hands around her own neck, just like when the Brume took possession of a highway patrolman and attacked her.

"Breathe, just breathe," Alexa murmured, dropping to her knees as the world spun. Blood rushed in her ears; bright spots danced before her vision. She fell into the mantra she used when she was alone during an attack. "It's not your fault. It's not your fault."

Sid arrived moments later with a damp hand towel and a water bottle. "Hey there, Naija tells me you're having an episode. Can you look at me?"

Alexa raised her head and gazed into the eyes of the one person who could always pull her back out of her broken mind.

"Good, now let's start some deep breaths." Sid wrapped her cold, sweaty hand into his warm, dry one. "Deep breath in, hold it, and deep breath out."

Alexa did as directed, her breath shaky and weak. She shoved away thoughts of Una, focusing on Sid's calm voice.

"You have to get help for this, Lex," Sid murmured, rubbing her back. "Promise me you will. What happens when we go out East? Promise me, Alexa, that this summer, you'll get some help."

"Sure, okay." Alexa gasped, knowing she would put off making an appointment again and again. She hated lying all the time. Would a therapist see right through her? As her heart slowed and her breath evened, only one thing in her life felt certain: following Sid to Boston would be the best choice she would ever make.

Chapter 7

Alexa's cell phone buzzed in her pocket but she ignored the notification. She stuffed another mouthful of shahi korma between her lips, thankful the food was willing to settle in her uneasy stomach.

Much to Alexa's relief, neither of Sid's parents had made a big deal out of her delay. They were too polite to ask questions once they all sat at the table. After the salad course, everyone seemed to have forgotten the incident.

"Dr. Diyani, this is just amazing," Alexa repeated for the third time. So far, the conversation had revolved around Sid and Naija's school day. Sid gave a detailed description of his Prom-posal that morning, beaming the whole time. Sid's parents smiled and nodded while Naija giggled in the corner.

"Please, I'm not in the office. Call me Ira," Ira said, sipping a glass of white wine.

"Honestly, I thought stuff like what you did, Sid, only happened in movies." Alexa fought the urge to grab his hand and tell him how much she loved him.

"You can blame Mateo," Sid said. "Last Wednesday, he announced you were going dress shopping this last weekend, and I better ask you to prom on Monday, or he would kick my a—er—butt."

Naija giggled. "You were going to say 'ass,' weren't you?"

"Naija!" Ira's eyebrows raised while Sid's father hid a smile. "You are not allowed that kind of language at the dinner table, young lady."

Naija bowed her head and pouted. "But Sid says it all the time."

"Sid, what kind of example are you setting for your sister?" Ira sat back in her chair, frowning at her oldest son, but her eyes sparkled.

"Sorry, Mom, won't happen again." Sid fought back a laugh by sticking out his bottom lip in Naija's direction.

"Did you find a dress, Alexa?" Ira's intelligent gaze seemed to take Alexa apart piece by piece.

Alexa nodded. "Yes."

"Something black?" Umar smirked, then must have realized he may have been a little too presumptuous. "I'm sure you'll look lovely in whatever you chose."

"Actually, it's *not* a black dress," Alexa said. "Mateo found the perfect dress, even if it's not the type of thing I normally wear."

"What color, what color?" Naija wiggled in her seat.

Alexa leaned toward her conspiratorially. "It's a surprise."

Najia beamed. "I love surprises."

Alexa's phone buzzed again and, once again, she ignored it. "Did either of you go to prom? I mean, before you met each other in med school?"

Umar's lips quirked. "I swear I didn't hit puberty until my sophomore year at Northwestern. And no one wanted to date the skinny Indian kid at my high school. Ira's experience was a bit different than mine. Didn't you go with the captain of the football team?"

Ira shrugged. "I did. I was prom queen too. I would have been a cheerleader if my mother hadn't thought it inappropriate. She didn't care much for the uniform's short skirts."

Sid said, "You should see the pictures."

"Have you figured out all of your prom night plans?" Ira said.

"We've got a short list of restaurants," Sid said. "The limo is already booked. And we're planning to crash at Ashley's place after prom. I can give you Ashley's parents' number if you want."

This was news to Alexa, but she didn't mind. She planned on going with the flow when it came to anything prom-related. They would probably go to some over-priced restaurant in Minneapolis, dance at prom, then head to Ashley's for the afterparty, which would likely include a lot of booze.

"I would appreciate that." Ira steepled her fingers. "You're an adult now, so I promise not to helicopter you all the time. And over the past six months, you've rebuilt our trust. It's only fair to let you live a little."

Of all the parents, Sid's were by far the most distressed over what had happened. While Alexa was in a partial coma, Ira and Umar pressed the police for a full investigation. After a long debate between the parental units, everyone agreed to keep the whole incident quiet. Shortly thereafter, a series of teenage drug overdoses within the community replaced any interest in three spoiled children gone missing from Riverview only to be found in Oregon.

"What are your plans for the summer, Alexa?" Ira fixed Alexa with her penetrating gaze.

"I'm thinking about getting a job." Alexa tucked her trembling hands between her knees. "My parents and I agree that it would be good for me. You know, following a schedule, being a good employee, developing work ethic, and all that stuff."

Alexa's phone buzzed again in her pocket. Was Mateo trying to get a hold of her? She didn't dare pull it out in the middle of dinner.

"And then off to college," Umar said. "You're going to the University of Minnesota, right? And what are you planning to study?"

Alexa and Sid exchanged a long look. Alexa opened her mouth to speak, but Sid squeezed her leg and cleared his throat. "Actually, she's planning to go to Boston University instead."

Ira and Umar stared at them. Ira appeared stunned, Umar confused.

"I figured if I wanted to study art, I should go where I can find some of the greatest art galleries in the world. New York City is only a train ride away if I want to check out the MoMa or the Guggenheim. I think I want to study art education. I hope someday I can be an art professor. Or maybe study art and psychology. Art therapy is fascinating."

"Oh, art therapy, huh?" Umar nodded, half-heartedly feigning enthusiasm.

"Do, uh, do your parents know, Alexa?" Ira smoothed her hair and threw back her last gulp of wine.

"I planned on telling them tomorrow." Alexa swallowed the tight lump in her throat.

Everyone lapsed into silence. Alexa glanced in Sid's direction, and he gave her a hopeful smile. Ira and Umar exchanged a couple more looks before Umar poured them another glass of wine. Naija was the only one unbothered by the quiet, munching on a piece of naan and humming tunelessly to herself.

Ira forced out a smile that didn't reach her eyes. "Is everyone ready for dessert?"

Umar jumped up like a man looking for an excuse to leave. "Let me get it."

"No, no, allow me." Ira's smile turned into a slight grimace, and she hurried back to the kitchen.

"Why is this such a big deal?" Sid whispered to his father across the table.

Umar sighed and settled back into his seat. "Your mother just doesn't want you to have any—uh—she wants you to be completely focused on school when you're at Harvard."

"Are you saying my relationship with Lex is a distraction?" Sid's voice rose in volume.

Umar shook his head. "Not at all. You know you won't have the time for each other that you have now. The two of you are effortlessly sailing through this semester, from what I can tell. But college is different. It's much more intense."

Alexa's phone vibrated again. Desperate for a distraction, she dug into her pocket and pulled out her phone.

"This is a great opportunity for Alexa too." Sid's jaw clenched. "Boston University is an excellent school."

"Why are you so mad at each other?" Naija whimpered.

Alexa punched in her passcode, her thumb too sweaty for the fingerprint lock. She read the three messages on her phone then reread them. Her hands shook as she tried to understand who would send her such intimidating messages.

Alexa Baxter.

You cannot avoid us forever.

We know what you know.

Ira returned to the dining room carrying the dessert course. "Who is ready for some gulab jamun?"

Everyone stared at each other for several seconds until Naija shoved her hand into the air. "Me!"

Chapter 8

Alexa couldn't stop flinching at every shadow, every glaring headlight as she drove home. Had her fears been confirmed? Had the MGA sent someone to spy on her? Maybe. Several times over the last few months, a creeping sensation slunk down her spine as if someone was following or watching her. She had blamed her paranoia on leftover trauma from Una and the Brume. How could anyone go through such a crazy experience and remain sane?

Una's death wasn't the end of the story. From the little Alexa had retained from the Brume's brief possession, follow-up was protocol. The MGA wouldn't take a mercenary's word without sending a team to verify the Brume's report. What Alexa knew about the multiverse could change everything on Earth—if anyone actually believed her. Were there others who also knew? Or could she be the only one?

Stopping at a red light, Alexa had to acknowledge that if she didn't have her strange new abilities, she would have eventually convinced herself none of it had happened. Even the strands of Una's hair in the locket she hid in her underwear drawer could be explained away if she really wanted to forget.

A car horn blared behind her. Alexa jumped and hit the gas.

Bearing her burdens alone had taken its toll, but what could she do? If she was right about being monitored—bizarre texts certainly didn't alleviate such concerns—then what next?

You can't avoid us forever.

Did they expect her to text them back? There was no way in hell. Before leaving Sid's, she had made a half-hearted attempt to block the number. She wasn't surprised when her phone couldn't perform the request.

We know what you know.

And what was that? How could anyone know her thoughts? She hadn't written any of them down anywhere, had she? The text exchanges between Sid, Alexa, Mateo, and her parents had magically disappeared several days after she returned from Oregon. What about the texts between her and Mateo over the last several months? At first, she had planned to tell Mateo everything when the time was right. But she later realized telling him anything could put him in danger.

She steered her Honda left and wove through a suburban neighborhood adjacent to her own. Sometimes, she hated how loopy and windy the streets outside Riverview city limits could be. Why not stick to a grid? Why make panicked people like her accidentally drive down a dead end when she just wanted to get home?

Turning into her driveway, Alexa realized she had to face the truth. She wasn't okay. She would never be okay, and trying to hold herself together might cause her to shatter into a thousand pieces. She parked and rested her head against the steering wheel. Maybe she should just text them back and get it over with.

Get *what* over with? What would they do to her if she sent them a message? Would they send someone to hunt her down like they did with Una?

Alexa shivered, looking at her rearview mirror, recalling a moment when the Bright One had stared back at her with eyes like galaxies.

You are the only one who can save me. Please do not give up on me, Alexa.

Alexa yelped when her phone vibrated in her jacket pocket. She hesitated a moment before digging out her device. What now? Her state of mind couldn't handle another cryptic text. Holding her breath, she scanned her notifications. Nothing to worry about, just Sid asking if she got home safe and sound. She dipped deeper into her notifications to find that the text messages had disappeared just like before.

Had the messages ever existed? Was she reaching a new level of delusion? Either way, sitting in her car trying to hold herself together wouldn't help. Like many times before, Alexa hid her fears behind a fragile mental wall and exited her vehicle. She had to hold onto the real, the tangible, and not let herself get lost in impossible memories.

Stepping into her warm, cozy home, the smell of cinnamon and vanilla filling her nose, Alexa's intergalactic worries fell aside. She entered the kitchen to find her mother pulling a tray out of the oven while Andrea nibbled a cookie.

"Hey, how was dinner with Sid's family?" Cynthia blew a lock of hair from her face as she laid cookies on a cooling rack.

"Mmm, are those Snickerdoodles?" Alexa's nose drew her toward the several dozen cookies spread across the kitchen counters. "What's the occasion?"

"Oh, I just felt like baking." Cynthia shrugged, sliding another tray into the oven.

"Oh, yeah?" Alexa tossed an uncertain look her sister's way. Her mother only baked when she was unhappy or stressed. Andrea winced and mouthed a word Alexa couldn't quite catch. Alexa shook her head, conveying her confusion. Andrea rolled her eyes, grabbed her phone, and texted out the message.

She knows about Boston.

Blood drained from Alexa's face. Two sets of unhappy parents in one night? She wasn't sure she had it in her. "Well, I've got a pile of homework to dig through—"

Cynthia banged the oven door closed. "So, I've never been one of those horrible mothers who digs through her daughter's sock drawer. I respect your privacy and your boundaries because you're an adult. But I did laundry today, and well..."

Alexa gripped the edge of the counter. She should have run when she had the chance. A tall glass of chardonnay sat beside the mixing bowls, and her mother took a gulp, much like Ira had an hour before.

"Mom, I told you I like to put my own clothes away." Alexa cursed herself for not having a better hiding spot. Of all the places to put her acceptance packet from Boston

University. Ensuring her parents hadn't seen it arrive in the mail in the first place had taken quite an effort.

"Your father is going to be thrilled." Cynthia shook her head, punching ten minutes into the oven timer. "East Coast school. One of the top universities in the country. I'm not going to lie. When I heard Sid was officially going to Harvard, I wondered if you might take another look at your options. But I never thought you wouldn't at least say something to me."

"It was a last-minute decision," Alexa said. "You know I had a hard time when I got back and, well, Sid really helped me get through a lot of it. So, when Sid told me he got early admission into Harvard, it was just ... something I had to do. Barely made it in before the application deadline."

"I wondered a little, especially with your SAT scores." Cynthia sipped her wine and sagged onto a kitchen chair. "When were you going to tell us?"

"Enrollment deposit is due May 1... so by the end of the week."

Cynthia blew a puff of air between her lips. "You know, I always thought you'd head West, like to Seattle or Portland."

"The birthplace of grunge music?" Alexa laughed. "Yeah, I sometimes thought that too."

"Does Mateo know?" Andrea said.

"Not yet. We haven't talked about going to college together in a while." In fact, he hadn't texted her yet that night. Once upon a time, he couldn't wait to get all the details about her and Sid. But that was before he knew she was a liar, would never tell him the whole truth, and couldn't forgive her for it.

Cynthia pursed her lips, deep in thought for a moment, and took another drink of chardonnay. She bobbed her head left, then right. "Well, of course, I don't want you to move away. I was honestly relieved you wanted to stay in the Midwest. Especially after ... But if you want to go to Boston, you should go to Boston."

"That's what I want."

"Okay, then." Cynthia put down her glass and opened her arms. "Then give me a hug before you hide for the rest of the night. And when your dad gets home from his work trip, you'll tell him the great news right away. Okay?"

"You bet." Alexa leaned into her mother's cinnamon-and-sugar embrace. At least her parents would be happy for her.

Cynthia kissed her brow. "And tell Mateo. I know things haven't been the same between you two for a while, but he needs to know."

The knot in Alexa's chest tightened again, but her mother was right. "I will."

Chapter 9

Cynthia was right. Alexa's father was thrilled about Boston University and didn't care one bit about her heading to the same city as Sid. "You're going to an excellent school. That's all that matters."

Her father's enthusiasm softened when she mentioned her hopes of studying art education or therapy. "You know, you'd make a great lawyer."

Alexa, Andrea, and Cynthia agreed Alexa would *not* make a good lawyer.

The rest of the week went as most weeks did. Alexa and Andrea drove to school. Alexa met Sid and his friends in the atrium each morning, went to class, took her notes, and focused on getting through her senior year. Alexa tried half-heartedly to find the right moment to tell Mateo about Boston University. However, the EME team seemed glued to Mateo's side, always twittering in the background. Alexa had all summer to tell him the truth. Maybe after graduation, she would find the right time.

No new ominous texts arrived, so Alexa did what came easiest: pretend everything was fine until something happened to remind her otherwise. She focused her energies on school, prom plans, and Sid.

Sid's friends, Ryan and Ashley, sorted out who would be a part of their pre-prom dinner party. They picked a nice but not too nice restaurant in Minneapolis. A stretch limo rental was confirmed, and Ashley's afterparty quickly became the most exclusive invite in town. Ashley's parents were the type to believe it was fine if their daughter wanted to drink, as long as she didn't leave the house when she did so. Alexa expected the party would digress into an epic drunk-fest, and though she wasn't much of a partier, if not on prom night, then when?

Sid didn't let go of his request for her to seek help either. He brought it up at least once a day when they hung out after school, finishing up homework at either of their houses. She danced around his suggestions, changing the subject (which was easy with so many end-of-semester distractions), but eventually, he lost his patience.

"Is it wrong that I want to help you?" Sid blurted out on a Friday afternoon while he worked on calculus problems and she read an article on the history of the Supreme Court for civics.

Alexa startled in her chair, pencil running in a wild arc across her notebook. "Help me?"

"Whatever you're going through, you're not getting better. You're good at hiding it from everyone else, but I can always tell."

Alexa began to say something, but Sid interrupted.

"And don't try to change the subject this time. What happens when we move to Boston? What if your panic attacks get worse?"

Alexa fought the urge to run up the stairs and hide in her room. "I—uh—I don't know."

"Here." Sid turned his laptop in her direction. "I did a little research and found some really good—"

"That's not necessary." Flustered, Alexa tried to refocus on her textbook. "My—uh—Mom and I were going to look over some options this weekend."

"That's what you said two weeks ago. Please, just take a—"

Alexa jumped up from the sectional. "Hey, I'm kinda thirsty. I'm going to go get a bottle of water."

"Lex, this isn't cute anymore." Sid snapped shut his laptop. "You promised. If you won't go to therapy for yourself, then do it for me. For your parents. Heck, for Mateo. He's worried about you too."

Alexa's cheeks burned. "Are you two talking behind my back?"

"No, it's just that...you two don't talk to each other anymore. Do you? What's up with that?"

"It's complicated." Her throat tightened. She had spent so much time lately avoiding tough questions. Perhaps Sid deserved a kernel of truth.

"That's okay." Sid set aside his homework, grabbed the glass of water beside him, and took a long drink. "I'm not going anywhere."

Alexa closed her textbook and clutched it to her chest. "You know how you don't like talking about what happened last October?"

This time, Sid squirmed. "Yeah. I just want to move on with my life. Nothing good came out of that ordeal, so why would I *want* to remember?"

"Nothing good?" Alexa clutched the textbook tighter.

Sid gave her his signature crooked grin. "You're the exception, of course."

"Well, Mateo's the opposite. I told him what I remembered, and he didn't believe me. He's sure I'm keeping something from him."

Sid leaned back into the overstuffed couch. "Don't take this the wrong way, Lex, but even I know you're not telling us the whole truth."

The warmth drained from Alexa's face. "What are you talking about?"

"I know you pretty well at this point. And you've never been a good liar. That's the other reason why I don't ask questions. I hate watching you spin whatever truth you choose to share with us."

She curled further into her corner of the couch. "Really? I...uh...well—"

"Hey," Sid reached for her, "it's fine. I don't care. Truly. But I think you should consider telling Mateo what actually happened. He deserves to know."

"What happened..." Alexa pictured the first time Mateo met Una, his eyes wide, jaw slack. He had barely believed what stood before him. "Take my word for it when I say there's a reason neither of you remembers what happened. Hell, I'm not supposed to remember either. If they found out ... I don't know what they'd do."

"They? Do you mean Una and Burt? I thought they were long gone?"

A dull throb built behind Alexa's eyes. "Never mind. I'm probably being paranoid."

Sid frowned. "Do we have to worry about Burt trying to find us? You made it sound like we'd never see him again. Or Una."

The throb blossomed into a stabbing pain. "I don't think we will. Like I said, I'm just being paranoid. Burt is long gone."

"Lex, why are you—"

Snap.

"Crap." Sid jumped up from the couch, dripping glass of water in hand.

"What happened?" Alexa leaped up too.

"Did you notice a crack in this glass before?" Sid hurried out of the room, leaving a trail of dribbling water behind him.

Alexa's headache immediately receded. "Not again."

"What?" Sid shouted from the kitchen. Alexa could hear him setting the broken glass in the sink.

"No, I didn't notice a crack." She rubbed her forehead and dropped back onto the couch. Saved by telekinesis.

Alexa's mom and Andrea walked through the front door, their bright voices echoing through the foyer and into the living room. Sid met them there, spurting out a series of apologies for breaking one of Cynthia's glasses.

"Don't worry about it, Sid." Looking fresh despite returning from another intense yoga session, Alexa's mom strolled into the living room with Sid at her heels. "I'm just glad you didn't cut yourself. I'm making lasagna if you feel like staying for dinner."

Sid returned to his place on the couch, dish rag in hand. "Thanks for the invite, but It's Fiesta Friday, and Naija would not forgive me if I missed it."

Andrea sauntered into the living room, also looking lovely despite her flushed, post-volleyball practice state. "You're such a nice big brother."

"Okay, well, if anybody needs anything, I'll be in the kitchen," Cynthia said.

Andrea surveyed Alexa, eyes roving from foot to brow once then twice. "You look tense, Lex. Did you two fight or something?"

Alexa flinched. "What are you talking about?"

"You may not notice, but you carry a lot of tension in your shoulders." Andrea shrugged and sniffed her damp practice gear. "Yuck. Oh, and, shit, I meant to text you earlier." Andrea grabbed her phone from her gym bag. "But my battery was almost dead. Someone with a fake Instagram is posting all the places Riverview seniors are heading for college."

Alexa dropped her pencil. "Why would someone do that?"

"Cuz everyone wants to know, silly." Andrea scrolled through her phone. "And someone figured out that you were going to Boston University. They put your name right next to Sid's and might have added a couple of heart emojis."

"How is this possible?" Alexa stopped breathing for a second. If Andrea had seen the post, then Mateo had too. "I thought only our families knew, Sid."

Sid winced. "I might have told Drew a couple days ago."

Alexa's voice sailed up several octaves. "Why would you do that?"

"He was giving me shit about long-distance relationships, and I … I'm so sorry. He promised he wouldn't say anything to anyone."

Alexa immediately whipped out her phone and called Mateo. She didn't dare send him a text at such a critical moment. She fought back tears when her call went straight to voicemail. Mateo always picked up the phone when she called, even if he was in the shower.

"This is bad." Alexa's stomach clenched. Five of the seven family pictures hanging on the wall opposite her went crooked. The other two vibrated on their hangars. "This is really, really bad."

Chapter 10

Alexa knew the exact moment she and Mateo's relationship began to fracture.

Last November, a month after their cross-country adventure with Una, Alexa and Sid had gone on several coffee dates. She sensed his interest was no longer academic. He gazed at her as if she was something special, something he wanted. She couldn't believe her luck. After years of quietly pining for him, the feeling was finally mutual.

Her relationship with Mateo, however, had grown strained. Alexa's back and neck tensed whenever he texted or approached her in school. They gradually spent less time together. She had sensed his creeping jealousy about her and Sid's new connection, but he never said the words. Around the same time, Mateo found a new friend group with Emma, Madison, and Emily. Alexa wasn't thrilled with his choice of friends, but she knew better than to say anything.

Until one fateful Friday night.

Since the beginning of their freshman year, Alexa and Mateo had spent Friday evenings together watching movies and eating junk food. Mateo had been uncharacteristically quiet at school earlier that day. He said little at lunch, choosing instead to scroll through his phone. It was the last time they ate lunch together in the art room.

That evening, Mateo arrived with a half-hearted greeting. From the worried expression on his face, Alexa sensed it was only a matter of time before he cracked. She had opened the popcorn and prepped the movie for streaming when he made a strange sound. Something between a yelp and a sob. She turned to her best friend to see tears and Urban Decay mascara pouring down his face.

Alexa didn't know what to do. She clutched the blanket draped over her shoulders instead of her weeping best friend.

"Aren't you going to ask me why I'm crying?" Mateo sputtered, dabbing at his eyes.

"Why are you crying?" Alexa scanned the room for a Kleenex or a towel or something to clean the mess on her friend's face.

"Because my best friend in the whole world is a liar."

"Oh, that." She sunk to the floor and leaned against the entertainment center.

"Does Sid know the truth?" Mateo bawled.

"No, he doesn't really care."

"Seriously?" Mateo shook his head, flicking away a damp lock of hair pasted to his cheek. "You mean he believes in this whole Una-and-the-bad-boyfriend story?"

"Sid wants to get back to as normal a life as possible. Don't you?"

"I guess." Mateo pouted. "Who was Una? Who was she? Why can't I remember her face?"

Alexa had pressed her lips together tightly while images of Una looped through her thoughts. Even if she told him the truth, he would never believe her.

"Alexa Baxter," Mateo snapped. "I deserve to know who Una is. Does she have a last name? Where was she from?"

"I told you. I met Una while record shopping at Electric Fetus. She liked nineties grunge, just like me."

"And you, of all people, were the only one who could help her?"

That part was mostly true. "All Una's friends knew her ex, and her ex knew them. She asked me for help because I was outside her circle. I wasn't traceable."

"Then why does the word unicorn keep popping into my mind when I try to remember Una?"

"Because she was wearing a t-shirt with a unicorn on it." The lie came so quickly that she almost believed it.

"And why do you remember stuff and we don't?"

"I have no idea—"

"Yes, you do, and that's the part that bothers me the most. Something awful happened, and you won't tell me. What if I have permanent brain damage?"

According to the bits of information the Brume had left behind, such a thing wasn't possible. At least, the Brume hadn't thought so.

"I've told you all I know," Alexa whispered, dropping her gaze to the floor.

"Fuck you, Alexa." Mateo jumped up from the couch, wiping tears from his cheeks. "I'm out. I can't look at you anymore."

"Mateo, please—"

Mateo's determined footsteps had thundered down the hallway, where he grabbed his coat and slammed the front door behind him.

Eventually, Mateo's frustration reduced to an annoyed simmer. They still hung out sometimes, but their once-deep, unconditional friendship seemed beyond repair.

And now, four, nearly five months later, Alexa sat in front of the coffee shop where he worked some school nights and every Saturday morning. She could see him buzzing behind the counter, making espresso drinks for a line of customers. She should give him the weekend to cool off and let his fury soften until Monday. Bothering him at work was the absolute wrong thing to do, but she had the nagging feeling that if she held off until Monday, he might permanently remove her from his life. Her going off to Boston University could be the final nail in the coffin of their dying friendship.

Alexa waited twenty minutes for the line of customers to diminish. When only one customer remained, she popped out of her car and hurried to the coffee shop door before she could change her mind.

Once upon a time, when she would visit Mateo during a shift, he would bounce on his toes and squeal with delight. Now, handing a spiky-haired woman her coffee, he didn't even acknowledge her presence.

The customer passed in a cloud of espresso and vanilla, and Alexa stepped up to Mateo's register.

"Welcome to Latte Da. Can I interest you in a blueberry cobbler latte?" Mateo's eyes were fixed to a point just above her head, his voice a flat monotone.

Yep, Mateo was super pissed. She stuffed her hands in her pockets so he wouldn't see them shaking, and kept her tone light. "Ugh, do people actually order that?"

"The Karens live for it." Mateo maintained his expressionless demeanor.

"Can I get my usual?"

"You have a usual?" Mateo turned to a sparkling young woman Alexa recognized as one of Mateo's favorite co-workers. "Meadow, apparently, this woman has a 'usual' order here, but I have no idea what she's talking about. I've never seen her in my life."

Meadow rolled her eyes. "I bet she wants a mocha latte with an extra shot of espresso and oat milk. Does that sound right, Alexa?"

"Yep, that's it."

"I'll get that started." Meadow nudged Mateo's elbow and headed over to the espresso machine.

"Anything else I can get you today, Miss?" Mateo pursed his lips, punching in her order.

"Maybe five minutes with my friend? Can we talk?"

"You mean Meadow, right? Because you can't possibly mean me."

"Please, Mateo. Five minutes, and I'll leave you alone for as long as you want."

"That'll be six twenty-five, *Miss*." Mateo held out his hand.

Alexa handed him a twenty. "You can keep the change if you give me five minutes."

"Trying to buy me off, are we?"

"Please. Just ... please."

"Ugh, fine. Meadow, I'm taking a cigarette break. Can you hold down the fort?"

Meadow sighed, handing Alexa her mocha. "Sure."

"Meet me out back." Mateo flipped his bangs out of his eyes and headed toward the back storeroom.

Alexa took a deep breath and hurried out the front door. She jogged around the building, mocha sloshing down her hand. She paused to lick up the mess, her heart racing with faint hope. There was a time when she believed nothing could come between her and Mateo. The multiverse had other ideas in mind.

Rounding the corner, Alexa found her best friend leaning against the coffee shop's back door with a straw between his teeth, blowing out an imaginary lungful of smoke.

"You had a lot of nerve coming to my workplace." Mateo fixed his eyes on a line of dumpsters, wrinkling his nose at the faint stench wafting their way.

"I'm sorry. I'm the worst. I had every intention of telling you before the news went public. Sid made the mistake of telling Drew. And what Drew knows, Ashley knows."

"And Ashley couldn't keep such a juicy tidbit to herself." Mateo gnawed on the straw, thoughtful. "The EME team told me as soon as they found out."

"I should have told you as soon as we told our parents."

"I guess I wasn't all that surprised. It wouldn't be the first time you withheld the truth from me. Why wouldn't you go to Boston? I see how you are without Sid, and it's frankly sad. Like a lost little bird."

Alexa braced herself against his words. "I love him, so it makes sense I would want to be around him all the time."

"You don't just love him. You're using him as a Band-Aid. Meanwhile, you're emotionally bleeding out everywhere.

And I don't know if I can sit around and watch it happen anymore. What will you do when he's too busy to help you? You have plenty of time to hang out now, but he's going to Harvard, for fuck's sake. You think he will race to your side when he's in the middle of class?"

"I've taken that into consideration," Alexa sputtered, fighting to stand firm against the truth he hurled.

"And why wouldn't you want to run away with the boy who doesn't question your panic attacks or the fact that you flinch at shadows? You think he's helping you, but he isn't. How can we help when you don't tell us what's wrong?"

"No one can help me." Tears burned Alexa's eyes. She turned to get the hell out of there, but Mateo grabbed her hand. A sob bubbled in her chest, fighting to be let out. Mateo was right. Running off to Boston would solve nothing, but she didn't know what else to do.

"Alexa, you need to tell someone, anyone, what you're dealing with." Mateo gripped her hand so tight her joints popped. "It doesn't have to be me, but you can't keep living like this."

"That's what Sid said," Alexa murmured, her voice coming out in stops and gasps. "But I can't—it's not safe."

"What's not safe?"

"I can't—you don't—it's dangerous for you to know what I know."

Mateo frowned, surprised. "Dangerous? Why?"

"I know things I'm not supposed to." Alexa looked up and down the service road behind the strip mall. Someone might be listening in on their conversation. She half expected to see one of the mysterious figures pop its head around a corner.

"Does it have to do with Burt? Is he, like, harassing you or something?"

She shook her head. "No, I haven't heard from Burt since the lake."

"Does it have something to do with Una? I know all this is Una's fault somehow. Is she still in contact with you?"

"Una is dead."

The straw tumbled from Mateo's lips. "What?"

Alexa flinched. Someone was watching them. She scanned the empty street, unable to shake the feeling.

"How did Una die? Did Burt kill her? Is that why he strangled you, because you got in the way? Lex, why didn't you tell me this before? Why didn't you tell the police? Oh, my God, I can't believe the words coming out of my mouth. This sounds like some kind of crazy murder podcast. But then, how did Sid and I lose our memories? Ugh! None of this makes sense."

Alexa didn't dare say more. She had already said too much. What if she finally showed him the hairs in the locket? Maybe if he touched the flaxen strands, everything would return to him, as it did for her. And then what? Sentence him to the same nightmares that followed her everywhere she went?

Her phone vibrated. She ignored it at first until it shook a second time, then a third.

"Lex, you have to tell me how she died." Mateo shook Alexa's shoulders, his eyes wild. "I'll go to the police with you. You don't have to go through this alone."

Alexa pulled out her phone.

"You're not seriously looking at your phone right now, are you?" Mateo snapped.

"I'm just. It's just ..."

Something had told Alexa that she ought to look this time. Three messages covered her home screen.

We will not tolerate this silence.

You have seven days to answer us.

Otherwise, we will take severe action.

Seven days. Funny, prom was in seven days. Alexa barked out a laugh, tucking her phone into her back pocket. The straw that fell from Mateo's lips spun like a propeller on the asphalt. She couldn't look away, shoving her fear, anger, and frustration into spinning the straw faster and faster while Mateo rubbed away tears.

"Alexa, what are you—"

The straw took flight, hurling through the air and skating into the sky. A gust of wind lifted the little piece of plastic higher, so high she soon lost sight of her strange miracle.

Mateo watched the path of the straw. "Lex, what the fuck?"

"I have seven days," she said and raced back the way she came. She expected Mateo to throw an epic fit behind her, but he said nothing. She stumbled down along the backside of the strip mall, the world receding around her. She dug out her keys, unlocked her car, and settled into the driver's seat.

Seven days. Alexa could hang on for seven more days, couldn't she? Be the Shadow girl, Queen of Darkness, girlfriend to Sid, bad friend to Mateo, and daughter to her parents. After those seven days? She would find out if she could survive her greatest fear: the world beyond her own.

Chapter 11

As Alexa moved through the next several days, time followed an inconsistent path. Moments could feel like hours while she was in class, trying to concentrate on lectures, assignments, and the occasional quiz she handed in half-finished. What was the point of doing well in school when her life might irrevocably change in a couple days? Occasionally, she surfaced from the haze, leaning into Sid, smiling at a joke made by one of his friends, or remembering prom was still around the corner.

The mundane world buzzed around Alexa as she sat perfectly still, afraid to do anything. If she did, she might admit the insane truth buzzing at the back of her mind. Her time had come. Those who once hunted Una figured out she knew things, that her mind hadn't been erased as promised.

What would they do to her? And who exactly was sending her the texts? Was it the Brumes? The MGA? Someone else? Alexa typed out several responses, losing the courage to send them each time. The previous text didn't disappear as the others had before. It remained in her notifications, persistently blinking each time she opened her phone.

They wanted a response. Expected a response. Perhaps the MGA existed in a different time than your average, impatient Earthling. What was a week in comparison to the vast multiverse?

Alexa expected Mateo to attack her with a flurry of questions at some point during the week, but he never did. They passed each other every day between third and fourth periods. She opened her mouth several times to say something, wishing for Mateo to confess ... what? But Mateo stared at her mournfully and whispered, "I'm here when you're ready. Or when you want my help."

Alexa nodded, her throat too thick to choke out words, and walked away. Next time.

On the fifth day of the seven-day deadline, Alexa decided to wait until the last moment to respond to the texts. She wanted to go to prom, after all. Even if pomp and circumstance wasn't her cup of tea, she didn't want to leave Earth before Sid twirled her across the dance floor in her beautiful dress. She deserved one last innocent teenage moment before the multiverse came to collect its due.

The morning of prom, Alexa unexpectedly found herself at one of the best salons in Riverview. Ashley's best friend had come down with a surprise bout of mono, which left a space open. Alexa decided since that night was possibly her last night on Earth, she might as well look good.

"You have such amazing cheekbones," the makeup artist cooed as she brushed on a shimmery blush.

"Thank you," Alexa murmured. This was her first time in a makeup chair, and the intimacy of the process made her a little uneasy. The whole week had been one queasy episode after another, bringing her to the night she had anticipated—and dreaded—for the past month.

"This is going to be the best night ever," Ashley squealed from the other side of the salon. "I look amazing." The willowy young woman raised her phone to take a pouty selfie.

"Yep, best night ever." Alexa muttered, ignoring the anxiety twisting her gut. A bottle of nail polish on the makeup table jiggled. She still hadn't figured out the key to keeping her emotions separate from her telekinetic abilities. In an attempt to calm down, she took a deep breath, held it for several seconds, then let it out when the makeup artist, Lilli, stepped back to check her work. The makeup artist—a combination of Cindy Lauper and Lady Gaga—surveyed Alexa's face from several angles.

"You have lovely eyes." Lilli grinned, appraising Alexa like an unfinished painting. "Is it okay if I bring them out a little more? Have you ever worn fake eyelashes before?"

"I never really wear makeup," Alexa admitted.

"Your friends are gonna flip when they see you," Lilli said. "Close your eyes. Let's glue these babies on."

Alexa did as she was told, no longer unnerved by the sensation of Lilli's careful touch but soothed by her attention to detail.

"You can open your eyes, hon. It's time for the big reveal."

Alexa turned to the mirror and peered into a face she knew so very well yet almost didn't recognize. "Oh, wow."

"I just sprinkled a little fairy dust on you." Lilli beamed. She gently placed a finger beneath Alexa's chin and surveyed her work. "Not that you needed it."

"Thank you, Lilli." The words caught in Alexa's throat.

"No crying, hon. It'll ruin your makeup. Have an amazing night."

"I will. Thank you." Alexa slid out of the salon chair, smoothed the front of her Nirvana t-shirt, hitched up the waist of her torn black jeans, and walked over to the three girls sitting in the lobby, deep in their cell phones.

"Uh, finally," Haleigh grumbled, flicking back one of her barrel curls.

"Oh, whoa, Alexa." Ashley, painted within an inch of her life, hair pinned back in a classic chignon, gaped. "You look—Sid's gonna die." She popped up from her seat. "Let's go. We only have an hour to get dressed before the limo arrives."

Alexa felt as if a fairy godmother had blessed her. She glided through her front door, glanced at her face in the foyer mirror, and couldn't help but giggle.

Cynthia popped into the front hall to check out what her money had paid for "Hey, Lex, how did it—" Her jaw dropped. Oh, look at you!"

"Lilli did a great job." Alexa grinned, pleased by her mother's reaction.

"You look beautiful. Hang on, can I take a picture?"

"Um, maybe later. I have to hurry up and get my dress on. I need you to drop me off at Ashley's in a half hour."

"Sounds good. Just yell for me when you're ready."

Alexa bounded up the stairs to her bedroom, feeling light as air. She pulled out her phone, ready to send Mateo a selfie of Lilli's fantastic work, but stopped dead in her tracks. A new message had arrived.

You are running out of time, Alexa Baxter.

"No," Alexa shuddered. She tossed her phone onto her bed as several books tumbled from the pile on her desk. One of the books fell open, pages flipping one after another. Her heart thundered.

They had promised her seven days, and her time had run out. What would happen if she decided to ignore them? What would they do?

Alexa held out her hand. All it took was a slight gesture for Starlight to fly across the room and land in her outstretched palm. What would the MGA do when they realized she could do things that no human should be able to do? It may be time to stop asking questions and find out.

Clutching her unicorn, Alexa grabbed her phone and typed, *What do you want?*

Instead of receiving an answer from her unseen antagonists, a text popped up from Sid. *I'm already at Ashley's house. When are you going to get here? Do you need me to pick you up?*

Alexa exhaled. Unseen creatures from the multiverse may be sending her threats, but it was still prom night. She texted back, *I'm about to put on my dress. See you in 20.*

Her mother had hung the dress from a hook on the back of her bedroom door. Alexa hurried over to the garment bag and pulled down the zipper. The delicate pink fabric shimmered beneath her trembling fingers. She pulled off her clothes, tossed each black item on the floor, and replaced them with the smooth, silky dress. She pulled up the zipper as far as she could, grabbed the shoe box containing the ridiculous heels Mateo had convinced her to buy, and dumped a few more items into her overnight bag.

Her phone buzzed several times as texts came in, but she didn't want to look. Not yet. For the next twenty minutes, she wanted to be nothing more than a teenager heading to her senior prom.

Chapter 12

Like Sid, Ashley lived in a large house overlooking the St. Croix River. Ashley's parents were executives at 3M, often jetting back and forth across the country, conveniently out of town. So Ashley's mansion was the party house for the popular kids of Riverview High.

When Alexa arrived, several girls from Sid's friend group were in the middle of a photo session on the front lawn. They flounced and bounced and posed like glittering pastel flowers, their skin just a little too tan and gleaming in the afternoon sun.

"Did someone hire a photographer?" Alexa's mom gaped, slowing their Range Rover to a steady crawl.

"Yep." Alexa double-checked her makeup in the mirror. Lilli had sent her off with a few items to maintain her look. Alexa's eyes looked huge against her shimmery cheeks. She touched the opal necklace her mother lent her for the evening, the pinks and purples in the stone matching her gown.

"You look beautiful, honey." Cynthia's eyes shone like she was about to cry. "Have lots of fun at dinner. I'll be in the stands for the Grand March. You have everything you need?"

"I should be good to go." Alexa lifted her battered backpack covered in 90s grunge band patches. She glanced at her phone one last time before tucking it into the front pocket of her bag. Much to her relief, the mysterious texter hadn't responded to her last message. She had done as they asked; now, she could only wait.

"Okay. Have fun. Be safe. I'd hug you if I wasn't worried about ruining your makeup. And please, be safe. Make good choices. You can always call me at any time if you need to come home or need help."

"I will." Alexa squeezed her mother's hand. "I love you."

"I love you too." Cynthia waved a hand in front of her face as tears fell. "Oh, my goodness. Go! Have fun with your friends."

Alexa gave one last reassuring smile, then pushed open the passenger door, gathered her skirts and, much like a trapeze artist, found her balance on the sparkly stilettos. She planned to wear the uncomfortable shoes until after the Grand March, then switch into her preferred Converse for the rest of the evening. She searched the lawn for Sid, but none of the boys were in sight.

A brassy voice burst across the lawn. "Is that Alexa?" The question came from one of the girls who were draping their lithe bodies against each other at the fountain near the mansion's entrance, posing for the photographer.

The photographer—a twenty-something woman dressed entirely in black with a neon streak of red through her dark hair—pivoted and snapped a picture of Alexa.

"Whoa, you don't have to do that." Alexa shielded her face with her hands. Unlike most girls her age, she didn't care for photographs. She was always caught in a blink, or her face involuntarily did something weird when she tried to smile.

"Oh my God, Alexa, you're wearing pink?" Ashley clopped down the cobblestone path between the fountain and the driveway. "Holy crap, you look amazing."

The four other girls gaped, shocked by her appearance.

Alexa tugged on her skirt. "I thought I'd try not to be the Queen of Darkness for once."

"You look fabulous, Lex." Ashley gave her a genuine smile. "You want to take some pictures with us? We were going to head back to the pool."

"Oh, no, that's okay," Alexa's cheeks burned at the girls' blatant stares. "Do you know where I can find Sid?"

"I think they're playing video games in the movie room." Ashley pointed a thumb toward the house. "I put you and Sid in the blue guest room downstairs. You know where that's at, right?"

It was Alexa's turn to be shocked. "We get a bedroom? Are your parents—"

"There's a bowl of condoms in the downstairs bathroom, too." Ashley nonchalantly scanned her phone.

"Bowl of—"

"Oh, Alexa, don't be such a prude." Haleigh giggled. "Ashley's parents are super progressive. They don't pretend that teens aren't screwing like rabbits."

"And my parents' policy is if you're drinking, you stay overnight. If you over-indulge, you clean up whatever messes you make or pay for a professional cleaner. And don't get sloppy. We're better than that, right?"

"Sure," Alexa said, once again feeling like a fish out of water.

"The limo is on its way. Can you tell the guys?" Ashley checked her reflection on her cell phone. "Let's head to the pool!"

Alexa followed the girls and the photographer toward the house. She had attended enough parties at Ashley's home to know her way around. Her feet were throbbing by the time she teetered through the soaring foyer. She tugged off her shoes before heading beneath the grand staircase to a short hall leading to the basement stairs.

She could hear the sounds of gunshots and explosions when she reached the bottom of the stairway. Ashley's brother—an avid gamer—had an elaborate system in the movie room that would rival any in Riverview.

Instead of heading to the movie room, she went down the hall leading to the guest rooms in Ashley's basement. She poked her head into several rooms until she found what had to be the "blue" guest room. Sid had already dropped his duffle bag on the bed. Alexa shivered as she dropped her bag beside his. She ran her hands over the duvet then rechecked her phone to see if the unknown number had sent her any new messages.

Nothing. Was all this a big mistake? If it had been a wrong number all along, Alexa had been worried about nothing. But then, how did they know her name? Was one of Sid's friends messing with her? Suddenly, the idea of multiverses and unseen agents surveilling her sounded utterly ridiculous.

Alexa turned back to the bed. She and Sid had never had a room to themselves for a night. They wouldn't have to anticipate their parents' schedule or steal a few minutes alone. Was she ready to take that step?

"Wow, Alexa?" Suit jacket in hand, Sid stood in the doorway, eyes wide.

Alexa fluffed out her skirt. "Hey, sorry, I was hoping for a big reveal moment, but, well, here I am!"

"You're wearing pink?" Sid surveyed Alexa from head to toe, his smile increasing in size. "You look really, really good in pink."

"It's Mateo's fault." Alexa blushed.

Sid took her hand and kissed her knuckles. "I'll have to thank him later. So, uh, I didn't know about the whole guest bedroom situation. Ashley's also turning the downstairs den into a slumber party if you're uncomfortable with all this."

Alexa took a deep breath and clutched his hand. "What if I'm okay with it?" Her head felt air-filled, ready to disconnect and float into the sky. "How often do we get a chance to be alone?"

"Yeah?" Sid ran a hand down her exposed back, and Alexa shivered. "But are you sure? Cuz I don't want you to feel like you have to. It's a huge deal for both of us."

"You love me, I love you." Alexa gave a nonchalant shrug even as her stomach quivered in anticipation. "It feels right to me."

Sid blew out a long breath. "Okay. But like I said. You can change your mind. I want both of us to be all in."

"And so can you."

Sid cupped her face in his warm hands and dropped a gentle kiss upon her lips. "I love you, Alexa."

"I love you, too." Alexa's heart thrummed in her chest—a tiny hummingbird threatening to burst out. She ignored the persistent whisper in the back of her mind, repeatedly asking why he loved her. Was it true love or the Brume's influence?

"Limo's here!" someone shouted down the stairs.

"Let's have the best night ever," Sid murmured in her ear.

"A night we'll never forget." Alexa grabbed her purse and shoes then followed Sid and the rest of his friends to the stretch limo.

Chapter 13

"**O**h, my God, is *that* Alexa Baxter?" A voice shouted from the crowd.

"Sure is." Alexa's cheeks ached from a night of grinning. She, Sid, and the rest of their posse had just unloaded from their limo and headed for the gym doors.

Alexa never wished to be a princess but felt like teenage royalty with Sid standing beside her. She enjoyed the reactions to her appearance. Compliments came from far and wide, even from people who had never spoken to her before. For once, she basked in their attention.

"Okay, I know it's cheesy, but do you want to get a picture?" Sid nodded to the glittering prom-goers waiting for photos before they lined up for the Grand March. The prom committee had hung a blue curtain and covered it with plastic seaweed, a fishing net, and a bunch of fake fish to stick with their "Sea of Love" theme.

"This whole thing is corny as hell, so why not?" Alexa laughed as a couple tangled themselves in the fishing net.

"I knew it." Mateo exited the crowd, his polished and plucked EME Team in tow. He wore a powder blue tuxedo stolen he'd taken out of his grandfather's closet. From his shiny patent leather shoes to the ruffled button-up dress shirt, Mateo looked fabulous.

Alexa held her breath. They hadn't spoken all week.

"I knew you would look absolutely amazing," Mateo gushed as he tugged Alexa from Sid's side and directed her to twirl around. "Look at those alterations. And your makeup? Holy shit, Lex, you are a goddess."

"I'm glad you picked it out for me." She swallowed the knot in her throat.

"I know that look on your face." Mateo elegantly brushed back his hair, studied Alexa for another second, then leaned close. "Don't worry. Tonight, we'll let bygones be bygones. I still have a whole summer to get the truth out of you."

Alexa pressed her lips tightly together and nodded, afraid if she said anything, she might break the spell everyone was under. Mateo's girl gang immediately swarmed her the moment Mateo stepped back.

"Yes, that's right. I'm the one who convinced our lady in black to wear pink," Mateo said loud enough for everyone nearby to hear. "I'm available for consultations if anyone is interested."

Eventually, it was Alexa and Sid's turn to have their picture taken. They settled on the classic prom pose—Alexa standing with her back against Sid as he wrapped his arms around her waist—then hopped into the line for the Grand March.

"This is why I don't wear heels," Alexa grumbled, leaning against Sid and rotating her ankles one at a time.

"I'm surprised you still have them on," Sid said.

"Ugh, I know," Alexa glanced in her purse, searching for the ibuprofen her mother had slipped into the inner pocket before heading to Ashley's that afternoon. "I know the pain of stilettos all too well," her mother had said.

Alexa's phone buzzed as she snapped the purse closed again. Out of habit, she pulled out her phone and read the screen.

Alexa Baxter, we apologize if we've frightened you. We only wish to speak with you. We know you remember the Bright One.

Alexa nearly dropped her phone.

"Everything okay?" Sid slid a hand down her back. "Are you cold?"

"No, I, uh, no." Alexa stared at the two messages, unable to look away.

"You're covered in goosebumps. Are you sure?" Sid leaned over to read the phone screen. "Who wants to speak to you?"

Alexa slapped the phone against her chest. "Uh...it's, uh...someone from Boston University. Um, Admissions, I think. I asked them some questions about housing."

"And they texted you? On a weekend night? Huh, crazy."

"I was put in contact with, uh, a student in the art department, and they're, uh, helping me figure out some things." Alexa smiled even as her heart raced and black spots danced across her vision. She would not have a panic attack at prom. *She would not have a panic attack at prom.*

Her fingers hovered above her phone. She needed to respond, but what the hell should she say? Of course, the texts weren't a misunderstanding. Who else would know about the Bright One? Not likely anyone else on Earth. This had to be the MGA.

"It's almost our turn." Sid wiggled and kissed Alexa's forehead. "If you feel overwhelmed, just look at me, and everything will be okay."

Alexa clutched his arm and messaged back, *How do you know what I remember?* Because how *did* they know her thoughts? No one should be capable of such a thing, even an advanced civilization.

Alexa caught her reflection in the trophy case next to the gym doors, her eyes round and huge against her pale skin. She sensed a building wave of panic—the surge, the crest, the desire to push it out and away from within.

No, not here, not here, Alexa silently screamed. She couldn't hold it back. Right before they were about to enter the gym, she let out her pulse of anxiety. Out of the corner of her eye, she saw several basketball trophies tumble over in the case, and a hair-line crack snaked across the protective glass. People gasped behind her.

"You ready?" Sid grinned, hugging Alexa tight.

Lights flashed, music blared, and onlookers roared from the bleachers. The release of anxiety helped. The tight compression building in her head and chest was entirely gone. She could breathe again.

"Ready," Alexa whispered but didn't squeak when the spotlight hit her and Sid.

A booming voice called out their names over the loudspeaker. "Our next couple is Alexa Baxter and Sidhit Diyani!"

Twenty minutes later, Alexa had dumped her stilettos in the corner of the gym and somehow ended up in a group dance with Sid, Drew, Ashley, and several others from their regular group. Ashley had distributed edibles among their posse right before the Grand March. A half-hour later, she and her girlfriends swung each other around, giggling wildly beneath the lights from the DJ station on the back side of the gym.

Alexa and Sid opted to stay sober during prom and save any substance-related debauchery for when they were off-campus. Since Alexa had released her invisible panic bullet into the trophy case, she could let go and enjoy the bliss of prom night. It was easy to forget her insane troubles while spinning in a pretty dress across the dance floor.

Alexa wasn't much of a dancer, nor was Sid, but that didn't keep them from bouncing around to the fast songs and slow dancing chest-to-cheek during the slow jams. Their group decided to head back to Ashley's after the crowning of the Prom King and Queen. Ashley and Drew were on the list of nominees.

"After this next song, we will finally crown Riverview High's official Prom Queen and King," the head of the prom committee shouted into the DJ's microphone.

"I'm going to grab some water, Sid." Alexa panted, waving her hands in front of her warm face. "You want one too?"

"Sure, you want me to come with you?" Sid loosened his tie and opened his collar.

"No, I got it. I'll be right back."

She hurried from the gym barefoot and made a beeline for the beverage table staffed by several Riverview parents. An unexpected yawn split her face as she surveyed the various soda and water offerings.

Mateo appeared beside her, still resplendent in his flawless 70's tux. "You have a lot more night ahead of you. Maybe you need an energy drink."

"Can your posse even keep up with you?" Alexa smirked. She had caught a few peeks of Mateo burning up the dance floor and even joined him for the *Macarena* and the *Cupid Shuffle*.

"Ugh, amateurs." Mateo waved his hand in front of his face. "You look like you're having fun with the royalty."

"I have surpassed expectations this evening and thus, they have accepted me into their court. At least for the time being." Alexa laughed. "You making an appearance at Ashley's tonight?"

Mateo shrugged. "I'm sure the EME team will want to go, and I promised to be their sober driver tonight. But there's always Uber, so maybe I'll let myself loose for once. You know, Lex, I haven't seen you so happy in a long time."

"I know," Alexa said, pushing away the persistent kernel of darkness at the back of her mind. She refused to think about the texts, Una, or the multiverse right then. She just wanted to be dull old Alexa in a pretty dress for a bit longer.

"Anyway, get your man a drink. We'll talk later." Mateo nodded to the rows of bottled water in front of them.

Alexa snatched one for her and one for Sid before Mateo could say anything else. She hadn't figured out what lie to tell him when he started asking questions again, knowing the next must be her most convincing. She hurried back to the dance floor and found Sid where she had left him.

"Here you go." Alexa handed Sid one of the water bottles.

Sid brushed away the film of sweat from his brow. "Thanks, you're the best." He pulled off his suit jacket and tossed it over his shoulder. "Whew, you really got some moves, Lex."

Alexa bumped him with her hip. "Liar."

He bent close to her ear. "So, rumor has it that if Ashley and Drew get Prom King and Queen, they will run a full circuit around her party tonight, naked."

Alexa grimaced. "Sounds floppy."

"Ha, right? Oh, here we go!"

All lights focused on the small stage built beside the DJ's table. The music faded to a dull roar, and Alexa fought off another yawn. She could barely see over the heads of the people around her. She cursed her height, not that she cared.

"Your phone keeps vibrating," Sid said. He had been gallant enough to hold on to her phone while they danced.

"Oh?" Alexa withdrew her phone from Sid's jacket, holding her breath, expecting to see a series of texts. Instead, her phone displayed three unanswered calls from an unknown number. Could they make phone calls too? Should she call them back?

"Ladies, gentlemen, and gender-non-conforming individuals of Riverview High!" the class president's voice boomed from the stage.

Alexa took a deep breath. Maybe she should call them back? If she gave them enough information, they would leave her alone for the rest of the night, and she could continue to enjoy her wonderful evening. She wanted to make love to her boyfriend, not worry about aliens.

"Hey, I have to make a call," Alexa said, her voice cracking.

"Yeah, okay, anything wrong?" Sid rubbed her back and frowned.

"Just my mom. She wants me to check in one more time." She hurried toward the gym doors before he could say anything else.

Alexa padded barefoot through the vast hall off the gym and into the atrium. No one was nearby. No one would be able to hear her conversation.

"Oh, God, oh, God. Just do it." She hit the call button, hovering beside the "Unknown" number. At first, nothing happened. She waited several seconds for some indication her call had gone somewhere and was about to give up when a series of tones chimed on the other end of the line.

A smooth, warm voice said, "We have received your transmission. Please wait for a moment while we connect you to your advisor."

Alexa paced in a slow circle while what she could only describe as elevator music played on the other end of the phone. The melodic series of clicks and tones meant to keep her calm only aggravated her further.

After waiting two minutes, she was ready to hang up.

A robotic voice broke through the synthesizer's moan. "Greetings. Is this Alexa Baxter?"

"Uh, yeah, that's me." Alexa stopped in place, trembling from head to toe.

"We appreciate you getting in touch with us. We have you scheduled for a full inspection in five Earth hours."

Alexa couldn't say a word. This couldn't be right. This couldn't be real.

"Are you still in attendance, Alexa Baxter?" The robotic voice asked in a perfect droning monotone.

"Five Earth hours?" Alexa glanced at the clock in the middle of the atrium. "That's, like, three in the morning?"

"According to our records, we will be prepared to inspect you at three ante meridiem, Central Standard Time. Your inspector will meet you at the Rift Door 20059."

"Rift Door 20059?" Alexa had a sinking feeling she knew which door they meant. "The door in the women's bathroom at the park? Where I found Una? But I thought it was only an exit door?" Her heart thundered. A Rift. The interdimensional doors within the multiverse's superhighway. Only someone deep in the multiverse world would know such a word.

"Regarding Rift Door 20059, we have modified the flow capacity. The Transportation Division of the MGA performed a series of improvements since the complaint filed by the Brume's Board of Advisors."

Alexa clutched her throat. "What does an inspection entail?"

"Your inspector will provide the details upon arrival. Be prompt. Late arrivals are unacceptable. We appreciate your timely response to our queries. This transmission will now terminate."

"But wait, what are you going to do to me?"

The line went dead and, according to Alexa's phone, the call ended. A long breath shuddered its way through Alexa's lungs. She leaned against the wall, fingers scraping the smooth, polished concrete.

So that was it? She had to go back to the women's bathroom in Birkmose Park and hand herself over to something called an "Inspector." What would they do to her? She anticipated something out of a horror film.

She sagged on her feet, nearly toppling into the wall. Darkness ringed her vision and threatened to collapse inward. She couldn't pass out in the middle of prom night, had only five hours left on Earth, and didn't want to lose a moment.

"Lex, hey, Lex, are you okay?" Hands grasped her arms. Mateo's concerned face floated into view. The EME team hovered behind him, whispering amongst themselves.

"Yeah, I just need to ... to ... catch my breath." Alexa leaned against Mateo, fighting to stay conscious.

"Hey, get her some water ASAP," Mateo barked at the girls. They immediately swept into action.

"I can't—I won't." Alexa bent over, resting her hands on her knees, and sucked breaths through her tight throat.

"Hey, I'm here, Alexa. You're going to be fine." Mateo rubbed her back.

"I'm ... I'm not going to be fine." Alexa coughed. "Mateo, there's something I have to tell you. I need your help."

Chapter 14

Mateo's jaw dropped. "Can you please say that again?"
"I have to go to Birkmose Park tonight at 3 am, and I need you to take me there."

When the EME team ran off to fetch her water, Alexa slumped onto the floor and twisted the hem of her skirt between her fingers. Sid would come bursting out the gym doors at any second, looking for her.

"I don't understand. You said this has to do with Una?" Mateo had loosened his tie and dropped his voice. "I thought Una was dead."

"It's hard to explain, and I wish I could tell you everything, but I can't. It's not safe for you to know. They might come for you, too."

"Lex, who is '*they*'?"

Alexa pressed a finger to her lips. "There are things I'm not supposed to know, but I do. And there are people out there who are worried about what I know. I was supposed to forget about Una like everyone else, but I didn't, and they don't like it."

"Can you be more cryptic?"

"I'm meeting these people at Birkmose. Tonight. I'm not sure what will happen, but I don't want to go alone. Someone needs to know where I've gone if I don't come back."

"Wait, wait, wait. Don't come back? Alexa, what the—"

"Just promise you'll take me tonight." Alexa pasted on a big fake smile when she saw the EME team returning with Sid in tow.

"Lex, you can't ask me to do that. Who am I taking you to meet? This is insane. Are you in danger?"

"I don't even know!" Alexa took a sharp breath, which dissolved into a sob. "I'm so sorry to ask you to do this, but I don't trust anyone else."

"Lex, you're ruining your makeup." Mateo pulled a silk handkerchief from his inner pocket and dabbed it beneath her eyes. "Not even Sid?"

"He'd never let me go."

"Lex!" Sid waved to her from across the room, tie loosened and the top buttons of his dress shirt undone. Alexa returned his wave.

"Here." Emily handed Alexa bottled water. "Got you the last one."

"Thank you." Alexa snapped off the lid. She could see the desperation in Mateo's expression and silently pleaded for him not to say another word.

"Everything okay?" Sid's gaze switched between Mateo and Alexa. "I thought you were calling your mom."

"Yes, and I didn't realize how dehydrated I was until after I called her." Alexa held up the water bottle before taking another swig. "And Mateo came to the rescue."

"What are best friends for?" Mateo tossed his hair out of his eyes and shot Alexa a brief, dirty look.

"Well, you missed it." Sid propped his hands on his hips. "Ashley and Drew were crowned king and queen. You know what that means?"

"I'm going to see more of Drew and Ashley than I ever wanted." Alexa forced out a laugh.

"Looks like people are starting to head out." Sid jabbed a thumb toward the steady stream of students heading out to various after-parties. "You feel up to standing?"

"I have to find my shoes before we go." Alexa held out her hand and let Sid lift her from the floor. The world swam before her eyes momentarily, but she regained her balance quickly. "Oh, and my purse."

"I can grab your purse," Sid offered. "I know your locker combo. Do you want to find your shoes, and I'll meet you by the main doors?"

"That would be awesome." Alexa reached up and kissed Sid's cheek. "Thank you. Love you."

"Love you too." Sid bounced off down the west side of the atrium and down another hall. Alexa watched him go, never tiring of the loose, easy way he moved through the world.

Mateo had already sent the EME ahead to grab their wraps and shawls from the coat check, leaving him and Alexa alone once again.

"How do you do this?" Mateo completely removed his tie.

"Do what?"

"Pretend you're okay when you say there are people out there who might want to hurt you?"

"I didn't say they wanted to hurt me." Alexa headed toward the gym, hoping her shoes were where she had left them. "They just want to talk to me, and that's all I know. If they ask, I'll tell them the truth."

"What truth?" Mateo hurried behind her.

"No one knows anything but me, and I'm not talking." Which was mostly true. Mateo knew a few things, but nothing too dangerous. Well, except for admitting Una was dead. What would the "inspector" think about that? Alexa's head ached from contemplating too many impossible things.

"Help me find my shoes?" Alexa dodged two silver-spangled juniors tottering on four-inch heels.

"Fine, Alexa, fine!" Mateo grumbled. "But this conversation is far from over."

Two hours and two shots of vodka later, Alexa wasn't feeling much better about her impending trip to Birkmose. She wandered among the swirl of teenagers who grew drunker and drunker by the hour as they danced, laughed, and enjoyed an evening Alexa ought to be enjoying, too.

Mateo hadn't joined the party yet, and Alexa couldn't stop pulling out her phone, hoping he would tell her when he planned to arrive. She drifted to and from Sid's side, desperate to remain calm despite the faint buzz of panic between her ears. He could tell something wasn't quite right. She forced a smile and tried to fend off his worries with frequent kisses.

A ball of tension had built in her gut. She had meant to avoid alcohol altogether—drinking wasn't her thing—but nerves drove her to the assortment of bottles across the kitchen counters. The first shot made her cough, and the hairs stood on the back of her neck. The second softened the strain between her shoulders. She was contemplating a third when Mateo finally texted.

I'll be there by 1 am. Emma had a situation with Jose Cuervo and needed to be put to bed.

Alexa decided a third shot of vodka couldn't hurt and returned once more to Sid, where he and his friends debated skinny dipping.

"If Drew and I jump in the pool naked, does that count?" Ashley pouted, already regretting her bet with her friends. Her crown sat slightly askew on her head, and her barrel curls had deflated into bulky waves.

"You made a deal. You can't back out now." Trevon, one of Sid's many soccer friends, gave Ashley's shoulder a friendly shove.

"Ugh, I'm not drunk enough for this." Ashley stormed over to the kitchen and started filling up plastic shot glasses.

"Did you have another shot?" Sid smiled down at Alexa and wrapped an arm around her. "You should have brought one for me."

"Sorry." Alexa sighed and leaned against him. The third shot was the winner. She felt as if she was enveloped in a warm wool blanket.

"You feeling a little drunky?" Sid tipped Alexa's face toward his.

"No, I feel good, actually. Really good. Like I'm wading through warm soup."

Sid laughed. "Soup, huh?"

Ashley approached with a tray full of shivering vodka shots.

"Hey, Ashley," Sid said. "Can I steal a couple of these?"

Before Ashley could respond, Sid took a shot in each hand and downed them one after the other. He coughed, stuck out his tongue, and laughed. Sid, much like Alexa, wasn't much of a drinker either. Prom night was bringing out the unexpected.

Alexa adjusted her dress straps. The magic the dress held faded since leaving the dance. She just wanted to throw on the black jeans and t-shirt she had shoved into her backpack and return to her natural state as the Queen of Darkness. She would not venture to the park in the middle of the night wearing a prom dress.

How long would the "inspection" take? Minutes? Hours? Would she be done by morning and have to pretend once again that nothing strange had ever happened? Maybe, if she was lucky, they would remove all the unwanted memories and crazy powers from her brain so she could once again be ordinary Alexa.

"I think I'm going to change," Alexa said above the blasting hip-hop music. She had meant to sneak off alone and quietly peel away the gossamer layers, but the alcohol had softened her head and given her a new, even better idea. She turned to Sid. "I might need help with my zipper."

Ashley slapped a hand to her mouth and giggled. Several of the boys in the circle of conversation grinned. Travon nearly choked on his beer.

"Yeah, you should help her with that." Drew smirked and punched Sid in the arm.

"Sure. Yeah. Okay." Sid blinked. The suggestion must have caught him off-guard.

Alexa had no idea what would happen to her in a couple of hours, but she *knew* what could happen right then and there. She took Sid by the hand, still riding the wave of vodka-fueled bravery, and led him through the crowd, down the stairs, and into their quiet little corner of the party.

Entering the bedroom, Alexa took a deep breath. Sid switched on one of the bedside lamps, filling the dark room with a gentle, golden glow. He tugged at the duvet, pulling it back, tossing it back up, then pulling it down again.

"Is, uh, the light okay?" he asked. There was a slight tremble in his fingers. "I know some people say to—"

"No, I want to be able to see you." Alexa turned on the other bedside light. The soft illumination highlighted the lovely curves of his face. No stumbling around in the dark. She wanted to remember every bit of him.

"I'm, uh, so I've got a condom." Sid opened the drawer on his bedside table and pulled out the small foil package.

"Safety is sexy."

Sid blushed, his cheeks bright red even in the warm light. "You're sure? Totally and completely sure?"

"I am." Alexa turned her back to him and pointed to the zipper.

Sid's usually loose limbs had tightened, and the tips of his fingers had cooled, making her shiver as he pulled down the zipper. The dress quickly fell away and puddled at Alexa's feet. She almost laughed. What was the saying? Off quicker than a prom dress?

Alexa looked over her shoulder and into the eyes of Sid, who was taking in every inch of her nearly naked body. He reached out to her again. This time, his fingers were warm as they slid down the curve of her back.

"You're beautiful," he whispered. "I love you."

"I love you too."

Chapter 15

In the movies, the characters always seem to fall asleep after making love, but Alexa was wired. Sid didn't doze off, either. He lay beside her, staring at the ceiling, a goofy grin splayed across his face.

He turned to her. "Do you feel different?"

Alexa shrugged, snuggling deep under the warm covers. She did feel a little different—both exhilarated and a little sad at the same time. Exhilarated because Sid had been so careful, gentle, and loving, and sad because she wasn't sure what would happen in the next few hours. She nearly admitted everything at that moment, every little thing she had hidden from him for the past six months, but she didn't know where to start.

"I do. A little. What about you?"

Sid rolled onto his belly, his nose inches from her own. "I never felt so close to you. Like we were almost one person. It was really amazing. And we could, like, do this again sometime, right?"

Alexa laughed at his eager hopefulness. Like a puppy with a treat sitting on its nose. "Yeah, we could do this again sometime."

"I would like that." Sid kissed her chin.

A roar of voices thundered through the ceiling above them. The sound began in the kitchen and migrated toward the back of the house. "Mmm, sounds like we're not the only ones getting naked."

"What a crazy night," Sid said. "Did you want to shower or, uh, maybe try to get some sleep or something?"

Alexa sat up. "I'm completely wired." She checked the little alarm clock on the bedside table. It read nearly one thirty in the morning. Mateo had probably arrived. Less than two hours until she headed into the unknown. "I think Mateo was stopping by tonight. I should see if he's here."

"This late?" Sid grabbed his underwear and tugged them on.

"I don't think anyone is sleeping tonight."

When another roar came from the kitchen, Alexa found her panties and grabbed her backpack. She tugged out her favorite band t-shirt—black with a big ZERO emblazoned across the chest.

"I should have been smart like you and brought a change of clothes," Sid grumbled, buttoning up his dress shirt.

"I knew I'd get sick of wearing a dress at some point." Alexa slipped on her black jeans and felt more like her old self than she had in days. She checked her phone. Mateo had sent her a text five minutes ago: *Are you two done yet?*

Alexa smiled, but it soon faltered. She wasn't ready for this part of the night, the part when she stepped away from everything safe and comfortable and returned to the cold, uneasy place where reality divided itself.

Hand in hand, Alexa and Sid headed from the quiet basement up to the noise and chaos on the main floor. In the time since they had left, the party shifted from mildly boisterous to all-out pandemonium. Someone had turned up the stereo. The bass throbbed against her eardrums. Empty bottles of hard liquor filled the kitchen sink while a dance party had broken out in the living room. Teenagers were grinding on a makeshift dance floor while the bodies of the passed-out or making-out littered the sectional.

The elaborate deck that led to Ashley's kidney-shaped pool was just as wild. People jumped in and out of the pool in various stages of undress. Drew sat on the diving board, completely naked, nursing a bottle of vodka. Prom dresses had been tossed across the lawn like used-up tissues, and someone was puking in the bushes.

"Holy shit." Alexa surveyed the madness, glad she had stolen her moment to disappear with Sid. She was tempted to drag him back downstairs, but she had to find Mateo in all that mess.

"Wow." Sid gaped. "I mean, I knew this would be a party, but wow. You sure you don't want to go back downstairs?"

"I have to find Mateo." Alexa wrapped her arms around him and glanced at the enormous clock hanging on the living room wall. It was nearly two o'clock. If she wanted to get to the park in time, she and Mateo would have to leave in roughly half an hour. She held Sid tighter. Was this it? Their last moment to hold each other? No, she couldn't think that way. The Inspector would do whatever they had to do to her, then she would return to her bizarre reality.

"Do you want me to help find him?" Sid peered down at her, a hand cupping her cheek.

She allowed herself a long look, memorizing the details of his face: his soft, dark eyes and their thick fringe of lashes, the way his hair always flopped into them, his full lips she loved to kiss over and over again, and the way he looked at her. No one had ever looked at her that way.

"You okay?" Sid frowned.

"Yeah," Alexa lied. She might never have the strength to leave if she held him too long. "If I was Mateo, where would I be?"

"Well, you know how he loves Beyonce." Sid pointed to the living room where Mateo, surrounded by sloppy drunk girls, executed several precision moves from the "Single Ladies" music video. "I'm going to check on my friends and make sure everyone is doing okay. That all right?"

"Sure. I'll be here when you get back." Alexa would wait until the song ended before interrupting Mateo's grand display on the dance floor.

Lost in the noise, she checked her phone for the hundred-thousandth time that day. A text she didn't want to see was among the various notifications on her phone: *Alert—adjustment to your inspector schedule. Attendance is now required at 2:30 ante meridiem, Central Standard Time.*

"No, no, no." Alexa scanned the writhing mass of teenagers, searching for Sid. She wasn't ready to leave. She had to hug him and kiss him before she said goodbye. Hopefully, she wouldn't be gone long, but what if they did something to her that made her forget him? If they did to her what they had done to Sid and Mateo? Would she still feel the same way about him? Scanning the many faces, she saw that his was nowhere to be seen.

Panic seized every part of her, freezing her in place. Until that point, she was almost able to set aside the reality of what she was about to do and who she was about to meet. As she stood in the middle of teenage chaos, the idea of unicorns, aliens, and multiverses seemed impossible.

Somehow, Mateo managed to find her after the Beyonce song ended. He emerged between the grinding bodies, wiping a thin sheen of sweat from his brow as he headed in her direction with a small smile on his lips.

"Of all people, I didn't expect you to be in the middle of—what's wrong, Alexa?" Mateo grabbed her hand. "God, your hands are so cold."

"I have to go. We have to go now," Alexa whispered, her words swallowed by the surrounding noise.

"What? Can you say that again?" Mateo wrapped his warm fingers around her cold ones.

"They changed the time. We have to go right now," Alexa shouted, glancing around to see if anyone could hear her. "I can't find Sid. I need to say goodbye."

"How long will this take?" Mateo shouted in her ear.

"I don't know," Alexa shivered. "I have no idea."

"Are you sure we shouldn't call, like, the police or something? If these are the same people who killed Una, aren't they dangerous? I was all for helping you out before, but I'm not so sure anymore."

"They didn't kill Una," Alexa said, though she was thinking, *no, they just hired someone to kill it.* What if they decided to kill her too? What if, after her "inspection," they decided she was too dangerous to live? Especially if they found out about her new abilities. Shit. She should have ignored her telekinesis, not attempted to control it. But how could they know, as long as she didn't break any mirrors in the Birkmose Park women's bathroom?

"Lex, think about this for a second. Is this a smart thing to do? Text these people, tell them you've changed your mind and want to meet them in daylight in a public place. Isn't that what they do in all the spy movies?"

Alexa let out a hollow laugh and checked the time. They had to leave immediately. Time was running out.

"Where did you park?" Alexa took one more quick visual sweep of the party before she gave up and headed toward the door. Sid would forgive her for disappearing for a few hours.

Mateo trotted behind her. "I'm practically on the road. There were so many cars. Hey, Lex, wait, seriously. Let's think this through a little longer."

Alexa couldn't be the scared little deer in the headlights. She had to face whatever was in front of her. She picked up her relentless pace, hurried through Ashley's front door, and onto the lawn where a cluster of kids were smoking weed.

"Hey, Queen of Darkness, you wanna hit?" a boy shouted from the group. The other stoners chuckled, muttering "Queen of Darkness" as she speed-walked her way down Ashley's long driveway.

Alexa ignored them. "We'll have to move fast. We only have twenty more minutes before I'm supposed to be there."

"Lex, I'm not sure about this." Mateo trotted to her side, matching her hurried pace.

"I'm not either but I don't have a choice. If I'm lucky, everything might be better after tonight."

"And if you're *not* lucky?"

Alexa wagged her head. "I just want to finish this and move on with my life."

Chapter 16

Alexa was unexpectedly calm while riding up the winding road leading to the crest of the St. Croix River bluffs. Between hopping into Mateo's car and driving through the inky-dark night, she convinced herself that this Inspector would likely assess whatever was wrong with her then remove all her unwanted memories as they had with Sid and Mateo.

"I don't like this," Mateo grumbled, white-knuckling his steering wheel. "Technically, the park is closed right now. How much time?"

"We've got five minutes." Alexa let out a held breath. Maybe she wasn't calm after all? "Not enough time."

Five minutes. Alexa clutched her hands, waiting for the inevitable panic attack to seize her. Her heart accelerated as the faint shapes of pines and oak trees materialized in the headlights. They reached the top of the bluff, the road curling in a tight turn and widening to allow those who came to Birkmose to park their car along the road and take in the amazing sights from the top of the river bluffs. The valley below was shaped by the headlights of vehicles cruising along the interstate to Alexa's left, and the speckling of residential lamps half-hidden among the trees below the bluffs. The river was a thick, black snake—a twisting glimmer.

"God, I hope the cops don't show up." Mateo shivered. "We're not supposed to be up here right now. Lex, I don't like this. Are you sure this is the right thing to do?"

"It's fine. Everything is going to be fine." Alexa got out and hovered beside the passenger door. She rechecked her phone.

Three minutes.

"You said they would be up here?" Mateo opened his window and scanned the darkness. "I don't see anyone."

"We're meeting in the bathroom." Alexa jerked her chin in the building's direction. Beneath the yellow glow of a single halogen lamp, the cinderblock bathroom reminded her of a tomb. And within stood a door that wasn't supposed to be there.

"You can't be serious?" Mateo let out a hollow laugh. "The bathroom? This is insane, Alexa. You can't go in there. Not by yourself."

"No, I have to." She walked around the front of the car and paused at Mateo's window. Her throat tightened. "Thank you for bringing me. I'm sorry, but I have to go."

"Wait!" Mateo opened his door and bounced out of the car. "Lex, this feels all wrong. Are you *sure* you're supposed to meet them in the bathroom? I don't see anyone. I don't see any other cars. What if we just left and waited at the bottom of the hill to see if—"

Alexa wrapped her arms around him and held him tight. "It's going to be okay. This might make everything okay." Before he could protest, she raced through the darkness toward the bathroom, arrowing straight to the women's side.

"Lex, you can't—"

She wrenched open the door, relieved to find it unlocked. The faint aroma of urine and bleach struck her nose and, suddenly, it was six months ago. She could almost hear the scuttle of Una's hooves on the concrete, trying to escape the accessible stall. *I need you to help me,* Una had cried out in a voice only Alexa could hear.

"Lex!"

"I'm sorry, Mateo." Alexa slammed the door behind her and turned the deadbolt. She snapped on the overhead light, a single lightbulb that provided little illumination. Using the flashlight on her phone, she checked the first two bathroom stalls, inspecting where Una's horn had ripped through the steel. The city park department had replaced the ruined partition over the winter. Any scrape or dent left by Una was long gone.

Her phone read 2:29. Any minute, any second, some kind of door, a door that looked like an ordinary cinderblock wall, would open and reveal...what? She had no idea what to expect. Una and the Brume were her only frames of reference. What else existed beyond the unseen doors to the rest of the multiverse?

"C'mon, c'mon, let's get this over with." She stared at her phone screen, waiting for the time to change, waiting for something to happen.

A knock banged on the bathroom door. "Lex, are you okay in there?"

Maybe Mateo taking her to the park wasn't a good idea, but she hated disappearing without anyone knowing where she had gone. What would the Inspector say or do if they heard Mateo banging on the bathroom door?

Light bloomed behind her. Alexa turned to see an illuminated rectangle the size and width of a door. The wall had become translucent as if someone had shone a spotlight through a thin fabric panel. The rectangle's light grew painful, and she looked away. The earth shuddered beneath her feet, and a tone—no, a detonation burst out from the glowing door, knocking her off her feet. The blast buffeted the bathroom stalls. Metal shrieked. The mirror above the bathroom sink shattered. Mateo cried out and then was silent.

"Ohmyholyshit." Alexa's ears rang, a high-pitched whine filling her head as she tried to sit up. She blinked, her eyes and ears throbbing. Her blurred vision made it impossible to see anything around her. Then, blinking a few more times and rubbing her eyes, she realized she wasn't alone.

A figure stood where the radiant door had faded into a weak glow. Alexa used the edge of the bathroom stall to get to her feet. A murmur rose from the figure as it glided her way, but Alexa's ringing ears made it impossible to hear what was said.

"I can't hear," Alexa said. She touched her left ear and felt a warm and sticky liquid trickling down her ear lobe.

The figure stepped closer, muttering words that didn't make any sense. Its breath glanced off her cheeks, smelling of bleach and, oddly, latex. Alexa rubbed her eyes, fighting to further clear her vision. A flash of light burst in front of her left eye, then her right eye, completely blinding her. She yelped. What was it doing to her? The figure tugged on her right, then left ear, and the high-pitched whine ceased immediately.

"Alexa Baxter?" a soft, reassuring voice murmured.

"Yes?"

"Your vision should clear any moment. I must apologize for the discharge. I sensed several others within our vicinity and needed to subdue them. I was able to project a protective shield around us to reduce the impact. However, such an experience can be quite unpleasant for those not used to it."

"Several?" Alexa scrambled to her feet, blindly reaching out in the direction she believed the bathroom door to be. "Did you hurt them?" She pictured Mateo on his back, knocked out cold in the park. And who else was out there?

"Negative. They have been rendered unconscious. The last thing we need is more distractions. As a representative of the Inspection Unit of the MGA, we thank you for your eventual response. There were concerns you might not comply, but we are pleased to see even an Earth-being can see reason."

"Are you my inspector?"

"Affirmative."

Alexa's blurred vision focused. The figure before her stood about a foot taller than her and appeared human. A face materialized through the blur. Alexa looked into the visage of an androgynous, beautiful person with pale skin and grey eyes. They had shortly-cropped pale hair, a pleasant but neutral expression, and wore a simply tailored, long-sleeved shirt and pants.

"You're not what I expected," she said.

"It is the policy of all Inspectors to take on the countenance of a being familiar to primitive species within the multiverse. Less advanced societies tend to become overwhelmed or frightened if you see an Inspector in their true form. Our general strategy is to avoid those from Earth at all costs, so we are taking extra precautions."

"You mean, this is not what you look like?"

"Certainly not." The Inspector gave her a pitying look. "Are you ready to depart?"

"Depart?" Alexa took a step back.

"We cannot have a proper Inspection," the Inspector glanced around the bathroom with disgust, "here." The human that was not human raised its hand and pressed fingers against Alexa's temple and below her ear. "This will help you safely process what you are about to see and hear. We call them Blinders. You must remain calm at all times. We understand that may be difficult for such a simple species."

"I know how to stay calm." Alexa's fingers fluttered to the places the Inspector touched.

"Please do not touch your Blinders. They are still processing. If you feel overwhelming distress at any moment, please let us know, and we will give you a mild sedative. Processing this inspection safely and quickly is paramount."

"How long is this going to take? People here will notice if I'm gone for too long."

The Inspector waved a hand to the glowing rectangle. "We expect this will not take long. Please close your eyes. This will feel strange to you. Do not panic."

"Where are we going?" Despite the Inspector's directive, Alexa's heart pounded in her ears. "And what are you going to do to me?"

"To the Primary Inspection Unit. Please take my hand and prepare yourself."

Alexa sucked in a sharp breath, fingers trembling as she placed her hand into the Inspector's. The creature's flesh was cold. As if she was gripping stone, the skin didn't give beneath her grip.

"Are you prepared?"

Alexa let out a long breath. "Yes, I'm ready."

"Excellent. Let us proceed."

Chapter 17

A lexa felt as if her body was being compressed and sucked through a straw. Her bones creaked. Her inner organs strained. Oh no, was she going to pee her pants? She exhaled and couldn't open her lungs to take in another breath.

"It's best to keep your eyes closed the first time you move through a temporal rift." The Inspector fastened its hand around her arm like a steel clamp, drawing Alexa's body through the elongated, compressed space. "You may find breathing difficult for a moment but do not worry. Your body is simply adapting to the shift in atmospheric pressure and interdimensional relocation."

The feeling of being squished intensified, as if Alexa's insides might start leaking out every orifice. What was the Inspector doing to her? She dared open her eyes only to see thousands of pulsing and flashing lights.

"Eyes closed," the Inspector repeated in its perpetually calm voice.

How could the creature stay so calm when their bodies stretched like taffy? Alexa's lungs screamed for air. Her ears roared as if the fists of the universe pounded them. She parted her lips to cry out, emitting a pathetic little whistle.

"Nearly there, Alexa Baxter. Maintain serenity."

As quickly as the pain grew intolerable, the pressure lessened, and her body reconfigured itself into its original state, from Jell-O back into muscle and bone. She gulped a breath of dry, sterile air and immediately started coughing. Movement flickered beyond her closed eyelids.

"You will take some adjusting to our atmosphere." The Inspector continued to lead her forward on an unseen path. "One step at a time. We have nearly reached the antechamber. Use caution when opening your eyes. Your Blinders will require a moment to reconfigure to this location."

Alexa could hear something whooshing open and the soft patter of footsteps around her. The air and space shifted. Sounds and voices grew distant and echoing, which told her they had walked from a small room to a much larger area.

"We have arrived," the Inspector said. "Congratulations, Alexa Baxter, you performed your first interdimensional travel. And you have not lost consciousness or evacuated your bowels. Excellent."

"I'm not sure about the latter." Alexa gulped. The vodka in her stomach threatened to come back up. She pressed a fist to her mouth.

"Do you require a receptacle for the contents of your stomach?"

"Not sure." Alexa sucked down another dry breath. She coughed then let out a phlegmy belch. "Whew. That's better. Nope. I think I'm good."

"We can put you on a ventilator if you cannot tolerate the discomfort. You are welcome to open your eyes again. We are at the threshold of the Primary Inspection Unit."

Alexa did as told and found the two of them standing in the lobby of what looked eerily similar to the Guggenheim.

"How is this possible?" she croaked.

When Alexa was twelve, her family took their first trip to New York City. She had begged them to take her to the famous art museum. The white cylindrical building Frank Lloyd Wright designed soared above her in perfect concentric circles. The structure's ceiling ended in an enormous skylight. A perfect reproduction, if her memory served correctly.

Around her, dozens of people who looked like the Inspector walked past but with subtle differences between their facial features, weight, and height. Much like the original Inspector, they wore their pale hair short and were dressed in simple long-sleeved tunics and loose-fitting pants a shade darker than their skin.

"I don't—how—where are we?" She gasped, shielding her eyes from the glass ceiling's sharp light.

"We understand your confusion." The Inspector blinked colorless eyes. Standing in a bright room, it appeared much more alien than before. Its pale skin had a faint blue tinge, and its pale, short hair had the acrylic quality of a Barbie doll.

"Your Blinder has converted what you see into a familiar environment." The Inspector's fixed smile remained in place. "What you perceive is an illusion. We have found that species such as yourself cannot process the truth of the multiverse, so we give you comfortable artifice."

"Oh, wow." The strange world tipped for a moment. Alexa rocked on her feet.

"Use caution." Her inspector wreathed a strong arm around her shoulders. "We can take a moment for you to compose yourself. The air here is more oxygen-rich than on Earth. You may experience euphoria."

The Inspector was right. Between her coughs, Alexa had the faint sensation of floating, like her feet didn't quite meet the ground. She desperately needed a glass of water. Did they drink water on other planets?

Standing in the middle of the building's lobby, the Inspector beckoned a group of what Alexa guessed were other Inspectors. The group studied Alexa, fascinated. One of them stepped away from the cluster and approached Alexa as she gasped for air.

"Is this what we think it is?" The Inspector's near-double leaned in, both delighted and perhaps disturbed by what it saw in Alexa.

"Affirmative." Alexa's Inspector nodded.

"And we did not feel the need to restrain it? Or render it unconscious?" The new Inspector sniffed and stepped back. "Such an unexpected aroma. And how small it is. How could such a fragile thing survive an encounter with a Bright One? We are perplexed."

"Alexa Baxter has been compliant and calm thus far. As you can see, restraints are unnecessary," Alexa's Inspector said. "And we are right. This Earth creature survived both a Bright One and a Brume."

"Perplexing." The twin cocked its head to take in Alexa from another angle.

"Indeed. Especially for such a simple base organism." Alexa's inspector also tilted its head.

"We look forward to your report." The twin inclined its head toward Alexa's Inspector and rejoined its group, who were whispering between themselves while they gaped in her direction. Nearly everyone on the building's lower floor had stopped to stare at her. She felt like an exotic animal in a zoo.

"You must not see many Earthlings around here."

"What you call Earth is designated a Class 609 planet. Under the MGA's banner, we avoid Earth at all costs, as you are not a member of our multi-galactic alliance. Your primitive species does not have the intellectual capacity to accept the joined resources and knowledge of the multiverse under the MGA's banner."

"How can I understand what everyone is saying?" Alexa's lungs no longer burned, but her tongue stuck to the roof of her mouth. Her head buzzed as she inhaled breath after breath of sterile air.

"You can understand our language due to the Blinder at your ears and temples. If I removed them, your brain would be unable to comprehend anything you see or hear."

"Whoa." Alexa was at a loss for words. The weight of her past day crashed around her. She staggered into the iron arms of her Inspector.

"I see you are overcome with exhaustion." The Inspector held her firmly but gently. "We expected as much. Multidimensional travel affects us all in different ways."

"I'm just—I can't—"

"We will take you to a place to rest." The Inspector easily lifted Alexa from the floor. Hundreds of voices tittered across the lobby, bouncing off the hard edges of the museum. Did they voice concern or disgust? "You must be fully conscious during your examination, or the results will be inconclusive."

"No, I need to get home," Alexa garbled as she faded into a half-sleep. "No one knows where I've gone. Sid. Mateo. They'll worry—"

"Leave your Earth-bound conception of existence behind." The Inspector carried Alexa across the lobby, heading up the Guggenheim's gentle ramp toward the heavens. "It is a construct and, like most, can be manipulated. When you wake again, we will see if we can reconfigure your mind like the other two Earth children. If all goes well, you will forget visiting the Inspection Unit."

That was what she wanted all along, wasn't it? To forget Una, the Brume, everything she didn't want to know? Yes, back to being an ordinary girl. No more broken glasses and mirrors. Just a normal eighteen-year-old human brain.

Alexa let go then and tumbled into a restful, empty sleep.

Chapter 18

A lexa stood at the edge of a body of water that reminded her of Lake Superior, except the water was mirror-smooth. The air didn't smell of sand or silt, and craggy rocks bit at the soles of her feet. Bright sunlight burned her eyes. The edges of the world continuously fell in and out of focus.

I am not ready to go.

A voice thundered through her mind but not her ears. A pillar of light ignited beside her.

"I want you to go." Alexa flinched away from her brilliant companion, Una, the shining, glorious, dangerous Bright One who stood beside her

When you forget me, it will be as if I never existed. No one left to mourn poor lost Una. One of the last of my kind. That is what they wanted. For everyone to forget us. Complete and utter eradication of my people.

"Everything is so hard for me," Alexa said, unable to bear looking at the small sun of a unicorn beside her. "I don't want this. I want to be normal. I want to be boring again."

You can never go back to before. Una tossed its head. Fire burst from its pink nostrils. *Let them try to rip me from your brain. I refuse to disappear. I am a part of you now, Alexa.*

"No, you're not." Even as Alexa said the words, she sensed Una's quiet rage when the resplendent beast quivered, snorting and pawing the rocks. "This was all a horrible accident. The fact we ever met was one big accident."

Or fate.

Alexa let out a hollow laugh. "I don't believe in fate."

A sudden wave crested and splashed at Alexa's feet. A chill seeped into her toes and legs and crept up her body. Goosebumps pebbled her skin.

Una dimmed. *They can try to cut me out of you. And they might succeed. You will miss me when I am gone, Alexa Baxter. I will leave a hole you cannot fill.*

"I'm sorry, Una." She wrapped her arms around her trembling shoulders. "It's better this way. I wish every day that I had never met you." The bone-deep chill threaded up her spine. "I should have left you in the bathroom. I don't know why I thought I could save you."

You nearly saved me. In the end, a lake got in the way.

"I'm not meant to know what I know. I don't want to break any more mirrors." The cold crystallized in Alexa's lungs until breathing hurt. Ice clutched her heart and stiffened her joints. The dry air prompted a series of coughs. Her body tipped back onto the shore. Beneath her, the rock altered to sand then changed to a hard slab of ice. The lake receded into a rising fog.

Please, do not forget me. Your memories of me are all that are left.

Una's star faded into the mist.

Reality shifted. The fog became smooth beige walls and a concrete floor. What room was this? No wonder she was cold. What happened to her clothes? Why was she covered in a thin sheet? Holy shit, did someone remove all the hair from her body? She peered closer. Yep. But why?

Alexa let out a low, deep groan and sat up, taking in every detail. She had been lying on a stainless steel examination table in what seemed to be but couldn't be an examination room in a clinic.

That couldn't be right. Where was she? What had the Inspectors done to her?

Tall, unadorned walls made up the windowless room. A large mirror covered the wall across from her, reflecting an image that didn't match her surroundings. Mirror-Alexa was surrounded by polished, stainless-steel walls and hundreds of blinking digital screens.

"Oh, shit." Alexa grasped the smooth plains of her now bald head. "And I was finally getting it to a length I liked."

A voice boomed from a speaker in the corner of the room. "Alexa Baxter?"

"Yes?" Alexa pulled the stiff, thin blanket tight to her naked body. She must still be in the Inspection Unit, but she had no idea how much time had passed or what they had done to her.

"We surveyed your vitals while you were unconscious," the voice continued. "As far as we can tell, everything is in order. Before we proceed, we want to tell you, first and foremost, we respect your right to exist. We intend to continue with this inspection without causing you any harm."

"Respect my right to exist?" Alexa peered at her reflection surrounded by glaring surfaces and flashing lights. Were the "blinders" they used to modify her vision glitching? Someone or something the size of an elephant stood behind the other side of the dark mirror. Were the Inspectors really that big? "Oh God, I don't like this. This is too much."

"Do you require a sedative, Alexa Baxter? You appear distressed."

"No, I'm fine. This is all just a lot," Alexa said, covering her eyes and taking long, deep breaths. Her fingers brushed a small metal disk on each temple. Those must be the Blinders. "Happy thoughts, Alexa, happy thoughts."

"However, we must warn you. We are not used to performing such procedures on such a nascent species. We must request complete compliance with every task we are about to execute. Otherwise, your health may be at risk."

"Fucking awesome." Alexa rubbed her eyes with one hand and clutched the sheet with the other. "You're not going to kill me accidentally, are you?"

"Absolutely not. We have prepared for all outcomes."

"So, what's next?"

"We have already done the first phase by determining your base composition status," the voice droned. "Next, we will perform a detailed scan of your neurological system. The scan should show us what went wrong when the Brume attempted to remove part of your memory. We intend to find what else may have been altered in the process."

"Altered?"

"You have attempted to hide it from us, but we know your unforeseen telekinetic powers."

She shuddered. "You saw that?"

"More times than you realize, Alexa Baxter."

"Is it going to hurt?" She couldn't tolerate sitting any longer in the sterile room. She wrapped the blanket against her shivering body and slipped off the slab, her bare feet padding across the cold concrete. The room smelled faintly of something similar to bleach. Her feet left prints on the otherwise polished floor. She nibbled on her bottom lip, hoping the Inspection would be as painless as a flu shot.

She stepped closer and closer to her reflection and pressed a hand to the glass. Her eyes appeared wide and frightened in the mirror. She looked genuinely bizarre without any eyebrows. Could the Inspectors grow them back after her procedure? Probably not the best questions to ask at the moment.

"We cannot anticipate," the voice boomed. "However, there is no other option. We cannot let a human of Earth continue to maintain your current knowledge or abilities. It is against several MGA edicts."

"So, just to be perfectly clear," Alexa's breath fogged the mirror, "you're going to remove all my memories of the Bright One? Each and every one? And the Brume? Nothing about them either?"

"Affirmative."

"And help me stop moving things with my mind?"

"Affirmative."

"Best news ever." Alexa drew a smiley face in the fog and shivered. "When can we get started?"

"Immediately, Alexa Baxter."

Chapter 19

A team of Inspectors entered the room. A horrible sci-fi torture device, roughly the size of a refrigerator with dozens of sharp steel arms, trailed behind them. However, in the next second, the apparatus elongated into a CT scanner. Should Alexa tell them her Blinders occasionally glitched?

"How are your vitals, Alexa Baxter?" One of the six Inspectors approached, wearing the same serene smile as every Inspector before them. "We are impressed by your demeanor. You appear to be adjusting well to the Blinders."

"Sure." Alexa eyeballed the false medical scanner as the other Inspectors prepared the device for whatever it was about to do to her. "I'll do anything to be normal again." She fingered the thin blanket wrapped tightly around her naked body. "Um, is there a reason you took my clothes?"

"We had to destroy them due to possible contamination." The Inspector began placing a series of little black discs in various places around her head, neck and, after tugging the blanket loose, along her spine. The discs pinched as they attached to her skin.

"Ouch. And shave me, too?" She reran her hand over her cue-ball scalp. "I can't go back looking like this."

"We will take care of that later, Alexa Baxter. First, we must scan you and decipher your irregularities. After observing your behavior on your home planet, it appears that the two male subjects who had contact with the Bright One do not remember their past interactions."

"You mean Mateo and Sid?" Alexa clutched the plastic blanket tighter. "How long have you been watching me?"

"Ever since we finished our Inspection of the Brume." The Inspector gave each of the dozen nodes attached to her skin a light tug. "They claimed to have completed full memory eradication. It is protocol for the Inspection Unit to confirm the claims of unreliable species."

"Unreliable?"

Behind Alexa, the five other Inspectors worked quickly to prepare the machine. The machine spun to life, emitting an ear-splitting whine. Alexa clapped her hands over her ears.

The Inspector tugged the disc on her forehead, shouting, "Mercenaries can never be fully trusted."

None of the Inspectors appeared bothered by the machine's horrid screech.

"From the observed confrontations between the Earthling called Mateo and yourself, he does not appear to remember anything."

"Observed confrontations?" Alexa dropped her hands from her ears once the screech diminished to a manageable whirr. So, they had been watching her after all. She wasn't losing her mind. "No, he doesn't remember anything. And I didn't tell him anything either. Even when he begged."

"A wise choice." The Inspector gave her a curt nod. "On a personal, perhaps unprofessional note, the fact you lived despite all the incidents the Brume reported is remarkable. That you convinced the Brume to allow you to live, even more so. Brume's typical protocol is to eliminate all evidence from a mission, especially lower life forms."

"Lower life forms," Alexa muttered bitterly.

"Precisely. How could such a simple creature live through interaction with one of the most dangerous beings in the multiverse?"

"Dumb luck, I guess." Alexa couldn't stop rubbing her hands over her shaved head. The sensation was oddly calming.

"Dumb luck?" The Inspector frowned, the first non-neutral expression since Alexa had met any of them. "What an odd phrase. What is 'luck'?"

"The Divider is ready for our subject." The tallest of the five Inspectors patted the place where Alexa was meant to lie down.

"Divider?" Alexa squeaked.

"Yes, to divide the normal and abnormal parts of your physical constitution. Please leave your cover on the table."

Alexa pressed the blanket to her chest. "Um, you mean—"

"Any form of garment will distort the Divider's scanners." The Inspector at Alexa's side held out a pale blue hand.

"But it's, like, freezing in here."

"We can modify the temperature to a more comfortable degree." One of the Inspectors walked over to a blank space on the wall. The creature placed its palm on the empty surface, and a panel immediately lit up. Within seconds, the floor beneath Alexa warmed.

"Is that adequate?" The Inspector beside Alexa took a corner of the blanket and gently but insistently tugged it off her.

"Yeah, that's better." She wrapped her arms over her breasts. The Inspectors didn't blink an eye at her nakedness, instead ushering her toward the long plastic slab that would slide into the CT scanner that wasn't a CT scanner.

She shivered despite the warmer temperature. "How long will this take?"

"Please lay down, Alexa Baxter." An Inspector held out a hand and helped Alexa onto the slab.

She anticipated another cold surface, but the hard table beneath her was smooth and warm. She shivered despite the warmer temperature.

Lights flashed. Motors whirred. The gantry rotated near her head, its rotation starting slowly before picking up speed.

"As long as required." An Inspector pressed a series of buttons next to the control panel on the gantry, its fingers moving too fast to see. "Please rest your arms at your sides and do not move."

The slab shifted, moving toward the spinning portal opening. If Alexa let her arms relax, there was a chance the gantry might take a finger or the skin off an elbow. The great disk continued accelerating as her body moved toward the machine's center. A loud whirr rang in her ears.

An Inspector shouted over the noise. "Do not move, Alexa Baxter! Lay perfectly still."

"You don't have to tell me twice." Alexa gasped, squeezing her eyes shut.

"And please, no speaking during the Inspection."

Alexa held her breath as her heart thudded in her chest, and a cold sweat broke across her skin. This was what she wanted, wasn't it? To forget Una, the Brume, running for her life, nearly dying beside Crater Lake. She prayed the Inspectors would remove her guilt, her nightmares, the moments when she couldn't catch her breath and almost passed out in the middle of class or at family dinner. No more breaking glass or random flying objects.

"Beginning Stage One."

But what if she lost what she had with Sid? What if the bits and pieces Una left behind were what connected them? What if the Inspector's procedure went horribly wrong, and she forgot all about Sid too? Would she still love him when it ended?

The chamber spun faster and faster, creating a whoosh of air so loud Alexa couldn't decipher the Inspectors' shouts. She didn't move. Didn't blink. Barely breathed. The inner edge of the gantry glowed hot and red all around her.

"You may feel a little pinch!" An Inspector bellowed into the gantry.

A hot knife drove itself through Alexa's left eye. Her brain seemed to melt into a hot, molten lump of agony inside her skull. An immense pain burst in the center of her head, and she couldn't stop the scream from ripping through her throat. Blistering agony shot down her spine and scorched her nervous system from head to toe. She couldn't control her body anymore or stop the convulsions shuddering every limb.

A voice much too quiet to be heard broke through her screams. "Move to Stage Two."

A surge of heat cleaved Alexa in two. She became bright. Electric. No longer flesh and bone but fire, eternal fire. Her screams died in her throat because she no longer had one. She wasn't a solid or liquid but a fiery cylinder poured out from the center of the sun.

"Completing Stage Two. Commencing Stage Three."

As fast as Alexa ignited, everything went dark just as quickly. She became no more than a tiny spark floating through space, moved within a vast void, growing smaller and smaller until her light went out—and died.

Chapter 20

Alexa had been in this position before: on her back, light burning her eyes, monitors beeping in the background, a painfully hard mattress beneath her battered body. However, she couldn't quite remember when or where. Shifting her weight, a bubble of pain popped behind her eyes, causing her to cry out. The air slicing through her mouth and nostrils was like a thousand tiny needles. She almost passed out again.

Voices murmured somewhere in the room where she lay. Were they voices? The rumbling tones punctuated by the occasional click or hiss didn't sound like any language she knew. She attempted to shift again, then realized it wasn't just pain holding her down. Her ankles and wrists were bound.

Panic—her old, familiar friend—filled her. She forced open her eyes and saw a series of dark and light blotches that refused to resolve into anything recognizable. The burbling voices grew louder, and an enormous shadow shifted from her feet to her shoulder. The reek of pungent antiseptic and melting electrical wires filled her nose.

The shadow pressed a sticky finger to her temple and below her ear. The dark figures altered in shape and size, becoming narrower and taller. The weird, garbled language of grumbles and grunts started to sound like English.

A figure at her feet spoke in a smooth, melodic tone. "Alexa Baxter is returning to consciousness. Should we subdue her again?"

"Negative." The figure hovering near Alexa's shoulder rested a cool hand on her arm. "Alexa Baxter may never wake again if she loses consciousness."

"Where am I?" Alexa twisted on the hard surface, testing her restraints. This wasn't a typical hospital. She wasn't even on Earth. What did she last remember? Pain. Incomprehensible pain. For a moment, as her body seemed to burn, she was confident she was about to die.

"Please remain calm, Alexa Baxter," the figure at her feet directed. "We should administer more of the relaxing agent."

"Negative. The relaxing agent could cause her to lose consciousness at this stage. She must remain coherent."

"What?" Alexa's throat and mouth were raw, tasted coppery. Her tongue felt like sandpaper. "What happened?" All of the crazy moments in her life leading to this point raced through her brain. "I still remember everything."

"We are waiting for the Executive Team to review your tests."

The figure at Alexa's side came further into focus. She recognized the original Inspector who had brought her through the door.

"They should arrive any moment."

Alexa tugged at her wrist restraints. "Why did you strap me down?"

"We were concerned for your safety." The voice at her feet shifted.

Alexa recognized the androgynous character from right before her "inspection." This was the one who had taken away her plastic blanket. Alexa dropped her chin and was relieved to see they had at least draped a sheet over her naked body.

Her fading panic returned. "Something went wrong, didn't it?"

"We cannot—"

A door at the other side of the room slid open. A group of Inspectors entered, whispering and muttering among themselves. Was this the "Executive Team?" Each held what looked like tablets of plastic or glass covered in blinking lights and scrolling text.

The two Inspectors at Alexa's side quickly approached the group. The agitated whispering continued. She could tell from the urgency in their eyes something hadn't gone as planned. The tallest Inspector, who appeared to be the group's leader from the deferential nods others gave him, shook his head and stabbed a finger over and over again on the tablet clutched in his large hands. Alexa caught the word "abnormal" among the low voices.

"Please, tell me what's going on?" She raised her head, gasping as intense pain behind her eyes sparked and filled her vision with bright points of light, winking in and out until her agony softened into a pulsing throb.

A half-dozen faces turned in her direction.

The leader let out a sigh. "Can one of you please remove Alexa Baxter's restraints?"

The other Inspectors snapped to action. One of them hit a button at the base of Alexa's bed, and the straps slid back into the polished surface. Another Inspector approached, holding a bundle of clothing, and started shoving socks onto her bare feet. Two inspectors trailed their leader as he strode to Alexa's right side.

Alexa rubbed her freed wrists. "What happened? Please, I need to know."

"The Inspection did not go as planned." The leader handed his tablet to another inspector. His bright, intelligent eyes bored into Alexa in a way the others hadn't. "And you died for a period of time."

"I what?" Alexa sat up and immediately regretted her choice. Her brain seemed to expand, pressing against her skull. The stars before her eyes burst and popped like miniature supernovas.

"You will want to move with more care. You're still fragile. We managed to revive you. The simplicity of your anatomical properties helped. If you were a more complex being, you would not have survived. We had to perform a bit of ... reconstruction. Restore fluids. Multiply a few million cells. Rebuild your frontal cortex."

"Reconstruction?" Alexa touched her face, searching her bone structure for any anomalies. Her skull was just as round and smooth as before whatever they had done to her before the inspection.

"Do not be concerned. Your skull is exactly the same as when you arrived here."

"But something went wrong?" She moved her legs and arms to see if anything was missing or ached unexpectedly. Except for her migraine, she appeared to be whole. "Is there another part to this exam? I thought you were supposed to remove my memories."

"As I said, there were complications." The leader let out a long whistling sigh and reached out a hand. The original Inspector who had taken his transparent tablet returned the blinking device. The leader scanned through a long list in a language she couldn't decipher. "We found what we were looking for and tried to remove it. We expected the process to be quite simple, but—"

"But?"

"We have not encountered anything like this before." The leader raised his tablet, showing a 3D image of Alexa's brain. "See this?" The leader pressed a button. A pulsating red blob with a series of twisting tentacles intertwined throughout her gray matter.

"What's that?" Alexa shivered, reaching a finger toward the image.

"This is what they left behind."

"They?"

"Somehow, the Brume and the Bright One have altered the neurological network within your brain. We noticed you had gained some peculiar abilities when observing you. You have some minor telekinesis, correct?"

"Yes? Is that a big deal?"

The leader pursed his lips. "The fact remains that we cannot remove your memories. And, while an Earth citizen in your condition is against MGA principles, we cannot terminate you due to the Treaty of—"

"Terminate?" Her breath hitched in her ruined throat.

"We could have easily done so when you died, Alexa Baxter. I understand you are a simple creature, but do not be an imbecile."

Alexa's cheeks burned, tired of the constant insults tossed her way by the inspectors. They were just like Una, like everyone else in her life, underestimating her time and time again.

"I'm not—I mean—-whatever." She swallowed her frustration. "So, what happens now?"

"As far as the MGA is concerned, we have completed the Inspection." The leader handed its tablet to the nearest inspector and gave her an insincere smile. "Our part in your case is over. It is now up to the Inspection Judicial Board to decide what to do with you."

"The what? When will I get to go home?" Alexa grasped the leader's arm. "I'm sure people already wonder where I am. How am I supposed to explain my bald head?"

"That decision is above my authority." The leader gave her a pitying look and gently removed her hand from his wrist. "Thank you for being compliant. We wish you well for the rest of your existence. A representative from the Judicial Board will arrive shortly and prepare you for transport."

"The rest of my existence? What the hell?"

"Be well, Alexa Baxter."

The group left without saying another word. The pulsing spots of light continued to pop before her eyes, but the headache receded an inch, leaving space for her to realize what had just happened. The Inspectors couldn't fix her. She was permanently broken. And she had the horrible feeling that whoever was in charge of her now would never let her go home.

Chapter 21

Alexa wasn't sure if she had been stuck in the room for minutes or hours.

How long had she been away from home? A day? More? Less? How long would her parents wait to call the police? How much would Mateo tell them? And what about Sid? She left him without explanation after their most intimate moment.

Pulsing waves of anxiety replaced Alexa's headache. She got up to pace the room. A wave of vertigo immediately warned her to sit back down. Her stomach rumbled. Her parched mouth ached for a glass of water. How long would they leave her in suspense?

Eventually, an Inspector arrived with her promised change of clothes.

"Hey, can you—"

The short, feminine figure skittered in, avoided eye contact, dumped the clothes at Alexa's feet, and raced back out.

"—tell me what's happening?" Alexa let out a string of curses as the door slid quietly closed behind the Inspector.

They had given her a simple, pale blue long-sleeved shirt and loose pants. The uniform was similar to what the Inspectors wore, only cut more like nurse scrubs. The fabric was a softer material, like cotton. A set of odd, numerical-looking characters sat over her heart. Her Blinders fought to translate the characters. First, they were all numbers, and then some letters were added to the jumble. They also provided her with a pair of ballet flats that fit unexpectedly well.

More time passed. Alexa's headache had softened enough for her to stand without feeling dizzy. She went to the door, searching for a doorknob or some sort of button that might open it, but found nothing. She was alone, completely and utterly alone.

Her throbbing brain began to whirr, her panic mounting as she circled the room over and over again. They weren't going to kill her. At least, she was pretty sure they weren't. She recalled that the death penalty was illegal in the MGA for the most part. There were legal loopholes, of course. That's why they had hired the Brumes to take out Una. Mercenaries kept their hands clean. Technically.

After Alexa made a dozen circuits around the room, her head filled with uncertainties, she fought the urge to scream, pound on the door, do anything to let out the mounting terror within. Her aching, empty stomach soon replaced her panic. When did she last eat? At the overpriced restaurant before prom?

Her breath caught as she remembered how Sid's eyes had glittered in the candlelight. He had held her hand, giving her the crooked smile that caused every part of her to quiver. She pressed her body to the cold wall, recalling the gentle slip of his fingers down her bare back.

Her two worlds crashed together. What would she say when she returned to Riverview? How long could she continue lying to her parents? To Sid? Mateo would never accept a half-baked story. How would she explain the lost hair, the lost clothes? Alexa ran a hand over her cue-ball smooth head, and her hunger immediately disappeared.

She wasn't going home.

The door slid open. An enormous, hulking figure walked into the room. Alexa flinched and, for the briefest moment, saw the creature as he was: a beast of horrible size, all muscle and clenching hands, with a dozen, unblinking eyes. Then he was a man again, holding what looked like a set of manacles in one hand. Two Inspectors squeezed in behind him, shooting the behemoth wary looks.

"Alexa Baxter?" The smaller of the Inspectors approached with their signature serene smile.

"Yes?"

"Hello, we are your Judicial Board Representatives. The Board has conferred with the MGA Judiciary Committee and agreed upon a probationary sentence regarding your unusual case. We have orders to put you into the custody of one of our Safekeeping Residences while they continue to examine your situation."

"Safekeeping Residence?" Alexa eyed the beast-man, who wore an expression alternating between neutral and menacing. The pleasure he seemed to take from the pronouncement intensified Alexa's mounting distress. "What's that?"

The Inspectors exchanged a look before the taller one said, "A secure place for those who have come under the MGA's scrutiny for various reasons."

"A secure place?" Alexa stared at the restraints just small enough for her tiny wrists.

"It is for your safety." The short inspector's smile verged on a grimace. "And for the safety of everything the MGA holds dear. You have some knowledge of the multiverse, but not enough for you to be a functioning, contributing member of our society. You must be kept in a protected place to maintain your well-being. As your case is complicated, the MGA will require a bit of time to figure out what to do next."

Alexa cleared her throat. "Can't I just go home while they decide?"

"Negative." The two Inspectors smiled even bigger than before, and the big man grunted, his squinty eyes finally resting upon Alexa. "The MGA cannot allow an Earth citizen to know what you know. It's against dozens of multiverse protocols. As it is still unsafe to give you a sedative at this time, we must ask you to remain calm. This Guardian will be transporting you to the Safekeeping Residence."

The Safekeeping Residence was starting to sound more and more like a prison than a hotel. "But people are going to be missing me. My family. My friends. You can't just make me disappear."

The shorter inspector said, "After everything you have seen, Alexa Baxter, you are too dangerous to allow back on Earth."

The Guardian approached and in a deep, gravelly voice suited for a beast his size said, "Come with me, Alexa Baxter."

"I won't say anything, I promise." Alexa backed away from the Guardian. "Please, I didn't say anything before, and I won't now. Please. Please!"

The tall Inspector's serene smile faded. "That is not entirely true. Is it, Alexa Baxter? We know you have told your Earth friend many things about your time with the Bright One. You have already said too much, and you will say more. Earth humans are not trustworthy creatures."

"Please, they'll be worried about me. They—"

The enormous Guardian let out a rumbling growl. "Are you resisting compliance?" He reached behind his back and withdrew a long, steel rod that reminded Alexa of a cattle prod.

She crouched, pressing her small body further into the corner of the room. Was there any way to escape? Could she get around the Guardian to the door if she moved fast enough? Maybe, but what would she do when she reached the door? There wasn't a knob or a handle to turn.

What about her "powers?" Alexa hadn't tried to reach for her telekinetic abilities since she entered the multiverse. Could she use them to push away the Guardian, open the door, and run? She grasped for the unseen power just behind her eyes. A splitting headache was her body's only response.

"I repeat, Alexa Baxter, are you resisting compliance?" The Guardian pointed the prod at her.

"I don't know." Pained tears trickled down her cheeks.

The prod popped alive, buzzing with electricity. "We have never used these on Earth humans before. Prepare for pain."

"No! No. I'll go with you." Alexa dropped her head and held out her wrists. The Guardian roughly grabbed her and slapped on the cuffs, which cut into her wrists. "These are really tight—"

"Silence." The Guardian hit an invisible button near the door, and it opened to reveal a steel box hovering an inch above the floor. The box was tall and wide enough to easily fit a person her size. A door built into the side of the box was open, ready to receive Alexa. The thing reminded her of an upright coffin.

"Inside." The Guardian pointed his cattle prod toward the unit.

Everything within Alexa resisted going into the tiny space. There were a series of perforations the size of her thumbnails along the box's sides. At least she wouldn't suffocate. Even as her mind screamed for her to stop, run, and find a means of escape, Alexa stepped into the chamber. The moment she entered the tiny space, the door slammed behind her, plunging her into darkness.

Chapter 22

S he wasn't going home.
They were tucking her away until they could decide what to do with her. How long? Days? Weeks? More.

Alexa folded herself into a corner of her cell, arms wrapped across her chest, holding in the panic that threatened to spill out any second. To distract herself, she finally examined her Blinders. The small discs were attached to her temple and behind her ears. The skin had grown sensitive around the devices. She considered ripping them off for a moment, then thought better of it.

"For my safety," she muttered, pressing the heels of her cuffed hands against her forehead. She rocked, her knees banging against the walls of the tiny cell. "I'm not going home."

The broom-closet-sized unit revealed little through the tiny circular vents above her head as she was being transported to the Safekeeping Residence. She sensed her prison traveling. Lights flickered. Voices rose and crashed against the container walls, then fell silent. At one point, they seemed to leave a building and roll outdoors. Sunlight burned through perforations, and the smell of exhaust and some sort of fuel filled her nose. She scrabbled her fingers along the walls, searching in vain for any way out.

Alexa's anxiety came in fits and starts. One moment, she felt as if she might crawl out of her skin. The next, sparks bloomed before her eyes, and she nearly passed out from the headache that grew into a migraine overwhelming her senses.

The wind and sun disappeared, replaced by a cool, dimly lit room. Below her, a massive engine roared, shaking the floor and filling her ears. The chamber lost any sense of time, place, or gravity.

"Fucking hell." She squealed when her aching bottom rose from the floor. Her throbbing head bumped the top of her cell. Floating in space, exhaustion replaced panic, and she fell into a deep, empty sleep.

When she woke, her container was on the move. Gravity had returned, and her joints screamed in protest. Her bladder started to throb in time with the hunger pangs from her empty stomach. She considered peeing on the floor for a delirious moment until the steel box's door s*wooshed* open. She slumped out of the door, every movement stiff and painful. Laying splayed across the cool floor felt so good.

"Resident Baxter?"

A pleasant-faced woman with short-cropped hair appeared above her. For a moment, Alexa's Blinders glitched, and she muffled a scream. The woman was, in reality, a slick, tentacled beast with clawed hands the size of her head. The surrounding room was dim and grimy, smelling of something rank and rotten.

"Holy shit," she spat, squirming away from the hideous beast. Then, the Blinders kicked back on, and Alexa appeared to be sitting in a black glass and concrete hallway.

A large, steel door stood behind her upright steel coffin. The enormous man who had brought her there was nowhere in sight.

"Welcome to Residence Darkstar. We are glad to have you join us." The woman, dressed in a simple navy cotton uniform with black combat boots, reached out a hand and helped Alexa sit up. "You must be exhausted from your journey. Here, this will help." The woman dropped a tablet into Alexa's hand.

The gray pill was the size of an antacid. Alexa nudged it with her finger. "What's this?"

"This will assist your transition." The woman wore the same serene smile as the Inspectors. Alexa couldn't tell if the blue tinge of the woman's skin was due to her outfit or the faintly strobing lights above them.

"Transition? Transition into what? I'm not supposed to be here."

"You are precisely where you are supposed to be, Resident Baxter. However, many of our occupants in the Safekeeping Residence arrive under duress. They are exhausted and hungry after travel, and you will likely have to evacuate your bowels soon. As a Guardian of this facility, I aim to keep you calm and secure at all times. Please, take it so we can move forward with your transition."

Alexa cursed under her breath, a fresh wave of dread pricking behind her eyes and creeping down her neck. The mirrored walls reflected a small, bald girl, too tiny and weak to stop anything that was happening to her. "What's it going to do to me?"

"Resident Baxter, you're displaying signs of distress. The tablet will help."

"Help? How?"

"As I said, ease your transition." A slight crease between the Guardian's eyes warned of lost patience.

Was this how Una felt when Alexa asked the Bright One to follow her out of the bathroom? Stepping through the door into a strange world where it didn't belong? But Una was a robust and powerful being who played possum, hiding its strength. Alexa was no one, nothing, just a fragile young woman.

The Guardian stepped closer and yanked Alexa to her feet. "I must insist, Resident Baxter."

"Fine." Alexa dumped the gray tablet into her mouth. It tasted like ashes and dissolved immediately. An unexpected belch bubbled up from her stomach in a puff of charcoal dust. "Ick, how quick does it—"

A sudden rush of euphoria wrapped her aching body in a soft, warm blanket of calm. All the tension and fear clenching her limbs slipped away, melting into the floor. She let out a long sigh and stumbled into the wall.

"Very good, your body metabolizes substances quickly. I am your assigned Guardian, Resident Baxter." The woman reached out a hand and helped Alexa to her feet. "You won't need these anymore." She pressed several unseen buttons on the shackles around Alexa's wrists. They opened, falling to the floor with a loud thud. "How do you feel?"

Alexa had tried edibles a few times with Mateo over the years. The last time, she ate too much of a brownie and curled up on the couch for hours, staring at the television without comprehending what she saw.

"It's like I took too much weed," Alexa mumbled, swaying.

"I am sorry, I do not understand this statement." The Guardian shrugged and smiled. "But that is to be expected. The Inspectors sent us all of your information, and I must admit, you are quite the enigma. However, we will do everything possible to accommodate your stay with us."

"How long before I can go home?" She tried to stand up straight as the black-and-gray world tilted.

"Are you worried about going home?" The Guardian's smile was warm as the sun.

Alexa blinked. No, she wasn't worried about going home. In fact, she wasn't concerned about anything for the first time in forever. Nothing mattered. Everything was fine, though she was a bit tired and still had to pee.

"Very good." The Guardian pulled out a device the size of a smartphone from a hidden pocket. "As your Guardian, I am always here to monitor you. Our goal at Residence Darkstar is to keep all our occupants calm and happy at all times. As you transition during your residency, we will begin removing all vestiges of your previous life. We find connections to the world outside of the Residence to be unconstructive to your personal and physical health."

"How long do I have to stay here?" Alexa tried to absorb what the Guardian was saying, but her thoughts came and went like eddies in a stream. For a moment, she was horrified by what the Guardian was telling her, and in the next, fascinated by her reflection's lack of eyebrows, she held back a giggle.

"That is yet to be determined." The Guardian scanned the device in her hand and nodded. "We will start with an updated scan of your vitals to check your post-travel composition. After that, I'll allow you a private moment to remove your digestive waste. Then I will give you a tour of the facilities and your primary living quarters. We will complete today's activities by introducing you to your cohort. The other Residents are very excited to meet you."

"Why?"

"We've never had a Resident from a Class 608 planet before. Please follow me. We have much to do."

Chapter 23

They did have much to do and, despite the absolute insanity of her situation, Alexa didn't mind any of it. Even when her Guardian stripped her naked and ran several scanners over her body, she didn't care. In her drugged state, every new piece of equipment, even the cold brush of air on her exposed skin, seemed to be happening to someone else.

The Guardian gave Alexa a new uniform in a different shade of gray and took her to her "living quarters." They walked down a long corridor filled with dozens of various rooms. Each empty cell contained a single bed with a mattress—no pillow or bedsheets. A simple metal table and chair sat on the opposite wall, along with what must be a lavatory or maybe a shower with a small privacy partition. The strange thing was that each cell was missing its fourth wall. Almost every action would be exposed to everyone else on her floor.

Oh, well.

"Here we are." They paused in front of one of the many identical cells. "As you can see, your cell does not yet have a proper label, but we will fix that in short order."

Alexa scanned the halls, noticing a combination of numbers and a single letter on a plaque at each cell door. At least she was pretty sure they were numbers and letters. Her Blinders kept glitching as it attempted translation.

"Now, do not be alarmed, but we activate a barrier field at night to keep you safe and contained while you sleep. The Residents here will not harm you. However, we prefer everyone to remain in their assigned place for evening retirement. Wandering outside your room during sleeping and rest hours is prohibited."

"Makes sense." Alexa nodded, entirely at ease. She stood in the center of the endless corridor, surveying room after room. None of them had any personal or distinguishing details other than the size of their bed.

"This wing is for the carbon-based Residents," the Guardian said. "You will remain with carbon-based residents for safety purposes. Those who are silicone-based or do not breathe oxygen are in different wings, along with another wing where we keep the special residents."

"Special residents?" Alexa flopped onto her bed to test out the mattress. A little stiff but manageable. Much better than the steel slabs she had laid upon in the Inspection Unit.

"Those who are not permitted to interact with other Residents," the Guardian said. "Not all Residents are suitable for group interactions. We've found that Residents need a little adjustment time before being introduced into the greater population. You may meet a few of them during your assignment rotations. We at Residence Darkstar believe a rigorous schedule prevents the pitfalls of boredom. Boredom causes smart Residents to do ill-advised things."

"What sort of schedule?" Alexa sat up and surveyed the remainder of her cell. She spied a series of perforations in a tight circle above a drain. "What's that?"

"You'll use this to stay clean." The Guardian pressed a series of buttons on the wall below the showerhead. "This is to adjust the temperature. This modifies water pressure, and you'll find sanitizing gel here. And here is the dryer." She pressed another button, and a blast of hot air ruffled the Guardian's short hair.

"That's so cool." Alexa stumbled over to test each of the various buttons.

Amusement curled the Guardian's lips as Alexa played with the dryer settings. "Everyone wakes, eats, exercises, performs assignment rotations, and rests with their cohort. We wish to keep order above all. Order keeps our Residents content. Right now, it is social time in the General Populace room. We will go there next so you can meet your cohort."

"Cohort?" Alexa switched off the dryer. "You mean I'm going to meet other—"

"Residents, yes." The Guardian folded her hands in front of her.

A bubble of anxiety broke through the pleasant haze, softening Alexa's brain. She was a prisoner. No matter their words and how cheerful her Guardian pretended to be, she was a prisoner in a faraway place. How did she go from a teenage girl enjoying a blissful prom night to a captive in an alien penitentiary? Was this where Una was supposed to end up? The Bright One preferred death rather than coming to this place. Why?

"Please, follow me." The Guardian strode down the hall in front of her, breaking Alexa from her reverie.

Alexa followed a few paces behind, ignoring her heart pounding in her ears. They walked through another set of doors, and with a *whoosh* of air, another wave of bliss soothed her juddering nerves. Why was she panicking? This wasn't a prison. Residence Darkstar was just a place to keep her safe while the MGA worked everything out. Surely, they would have the technology to fix whatever was wrong with her, remove her memories, and send her home again. They probably had a big group of scientists working out all her problems right then. All she had to do was come up with another brilliant lie about where she had been for whatever time she was gone. Her parents would probably ground her again.

They entered a junction in the hallways. Five massive doors stood in an arc in front of them. Despite Alexa's Blinders, she couldn't decipher the signage. Each door was labeled with numbered and lettered signage in a tricky font. The letters were geometric stacked symbols that almost reminded her of Korean.

"What language is that?" Alexa pressed her fingers to the foot-tall symbols etched into the wall.

"Multiverse Standard." The Guardian went to the door furthest to the left and opened it to reveal an enormous room filled with the voices of other creatures. "I see your Blinders are still getting used to your brain patterns. They will eventually sort themselves out, and you'll be able to read anything in front of you. Come and meet your fellow Residents, Resident Baxter."

Alexa and the Guardian entered a room the length and width of a football field. Twenty-foot-high concrete walls stood on each side, capped by a vast, arched glass ceiling, exposing the brilliant heavens above. The sky was purple, and pink feathered clouds like mare's tails brushed across the amethyst expanse. A faint sun shone through the cloudy haze. The curve of several gigantic, pale-yellow moons clustered at the far edge of the ceiling.

Alexa's cohort was less impressive than the sky. She was disappointed to find more blue-tinged humans in a wide variety of sizes and features. They sat at a cluster of steel tables, playing odd alien games, reading from glowing tablets, or staring blankly at the sky above. A Guardian hovered near every area where the Residents congregated, a faint smile upon each of their lips.

All conversation ceased the moment Alexa entered the room.

"Everyone still looks the same," she lamented. They were all dressed in the same drab uniform as Alexa, but she noted the different silhouettes among the group. They were tall, curvy, squat, thin, and petite. Some had long blue-black hair, some had facial hair, and some had no hair at all, much like Alexa. One particularly colossal man sat in an oversized chair near the back of the room, fingering what looked like a flute.

"You can thank your Blinders for what you see." The Guardian tapped her temple. "Your Earth citizen mind would be unable to process what is actually in this room."

Alexa chuckled. Yes, the last thing she needed was to see the reality of her horrible new circumstances. She had glimpsed the Guardian's true form for only a moment, which terrified her.

Several of the Residents rose from their seats, eyes wide with fascination. What did they see when they saw Alexa?

They also wore Blinders at their temples and below their ears.

A short, round man with beady eyes approached her first, hands clutched to his chest. "Is this the one you were telling us about?"

The Guardian nodded, resting a hand on Alexa's shoulders. "Yes, this is Resident X485, formerly known as Alexa Baxter. X485, this is Resident M356. From this point forward, as we integrate you into your cohort, you will begin to call yourself X485. We find it's best for the Residents to let go of their former selves. You can call me Guardian X or just 'X.' There are many Guardians, as you can see, and we each have our own letter."

That same bright, white bubble of anxiety Alexa felt before struck her again. She couldn't use her name anymore? That didn't seem right. Her Guardian studied her reaction, narrowing her eyes as she took in Alexa's response.

"It appears you may need another dose, X485." Guardian X dug out one of the grey tablets, dropping the pill into Alexa's outstretched hands.

"I'm sure I'm fine." Alexa held the pill momentarily, turning it over in her fingers.

X tightened the hand on Alexa's shoulders. "I am waiting, X485."

As a familiar surge of anxiety collected behind Alexa's eyes, she swallowed her medication. The reaction was almost instant. Her distress evaporated as quickly as the tablet on her tongue.

"We've not had a new Resident in forever." The small man's eyes gleamed with anticipation. "And definitely not one like you."

"Like me?" Alexa beamed. She loved the idea of being unique.

"M356, please introduce X485 to the rest of the Residents." X waved a hand to the Residents crowding toward Alexa on all sides. "I have some information to input, but I shall return as soon as my work is complete, X485."

"Can I be Alexa a little longer?" Despite the cascading waves of happiness, Alexa wasn't ready to be a series of numbers.

Face tight, X tightened her hand on Alexa's shoulder to the point of discomfort. "Only for a little longer. Integration and assimilation are necessary for your success at our Safekeeping Residence. Do you understand?"

"Of course." Alexa nodded, grinning at the myriad of Residents heading toward her. So many new friends to make.

"Excellent. I shall return shortly. Be good. Be calm. Make friends." Guardian X rested her palm on a small black glass panel at the door, and the enormous steel wall opened just enough to let her squeeze through.

"We are so very excited you are here, X485." M356 practically bounced on his little feet. "We have never had a new arrival from a Class 609 planet. Is it true you have never left your world until you came here?"

The group of Residents stared openly at Alexa in a mixture of awe and fascination.

Alexa nodded. "Yep, I'm from Earth. Have you heard of it before?"

M356 eyes widened. "Yes, it is a notorious place. Please, come meet everyone."

Chapter 24

Alexa was overwhelmed by the number of new faces and "names" to learn. Trying to keep track of M356 versus D958 was impossible for her addled brain, so she silently began giving nicknames to those who spoke to her most. M356 became Murphy because he reminded her of her grandmother's overweight Labrador of the same name. They both had the same warm, hopeful eyes and people-pleasing demeanor.

A string bean of a woman constantly stood at Murphy's elbow, reinforcing everything he said with a nod, sigh, or cluck of her tongue. Her name was D958. Alexa named her Deedee.

Usually, being the center of so much attention would overwhelm her, but riding high on drug-induced happiness, Alexa was more thrilled than anxious. A creature from a backwater planet made one an object of fascination. They found something else intriguing, but she couldn't quite put her finger on it. The Residents moved around her like a bubble of oil in water, never quite touching her, never looking away, as if they regarded her as a bit too dangerous.

Most of the Residents followed in a loose crowd behind Alexa as Murphy pointed out all the finer points of their room. While Murphy explained the game area and the library, Alexa couldn't help but notice some of the Residents had yet to approach her.

One huge, bug-eyed woman stared at her with a look of horror until a Guardian approached and placed one of the gray pills on the woman's tongue. Another sat at a table by himself, tablet in hand, pretending not to stare but unable to hide his confusion. And one tiny resident who looked more like a child than an adult scrambled over to a Guardian and demanded in a rush of words to be taken out of the room at once. They were also given another grey pill and were soon crouched over a table, drooling.

"What's their problem?" Alexa giggled, amused by the varying reactions. She stared at the one who sat alone at a table. Through her Blinders, he appeared to be an older man, perhaps in his fifties, with an unkempt beard.

"We all have our prejudices." Murphy shrugged and waved his fingers toward the older man. "That there is Z128. He has been here the longest of us all."

Z128 shook his head once and returned to his tablet. A Guardian approached and tapped his shoulder, murmuring something into his ear. Z128 immediately forced a grin and said in a booming baritone, "Wrapped up in my book. This part is my favorite."

Alexa wanted to give him a name too, but Murphy quickly ushered her to another part of the General Populace room.

"And here is where we play digital experience gaming when the network is functioning." Murphy waved to the blank screens on the wall. "You have to sign up for those privileges ahead of time. However, the analog games are first come first served." He pointed to the scattered items left on several tables. They were a mixture of games that reminded Alexa of cards, chess, dice, and mahjong.

"Looks like fun." Alexa picked up a plastic card, the various symbols reminding her of Egyptian hieroglyphics. "You'll have to teach me."

"That would be our pleasure." Deedee bobbed her head, clutching her hands to her narrow chest. "We are so excited to have a new arrival. And one so exotic."

"And brave." Murphy bounced on his toes. He glanced around once before leaning in and whispering, "So, is it true?"

"Is what true?" Alexa also leaned forward as more and more of the other residents clustered tightly around her.

"Did you destroy a Bright One?" Deedee, eyes wide, licked her thin lips as if hungry for the truth.

Despite the drugs fuzzing her brain, Alexa flinched. Even on the other side of the multiverse, she couldn't escape Una. The surrounding Residents seemed to hold their breath in anticipation of her answer but she had no idea what to say. She didn't like the idea of being considered a killer.

"Residents, we are gathering too close together." The Guardians, at the end of the room, circled the crowd. "X485 will be with us for a while. You do not have to ask all your questions at once."

The Residents smiled and nodded to the Guardians, doing as they were told without complaint. Everyone drifted away to what they were doing before Alexa arrived. She instinctually followed Murphy and Deedee. They were pleased to add her to their circle, taking up the plastic cards Alexa had fingered moments before.

The Guardians returned to their posts, eyes flicking from one side of the room to the other. Even though the Residents had returned to their activities, many continued staring at Alexa.

"Does the attention bother you?" Murphy laid down two cards, causing a large man with thick lips and a narrow nose to laugh. The big guy dropped his head into his hands as he chortled wetly. Alexa noticed a significant dent in the back of his bald head. "If you're anxious about all the attention, the Guards will give you another dose of Serenity whenever you want it."

"Serenity? Is that what you call it?"

"Happiness above all else." DeeDee sighed and laid down her own set of cards.

The large man giggled again, wiggling on his seat like a toddler.

"I was such an unhappy creature before I came here," DeeDee said. "Always fighting. Always warring. Now I have order in my life and endless contentment."

"And I was constantly blowing up buildings." Murphy slowly shook his head. "Such a waste of happiness."

"Why did you blow up buildings?" Alexa found the idea absurd. Why blow up anything? It only hurt others and made a terrible mess.

"Who knows," Murphy said. "I am so much happier playing games and spending time with my friends. It no longer seems important."

Alexa sat and absorbed the card game's progression, sensing a subtle organization in her chaotic thought patterns. Her state of bliss flattened, leaving her to see the room she sat in with clear eyes. She was a prisoner surrounded by dangerous alien creatures, and there was no way out. No end in sight. She was at the beginning of a truly horrible nightmare, far from her family and everyone who loved her. A tight knob formed in her throat, and her breathing hitched. No one at the table appeared to notice the change. They continued to play their card game joyfully.

Someone passed behind her, so close she could smell their sour breath. Alexa glanced up and over her shoulder. The grim-faced Z128 stared at her for a sharp moment, his eyes intelligent and bright while the others' eyes looked clouded with drugs. He pretended to study the card game.

"Who is winning?" Z128 crossed his arms over his chest.

"I have no idea. I don't understand the game." Alexa glanced across the room to see if any of the Guardians noticed her shift in behavior. One with a large black "G" on her chest smiled when their eyes connected. Thankfully, another wave of Serenity crashed against her rising anxiety. Alexa gave a grateful sigh and waved to Guardian G. The Guardian returned a tight smile and continued surveying the room.

"I am sure M128 will be happy to show you how to play." Z128's dark, intense eyes had intimidated Alexa a moment before. Now she wondered why he had to be so severe. Didn't he want to have fun like everyone else?

"Oh, yes, would you like to learn Save, X485?" Murphy, now excited, leaned forward, showing her his fan of brightly-colored cards. "It is very, very simple. Even C299 can play, and he has significant brain damage from when a group of MGA agents tortured him for six whole months!"

Alexa blinked, the drug haze clearing once more. "Tortured?"

C299 was the giggling man with a dent in the back of his head. His round body, lopsided grin, and unfocused eyes reminded her of the Three Stooges. Why not call him Curly? His giggling was infectious, and Alexa couldn't fight her own wave of pealing laughter. Soon, everyone at the table but Z128 had burst into laughter.

"So, this is the Bright One killer," Z128 murmured so low Alexa barely heard the rough sandpaper of his voice.

Alexa's giggling simmered into the occasional snort. "Killer?"

Z128's smile made Alexa uneasy, but another gentle wave of joy slipped over her itching brain, suffocating her worries. So what if the wizened man's gaze penetrated her very core? He couldn't hurt her. Her days of looking over her shoulder were over. She was caught, trapped, and locked up far from home.

"Oh, we've all done our share of murdering and torturing." Murphy shrugged, handing out a new hand of cards to everyone in the circle. "Right, Z128?"

"Welcome to the edge of the universe, Earth human." Z128 patted Alexa's shoulder. "You're stuck here like the rest of us. Until the end of your days."

"Till we die!" Curly bellowed, tears pouring down his face.

Chapter 25

"**S**ave" turned out to be an alien version of Go-Fish. Alexa and her bizarre new companions played for hours, riding the gentle euphoric waves of Serenity. From time to time, the joyful mental fog cleared, and Alexa noticed the other Residents hovering along the circle of their table. The Residents stared at her until a Guardian eventually intervened. Several attempted to start a conversation, only to be shooed away by Murphy or Deedee. Curly even growled at one of them at some point and was immediately served another dose of the gray pills.

A few minutes later, drool dripped from Curly's gap-toothed grin. His eyelids grew heavy around his red-rimmed eyes. Two Guardians helped him from the table and gently guided him to one of the several pale blue couches lining the back of the room, their pleasant expressions unwavering.

What a strange existence. Drugs, card games, and naps, all under the watchful gaze of the Guardians. *This* was what terrified Una? Such a strange, silly Bright One.

Time passed in an undulating blur. Alexa, Murphy, and Deedee conversed for hours while playing Save, but Alexa couldn't remember a word they exchanged. She hummed tunelessly as the edges of her vision fuzzed, focused for a moment, and then softened again. By the time the

Guardians announced dinner, the sky had turned a deep nighttime blue. Staring at the star-speckled ceiling, Alexa tried to recall their conversation and when exactly Curly had ended up passed out on the other side of the room, but then she decided it didn't matter. She hadn't eaten for several days, after all. Now ravenous when the Guardians set down a tray of grey oatmeal and a glass of water, she shoveled spoonful after spoonful of the tasteless goo into her mouth, not caring that it had little flavor. At least she would have a full belly.

Murphy and Deedee laughed at how quickly she ate her porridge.

"You remind me of a..." Murphy said several words that didn't make sense.

"You are so right." Deedee bobbed her head, languorously spooning goo into her mouth.

Satiated, Alexa let her head drop back so she could admire the massive pink moon taking up half the glass ceiling. The porridge settled rock-like in her gut as she hummed her made-up tune again. Nothing like her mother's delicious cooking. Her mom could even make beets and brussel sprouts appetizing. Not that she would ever enjoy her mother's cooking again. She slumped in her seat, staring at the phlegm-like residue from her dinner, and gagged.

"Are you well, X485?" Deedee peered over her bowl with big, dilated pupils.

Alexa's chest ached. Her mother. Alexa had left without saying goodbye. How stupid of her to assume everything would be okay when she followed the Inspector off-world. And what about her sister or her dad? She hummed another bar to calm herself and immediately recognized the song.

"Into Dust." The same song crooned by the glee club at Sid's prom-posal.

"Sid," she whispered.

"X485?" Murphy wiped away a smear of the oatmeal from the corner of his mouth. "Do you need Guardian help?"

"No, I just ... " The pure, ignorant bliss filling every facet of Alexa's being disappeared, leaving behind a hollow shell. She tried to sit up straight, but her body refused to obey.

Guardian X appeared through the breaking fog. "X485, do you need assistance?"

"I just miss my mom. My family. When will I get a chance to appeal my case? Do I get a lawyer?" Alexa shook her head to clear it as her body seemed to melt into the table.

"What's a lawyer?" Murphy gurgled.

"Sounds like you need another dose." Guardian X's serene smile tightened. She dug into her pocket and pulled out a bottle of the gray pills.

"No, no." Alexa pulled away, accidentally knocking her empty bowl to the floor. The sound of the bowl bouncing on the concrete rang through the room. Dozens of eyes rose from their dinner. Z128 turned in the seat at the table next to her, giving her that long, penetrating look none of the other prisoners had. Why wasn't he high on drugs like everyone else?

Alexa tumbled from her seat, smacking her elbow against the floor. The sharp pain cleared her brain of whatever was left of the Serenity. Her Blinders glitched, and she saw the monsters surrounding her for a horrible, seemingly unending moment. Beasts of all sizes and shapes, covered in fur, scales, and slimy flesh. They burbled in strange languages, their clawed hands reaching toward her.

Alexa shrieked, scrambling to her feet. She blinked, and her Blinders were restored. Once more, she stood in the sterile prison, and the Guardians rushed toward her from every direction. Laughter roared. The other Residents—no, prisoners—howled in laughter at her horror.

"Take her to her room," Guardian X directed the two other Guardians, who pulled Alexa from the ground. "She's having adaptation issues."

"Please, I want to go home," Alexa cried into the Guardians' stern faces. "I didn't get to say goodbye to my mom."

"Please be calm, X485. What you are experiencing right now is perfectly natural."

They half-carried and half-dragged Alexa toward the room's giant door. Her fear compounded, welling in a torrent, knotting her chest, gathering at the front of her brain. The air shivered. Was her telekinetic power not gone after all? This time, it came in a rising tumult so powerful she couldn't restrain it—hot, bright electricity burned between her eyes. The coalescing power had to go somewhere, so she shoved it forward, right into the enormous sliding steel door.

Alexa's unseen force struck the steel, ringing the door like a giant gong. The sound shuddered through the room, causing each creature to bend over and grasp their ears in pain. Alexa's Guardians dropped her, their hands clapping against their heads and mouths twisted in discomfort. The incredible sound faded, leaving a high-pitched ringing in Alexa's ears. She sat up, awestruck by what she had just done.

At the same time, Guardian X crawled to her feet, her usually tranquil face twisted with indignation, and shoved something sharp into Alexa's arm. The sudden poke reminded Alexa of a flu shot.

The sterile yet grim world flickered before Alexa's eyes. Reality faded along the edges of her vision. She knew she was about to lose consciousness at any moment and, this time, she welcomed it. Mazzy Star's warm, dark voice curled across the universe as Alexa closed her eyes.

"Turning into dust," she uttered, then fell into a dreamless sleep.

Chapter 26

Alexa laid back on the smooth rock, staring into the blistering bright sky. She plunged her feet into the lake and flinched, realizing she wasn't alone. Una gleamed beside her. The light from the sun refracting off Una's coat turned the small beast into a miniature supernova. She had forgotten how small Una was. The Bright One had grown in her memory.

They will never let you go. The unicorn, who wasn't a unicorn, heaved a long sigh. *Goodbye, Sid. Goodbye, Mateo. Goodbye, Riverview.*

Alexa frowned. "Who won't they let me go?"

You wondered why I would prefer to die. Now you will find out.

"But I don't wanna find out." A knot of pain pulsed behind Alexa's eyes. Beside her, the Bright One shifted in and out of focus. "Una, how are you here? With me?"

I am not. The unicorn leaned in, brushing its mole-soft muzzle against Alexa's cheek. Una's breath smelled unexpectedly stale. *But, I will never leave you.*

"Una, I—"

A throbbing *bong* sounded across the lake. The sun withdrew into the sky, taking all light with it.

Wake up, Alexa Baxter. Una dissolved into the encroaching darkness.

Alexa's head was so heavy. She closed her eyes, the twinge in her forehead ripening into a nasty headache. She clutched her skull, pulling her knees to her chest. Even opening her eyes took effort. How many shots of vodka had she downed before passing out at the party? Sid must have carried her to bed, but she didn't remember the guest bed mattress being so firm. She reached across the bed, searching for her boyfriend's warmth. Her fingertips hit a cold, hard wall.

"Sid, where did you go?" Alexa croaked, throat parched, mouth tasting of unfamiliar chemicals.

The sterile world came into focus. She wasn't in Ashley's basement sleeping beside the boy she loved. She lay on the stiff mattress in her "Resident's" cell. Was this her new life? Trapped in an alien prison subsisting on mush and a lovely drug called Serenity? Did that make her an addict? Her parents would be so disappointed when they found out. If they ever found out. Picturing her parents' faces as they received the terrible news via text made her giggle. Thank goodness for the drug-induced fuzzy halo surrounding even unpleasant thoughts.

Her bladder ached, forcing her to rise out of bed and move her stiff body to the round hole barely hidden behind a steel partition. Unlike using the toilets back at home, she had to crouch over the hole and shove her hands against the enclosure for balance. If she wasn't high, this would have irritated her. Under the influence, she giggled the whole time, even when it took too long to sort out how to clean herself and flush away the waste.

Finished, Alexa staggered back to her bed, slumped onto the foot of the mattress, and took in her surroundings. Two

Guardians stood outside her cell. She was relieved to see they looked human again. Someone must have fixed her Blinders while she was out. Even Serenity couldn't stop giant aliens from being terrifying. From her position, she could see other Residents in the other cells without the Guardian detail. She recognized one of them: Z128.

The scowling man deserved a better name than that. In her dazed state, she considered several nicknames: Zachary was obvious, but Z128 was much too severe for Zach. Zane? Zander? Zebra? She snickered at the last one and gazed blearily in the grumpy man's direction. He raised his head, a cold, hard look in his eyes. That wasn't right. He ought to be drugged out of his gourd just like her. What was his fixation with her anyway?

Alexa stuck out her tongue at him. Z128 let out a world-weary sigh and paced the edge of his cell. For whatever reason, his reaction struck Alexa as hilarious. A laughing attack seized her. She fell back on her bed, holding her belly. The illuminated ceiling shimmered, pulsing like the northern lights, the pattern so mesmerizing she didn't notice Guardian X standing over her until the woman cleared her throat.

"You're finally awake, X485." Guardian X's jaw clenched despite her smile. A noticeable detail but not worth worrying about. Alexa had caused quite a commotion in the General Populace Room. She expected to receive a sharp talking to.

Wait. What had she done? Is this why she couldn't remember when returning to her cell? There was a moment of panic.

"What did I do?" Alexa's chest clenched, a fleeting feeling of loss breaking through the drug haze. Had she dreamt of Una? The unicorn's memory hung in the back of her mind—a shining dream. Focus, Alexa, focus.

"That was quite a performance." Guardian X's gloved hands clenched and unclenched as if fighting to keep them from doing something violent. "Your mental aberration was thought to have been removed during Inspection. Clearly not. In fact, it appears to have grown in strength. And the Serenity doesn't seem to subdue your abilities either. Much like our failure to remove your memories due to your primitive state, the Serenity may work differently for your composition."

"I feel wonderful now." Alexa stretched out on her mattress and yawned. A tiny voice in her mind told her she ought to be cautious. Her Guardian was furious, but the drugs told her not to worry about it.

"Yes, we gave you a stronger dose and will continue to do so. Meanwhile, I'm keeping you under constant observation. It was a mistake on my part to introduce you to the general population right away. We think you need more time to transition into your new life here. However, we also know that isolation does not bode well for a Resident's state of mind. Therefore, you will be put on a different schedule, away from the others, for now. You will be in the company of a Guardian at all times. Also, we'll begin your assignment rotation starting this evening. A little physical exertion is important to maintain wellness."

Alexa tried to absorb everything the woman said, but the words passed through her ears like a sieve. How could she focus when the lights above her were putting on such a glorious show?

"Guardian D will join you shortly and take you to your first work assignment. As you adapt to your new dosage of Serenity, you may find it difficult to concentrate on a task. Don't concern yourself. Work as best you can."

Alexa yawned then nodded, only half-listening. She waved her hands over the lights, delighted by how her fingers appeared translucent if she moved them quickly enough. Guardian X must have left at some point because the woman was gone when she rolled onto her side, worn out from her hand dance.

She pulled her knees to her chest and dozed, her thoughts a useless jumble circling round and round. Between naps, a line of Residents walked in an orderly line past her cell at one point. She closed her eyes again, and the corridor was empty of Residents the next time she opened them. In place of the Residents stood a smiling Guardian. Like many Guardians, this one's gender was impossible to place.

"Hello, X485. I'm Guardian D."

Alexa returned the Guardian's serene smile. "Hello, Guardian D."

"I'm going to assist you with your work assignment." The Guardian pressed a panel outside her cell. The slight quiver of electricity coming from the unseen barrier field vanished. "Please, come with me."

They walked down several hallways, taking so many twists and turns Alexa lost all sense of direction. Luckily, the thick fog of her Serenity dosage had lifted an inch, making coherent thought possible again.

"Where are we going?" Alexa said as they passed another poorly lit hallway. How big was the prison? They had been walking for at least ten minutes, and still, the building had no end. Was this where they kept *all* of the dangerous people in the multiverse?

"You should consider yourself fortunate. Not many Residents receive such a special assignment so soon upon arrival. However, we Guardians felt this was the perfect one for you."

They paused at one of the large hallways. A massive steel door blocked this one. Several bright signs covered the entrance. Alexa's Blinders translated: *Warning: Supreme Security Unit, Use Elevated Caution. No Unauthorized Guardians Allowed.* Guardian D pressed their hand on a flickering screen, and the massive doors parted at the center. They were at least six inches thick. The doors' track moaned, straining to open the vast slabs.

The Guardian's serene face grew severe. "Before we go in, I must warn you. This is where we keep the most dangerous of all our Residents. They cannot stay with the general population because they have proven impossible to integrate. They all had their chance and chose to disobey."

Alexa's insides curdled, but she knew better than to show her fear. "What do you want me to do?"

Guardian D's smile returned. "We haven't properly cleaned the corridor outside their cells in a while and thought it would be the perfect task for you, X485."

Alexa followed the Guardian into the massive hall. The room was elliptical, unlike all the other cell blocks. A dozen doors lined the perimeter of the central pathway. Each cell door was made of the same thick steel as the front entry, with only a tiny window roughly head-height to show what monsters lay beyond. The space was quiet, too quiet for Alexa's liking.

"As you can see, we have some grime buildup that requires removal." Guardian D waved a hand to various sections of the room.

The space appeared spotless to Alexa, but she smiled and nodded.

"We come in here daily to see if the Residents are in reasonably good health." Guardian D crossed to the opposite side of the circular room and hit several buttons beside the cell door. The door whooshed open, revealing a space the size of a walk-in closet. It contained a slab for sleeping and a hole for waste removal. "They have automatic feeders, of course, and are given a specially modified dose of Serenity to keep them compliant. Unlike the rest of the population, they are simply too dangerous to integrate. So, we have no choice but to keep them isolated at all times. Also, we have a recently evacuated cell that could use a thorough cleaning. The Resident expired some days ago."

Alexa involuntarily shuddered, then held her breath, worried the Guardian might have caught her lucid moment of discomfort.

"This cell was for a resident about your size." Guardian D turned, their smile taking a cruel edge. "Here." They stepped out of the cell, opened a side panel, and withdrew a device that looked unexpectedly similar to a vacuum hose. A retractable tube was connected to the inner wall of the small closet. "You'll use this to remove the dust and dirt. The hose here is long enough for you to reach every section of the hall.

"After you clean everything on the floor level, I'll bring you an elevation rig so you can get to the ceiling. Whatever you do, do not engage with the Residents here. Not that they'll hear you. The cell walls are much too thick. You'll work here until I return to get you. Any questions?"

"I thought you were staying with me?" Alexa quivered.

"I'm securing the door behind you. You'll be perfectly safe."

Alexa turned over the vacuum hose in her hand. "How do I start this thing?"

Guardian D pressed a round red button above the retractable hose chute. The vacuum jumped to life. "Start with this cell first. The Resident was in there for many, many years, and it needs a thorough cleaning."

"Okay, will do." Alexa nodded, unwilling to fully step into the small room with the Guardian present. What if they locked her in? She gave the Guardian a false smile and vacuumed the area around the cell door.

"Do a good job, and we'll give you a treat with your next meal." Guardian D turned on their heel and headed toward the cell block's main door. "Unfortunately, I have to lock you in here with the Residents. You understand, of course."

Alexa fought the rising panic in her gut. "Of course."

The enormous doors closed. She inhaled deeply and sagged against the cell's doorway. The Guardian's threat, however subtle, was clear. If she wasn't compliant, she too could end up in one of those cells—alone, pumped with drugs, and left to rot.

Chapter 27

Roughly a half-hour into vacuuming the closet-sized cell, the Serenity started to wear off. The pleasant fog receded and left an electric spark of anxiety in its place. The cell was so small. How could a creature live in there without losing its mind? What if *she* ended up in a cell like that?

A shock wave of panic seized Alexa, and she scurried out of the room. Had she cleaned it enough? Did it matter? The cell was spotless before she started to vacuum its invisible coating of dust.

Collapsing to her knees, fighting for breath, she searched for a distraction. She hummed, "Into Dust," but that reminded her how much she missed Sid.

A *thump* came from within one of the many cells, startling her.

What sort of creatures ended up in solitary? The cells were all more or less the same size, with a small viewing window at eye level. Some doors were larger than others; one was covered in rivets and steel straps to reinforce it further. Alexa climbed to her unsteady feet to get a better look.

Fascination and horror drew her toward the cell nearest her. Before she reached it, she glanced up, searching for tell-tale signs of surveillance devices. They must be watching her at all times. This was a prison, after all, wasn't it? What would happen if she looked inside? Guardian D told her to clean the corridor, not avoid the prisoners.

Alexa pretended to vacuum more invisible dust at cell door. Wait. She was moving too fast, with too much purpose. She was supposed to be stoned and happy. If only she had taken that acting class with Mateo two years ago. Anyway, she had been performing for months, pretending to be just fine even while horrors spun through her thoughts.

Gradually, she fake-cleaned her way to the nearest cell window. A tiny person huddled in the furthest corner of the room, their back facing Alexa. The nobs of their bent spine stood out against their thin prison garb. She hadn't expected something so allegedly dangerous to look so pathetic. Did they all look so sad?

She continued to clear away unseen dust, sticking the hose attachment into every corner within reach while glancing through each window. With her Blinders, she saw the Supreme Security occupants as various shapes and sizes of human, much like the rest of the Residents. Most appeared drugged out of their mind, sleeping or drooling in the corner of their cell. One of the Residents was writhing on their cell floor, mouth stretched open in a silent scream.

As Alexa looked at them one by one, the lump of dread in her gut swelled. She fought through her increasing alarm and the tingling at the front of her brain. The last thing she needed was another telekinetic incident.

More time passed. Minutes. Hours. Alexa reached the last cell, the one covered in extra reinforcement, and glanced through the window as she had with the others.

"Oh, shit." She shoved a fist against her lips as two clear, intense eyes stared back at her. Her Blinders showed her an average-sized, slender young man with a blazing blue gaze. Unlike the others, he was coherent and furious.

Something about him was oddly familiar. She quickly went through the gestures of cleaning around his cell. When she dared a glance over her shoulder, she fought the urge to shriek. The young man had pressed his nose to the window, his breath fogging the glass. The absolute rage in his expression made her want to bang on the main cell block door and beg to be let out. A subtle rumble of power radiated from him.

Invisible talons plucked through her brain. She yelped, slapping a hand to her mouth before the scream building in her throat could work its way out. The feeling was horrifyingly familiar. She dared meet his eyes. His fierce, radiant blue eyes.

Eyes just like Una.

I see you, Simple One, the Bright One who looked nothing like a Bright One, whispered in her mind.

Alexa gasped. She had forgotten how strange it felt to have someone invade her brain. The Bright One's unspoken words filled her ears, playing over and over on repeat. She nearly dropped her vacuum as she hurried to the opposite side of the room. Suddenly, the little, open cell didn't seem so scary. What would the Guardians do if she hid in it? Would they laugh and lock her inside? If the Bright One had any clue what she had done to Una—

Can you hear me, Simple One? A faint thud knocked against the Bright One's door. Alexa instinctively looked in his direction. The Bright One pressed his cheek against the glass. *What are you? You seem to know me. You have communicated with one of my kind before. How is that possible?*

Una was a fierce and sometimes downright terrifying creature, but the beast glaring her way was on another level. Did Guardian X do this to her on purpose? Were they watching her now from the other side of a hidden camera, laughing at the silly, terrified Earthling?

Alexa returned to the empty cell, scrubbing in the deepest corners while her heart banged like a bass drum. What she wouldn't give to have a dose of Serenity to take the edge off her panic.

You cannot hide from me, Simple One. The Bright One smacked his cell door again. *If you have known my brethren, you know what we are. How can you know us?* One more bang droned through the cavernous room. *How can you know us?*

Alexa breathed deeply, closed her eyes, and scrubbed at yet another invisible patch of dirt in the furthest corner of the isolation cell. All remnants of the mind-numbing Serenity was long gone. The dry, sterilized air caught in her throat. The powerful scent of disinfectant filled the tiny room. Had the previous occupant died in this cell? How long had the body laid there before the Guardians knew it was dead?

Keep pretending you cannot hear me, the Bright One jeered from his cell. *These walls cannot stop the sound of my voice.*

Terror blurred Alexa's vision. She continued to scrub and suck, scrub and suck at nothing but pristine steel walls with the vacuum. Once upon a time, she had endured both a Bright One and a Brume in her mind and survived. She could do it again.

Come out, come out, Simple One. I only want to talk. No harm in talking, right?

The enormous doors leading into the restricted unit *whooshed* open. Alexa jumped up and stumbled out of the cell, praying a Guardian had returned to take her back to her own large, spacious compartment, far, far away from the Bright One.

"How is your work progressing, X485?" Guardian D glided into the central corridor, looking fresh and unbothered as always. They scanned the room. "Ah, I see you've done an excellent job so far, but there's much more to do. Are you well, X485? You appear pale?"

"Just a little hungry, that's all." Alexa forced a smile. The vacuum hose lay in a tangled heap all around her.

"Of course you are." Guardian D's serene smile widened. "I hope the Residents here didn't give you any trouble."

"No, no trouble." Alexa glanced toward the Bright One's cell. All she could see was the faint smear his cheek had left behind on the glass. She couldn't say why, but she knew telling the Guardian she could hear the Bright One was a bad idea.

"Excellent. Now, retract your suction device, and we can be on our way."

Alexa waved her hand at the loops of hose. "I don't know how."

"My apologies. It is quite simple." Guardian D walked over to the open closet door, turned a knob Alexa hadn't noticed in the upper left corner, and stepped back. The length of hose retracted back into the closet with a sharp *whoosh*. "Now you'll know what to do when you return for tomorrow's shift."

Alexa wavered on her feet. "Tomorrow? I have to come back tomorrow?"

"Of course, this is your work assignment. Each assignment lasts for ten days minimum."

"Oh. Great."

"Let's take you back to your cell. You look exhausted, X485."

As Guardian D led Alexa from the room, the Bright One whispered, *We shall meet again, Simple One.*

Chapter 28

Much to Alexa's relief, she was allowed to eat her porridge alone in her cell with a healthy side of Serenity while everyone else went to the General Populace Room. Carrying on any meaningful conversation would have been impossible while the Bright One's harsh voice repeated in her head.

These walls cannot stop the sound of my voice.

Could he reach her in her cell? And how did she know the Bright One was a "he" and not an "it" like Una? This one seethed with rage and hatred and didn't project an ounce of vulnerability. Una always carried a soft undercurrent of power, but the creature in the cell was more like a nuclear bomb.

Halfway through Alexa's sad meal, the drugs kicked in. The writhing anxiety and the Bright One's voice faded away. She finished her dinner and promptly fell into a series of strange, twisting dreams.

Una was a feature, of course, plunging horn-first in and out of various dreamscapes. Alexa was running from a cloud monster in her parents' backyard. Then she lay in the back of her Honda Civic, Sid at the helm, Una with its horn stuck in the ceiling. Mateo had languorously offered her a Twinkie before the car window shattered behind him, and he was sucked out into a sky as radiant and blue as a Bright One's eyes. After what felt like the passage of years, Alexa stood next to Crater Lake, gazing down at her reflection while Una drowned in the distance. Alexa cried out to the unicorn, but her voice was no more than a plaintive whisper.

When she woke, she knew precisely where she lay. Once more, the Serenity had run its course, leaving her empty. Her arms and back ached from hours of scrubbing at invisible dirt, and her tongue had the rough texture of sandpaper. Sensing someone was staring at her, she rolled onto her side. Z128 stood at the open wall of her cell, just beyond the invisible field. He parted his lips to say something, but a Guardian walked past.

Alexa ought to call him Rusty, just like an old friend of her grandfather. He reminded her of the wizened Polish farmer with an equally grumpy disposition. Alexa couldn't understand Z128's fascination with her and wouldn't know until the Guardians decided to let her back into the general population. From the open wall of his cell, Z128—now Rusty— gave her an odd, crooked smile, then turned and disappeared from her view.

Alexa curled into a ball and wished for a glass of water. Once, such a desire was easy to come by. Walk into the kitchen, turn on the faucet, and pour water into a nice, clean glass. Perhaps all she had to do was ask. After the quiet threats made earlier that day, she hesitated to call out to the Guardian slowly walking down the hall outside her cell.

"Excuse me?" Alexa slid off her bed, her head aching the way it did after spending too much time in the sun. "Would it be possible to get some water?"

The Guardian—yes, Guardian M—paused momentarily, smile unwavering. "Yes, X485. How are you feeling? Did you have a good chore rotation?"

"I did." Alexa shivered when the Bright One's intense gaze flashed through her thoughts.

The Guardian narrowed her eyes. "Do you need another dose? You seem a little unbalanced."

Alexa pretended to yawn. "I just woke up. Weird dreams."

"Very well. I will get you some water after my round." The Guardian continued her tranquil way down the hall.

"If you smile enough, they'll never know." Rusty had returned to the front corner of his cell and half-turned to monitor the Guardian's progression down the hall.

"Know what?"

"That you're sober as I am." Rusty flicked his fingers at the invisible cell wall. The wall sparked, rippling like a drop of water in a pond before becoming clear again. "And you belong here no more than I do."

Alexa blinked, startled by Rusty's sedate speech. When was the last time she had a truthful conversation with someone?

"I've been here for so long, they don't even notice anymore," Rusty said. "If you're careful, eventually they won't notice you either. Unless you want to stay drugged. Most of the others like it that way."

"Why are you here?" Alexa walked up to the invisible barrier.

"I said a few things the MGA didn't like. Then I said a few more. The MGA doesn't care for independent thinkers, those outside acceptable society, or those who break the mold. Like you, X485."

"I'm no one."

"And neither am I." Rusty crossed his arms over his chest. "It wasn't my fault when others caused chaos in my name, just as it isn't your fault that you can move things with your mind."

Alexa flinched, recalling the great, rolling *boom* from the General Populace Room door. Until then, her odd gift had seemed small, but something had opened within her when she threw her intention against the steel structure. When the Inspectors had pieced her back together, did they also cause a shift in her powers? No wonder the Guardians wanted to keep her drugged.

"They'll start putting the Serenity in your water, food, and even air you breathe. I've developed a tolerance to it over the years, but I've become such a docile, quiet thing they hardly know I exist anymore. If you want to stay drugged, stay drugged. I can't blame anyone here for reaching toward oblivion. If, however, you want to work on developing those abilities of yours, you'll need to stay present."

"How can I develop something I don't understand?"

"You probably had a full life before you came here, didn't you?"

Alexa shrugged, fighting back a swell of homesickness.

"In here, we have nothing but time. They have stripped everything away. All that's left is endless, empty time. They'll keep a tight watch on you for another week, maybe two. If you stay quiet and compliant, they'll worry about the other big bads in this place. So, when they stop watching, use your gift. Start small. When no one is looking, try pulling a bolt out of a wall or moving something small from one place to another."

"Why are you helping me?"

"Like I said, you don't belong here. They want you to rot away, become as forgotten as I am. But maybe this isn't the end. Maybe, with my help, you could become quite powerful."

Alexa snorted. "Me, powerful? I don't think so."

"Why not? You survived a Bright One. Who knows what else you're capable of doing."

Alexa had spent so much time being frightened —by what she knew, of the unwanted power within her, of the multiverse coming and taking her away—that she never considered her strength. She had survived the unsurvivable. The MGA's reckoning had arrived, taking her from everything she loved, yet she survived. Maybe she was strong, after all.

Guardian M returned, a ceramic vessel in hand. When Rusty caught a glimpse of her, he casually strolled toward the back of his cell, picked up a tablet beneath his bed, and pretended to be absorbed in whatever flickered across the screen.

Why, Alexa wondered, didn't she have one of those?

"Here is your water." Guardian M pressed several buttons on a panel next to Alexa's cell—a small, glowing square opened in Alexa's invisible cell wall. The Guardian stuck her hand through the window, and Alexa grabbed the smooth, white vessel.

"Do I get one of those?" Alexa jerked her chin toward Rusty, who was pouring over the glowing screen in his hand.

"We're developing a special tablet for you." The glowing square closed the moment Guardian M withdrew her hand. "Unlike our other Residents, your understanding of the multiverse is uneven. What is permissible for one like yourself is something that requires careful consideration."

"Why is that?"

"We are unsure if your brain could process the multiverse's popular entertainment." Guardian M gestured toward Rusty, who appeared wholly absorbed in whatever danced across his screen. "Or understand our collective culture. There are over a thousand systems represented in the MGA. And it is a great privilege to be a part of it. Something your planet will never achieve. The multiverse as we know it simply isn't made for primitive beings such as yourself. That's why your Blinders are so important. To be honest, we are quite surprised you haven't suffered heart failure or a seizure."

Alexa sensed an almost malicious quality to Guardian M's admission. Were they hoping she would die and end all their troubles?

"You shall follow a similar routine tomorrow. I suggest you drink your water and rest. Every day must be quite overwhelming for you, X485."

Guardian M turned on her heel and drifted out of Alexa's cell block unit, leaving Alexa to worry just how long she might survive the "Safekeeping Residence." Perhaps Rusty was right. If she could find a way to control and harness her telekinetic abilities, she might have a better chance of staying alive.

Alexa pulled the stopper from her water vessel and sniffed. Smelled close enough to water. She walked over to her bed and slumped onto the firm mattress. After the day she had, all she wanted to do was fall back into the drug's warm oblivion. She took a big gulp, lay on her bed, and considered Rusty's proposal until she fell into a restless sleep.

Chapter 29

Alexa had enough Serenity in her breakfast that she didn't have a care in the world by the time her Guardian showed up. She followed Guardian X to her work assignment with a smile on her face and a song in her heart. Guardian X appeared mildly concerned by her level of inebriation but didn't say anything, even when Alexa stumbled over her feet and fell headlong into another passing Guardian.

"May need to watch her dosage." The passing Guardian grinned and helped Alexa to her feet.

"Yes, we're trying to figure out what works best." Guardian X frowned—a rare facial expression. "I think we'll find a balance in the next couple of days."

The world tipped left, then right. Guardian X finally put out an arm to steady Alexa, her frown deepening. "Perhaps we should return you to your cell."

"No, no." Alexa waved away her Guardian's assistance. "This is fine. I'm fine. Walking is fine."

More amused than worried about her inability to walk straight, Alexa calmly wobbled down the corridor. The overhead lights flared, warming her face like dozens of little suns. Her fears of returning to the same cell block as the Bright One was a brief, passing thought in her otherwise empty head. Could she remove her head from her body and float like a balloon up to the ceiling?

"As before, take your time." Guardian X paused before opening the door to the isolated cell block.

The warning signs blinked neon, warning her of "danger" and to "use caution." Whatever, the super scary Residents were locked behind foot-thick slabs of steel. They couldn't hurt her.

Guardian X placed her hand on the identification panel. "And don't let the Bright One frighten you."

Alexa blinked. For a confused moment, she wondered if Guardian X meant Una had been moved into the empty cell. Was the unicorn alive? Had its body been pulled back together?

"He tends to make a bit of noise now and again, but even a Bright One can't break through the walls we constructed for monsters like him."

Alexa's clouded brain cleared for a moment. "Oh, is that what he is? I couldn't tell with the Blinders."

Guardian X narrowed her eyes. "Did he try to speak to you?"

"Nah." Even high, Alexa knew better than to tell the truth. "Just gave me a dirty look."

"He doesn't speak to anyone, so don't worry your simple little brain. He may bang on a wall or two but can't escape, so you have no reason to be frightened."

"I've survived worse." Alexa snickered. Locked in the Supreme Security unit with the most dangerous creature in the multiverse? Hardly a reason for anyone to panic.

The enormous doors *whooshed* open. "Yes, I suppose you have, X485. Do you need me to show you how to operate the suction device?"

"Nope." Alexa shook her head so hard she nearly fell over.

"Very well. Continue where you left off. We'll give you a lift for higher areas starting tomorrow. I shall return in a few hours."

"Okay, cool," Alexa scampered over to the vacuum's closet and let out a long sigh when she heard the Guardian leave. Alone at last.

The door to the empty cell was closed. But was it empty? Yes, vacant and waiting for the next dangerous occupant.

Alexa passed several blank, drooling faces. Yesterday, their incoherence tightened her bowels. Today, they amused her to no end. She hummed along, losing her balance now and again when her feet became entangled in the vacuum hose. How long was the hose? Did it have an end? She pulled and pulled, the tube looping around her in serpentine heaps.

Such a pathetic creature. Why would they put such a simpleton with us?

Alexa flinched, locating the Bright One's cell. "Shh, I'm trying to work here."

The Bright One stood at his cell window, light pouring from his pale skin. If Alexa didn't know better, she would have thought they were the same age. He could be just another boy from high school, only with crazy eyes. Tossing a hose loop over her shoulder, Alexa lumbered to the Bright One's cell and commenced cleaning. So what if he was trying to intimidate her? So what if his voice sent an odd thrill through her just like Una's had?

"Una, poor, poor Una," Alexa murmured. "I tried. I really tried, but I couldn't help it."

The Bright One slapped his hand on the glass. *Get away from my cell. I do not want you near me. Leave me to rot in peace.*

"I can't help you either." Alexa wagged her head, suctioning the ridge around the viewing glass. She sniggered, but her laugh caught in her throat. A wave of sadness broke through her drug-induced bliss. "I can't help anyone, not even myself."

What are you doing here, Simple One? How in the multiverse is such a pathetic creature considered dangerous? Has the MGA taxed or blasted everyone into compliance? Has existence become so altered that something as lowly as you frightens the government?

"I don't belong here." She dropped the vacuum. A dull throb pulsed across the front of her skull, a tell-tale sign the Serenity was wearing off. "I should have left Una in the bathroom. How could I be so stupid to think I could help it?"

The Bright One pressed his nose against the glass. *Una? Who is Una? Was Una the one to break into your mind?*

"Una was much nicer than you. Well, not that nice." Alexa rubbed the sides of her head, her parched mouth aching for a glass of water. Her withdrawal symptoms were getting worse each time. "I know it tried to be nice, but Una was scared. I was scared too. And the Brume was too powerful."

You must be talking about a Bright One. The name sounds familiar. Una ... Una ... What did the Bright One look like?

Alexa giggled. "Like a unicorn. Duh."

I do not understand. What is a unicorn?

"Ugh, not you too." She bent to pick up the vacuum nozzle. "A unicorn is, like, a white horse with a horn growing out of its forehead."

What is a horse?

"And you call me stupid. I may be a lowly Earth-person, but at least I know what a horse is." The thick fog roiling through her brain cleared further. "No, of course, you wouldn't know. I'm the weirdo here, not you."

The Bright One stopped pacing the small cell. From the lift of his chin and excellent posture, Alexa felt that this Bright One had come from a place of privilege. His disgust and dismissal of her were worse than Una's mild condescension. Alexa wondered why the Blinders presented the Bright One as male. Did Bright Ones have different genders?

Did you mention a Brume? The Bright One's eyes blazed behind the smeared glass, but his voice remained calm. *That is how they got me, too. Did Una refuse to go with them? I should have done the same. Death is better than this awful place.*

"And I ended up here instead." The realization hit her. She stood where they intended to cage Una; Una had let the Brume destroy it. Alexa picked at her aching forehead. "Hey, why aren't you all drugged up like everyone else?"

Their tranquilizers do not work on me. They have tried many times to make me as much of a vegetable as everyone else in this block. I see how it vexes them, which is my one delight. They built this prison to contain all the unwanted creatures in the multiverse. There is a reason they never open my door. A reason my food comes through a hole in the wall. A reason they send in an idiot to clean.

"Hey." Alexa half-heartedly slapped the Bright One's door. "I'm not an idiot. I did survive Una and a Brume, so I can't be all that stupid, can I?"

The Bright One shrugged. *So you say. I sense from the modifications in your mind that one of my nation once communed with you. Why they did not destroy you is ... unclear. To connect with a creature as lowly as you is beneath us. This Una should have crushed you when it realized you could not save it.*

"If I'm so beneath you, why are you speaking to me at all? By the way, my name is Alexa, if you care."

When the Bright One didn't respond after a moment, Alexa returned to her half-hearted vacuuming. Her headache continued to pulse. She preferred the pain over Serenity's giddy emptiness, especially in the presence of a Bright One. He couldn't hurt her; he could only throw empty threats and insults.

Alexa cleaned in silence. The Bright One didn't utter another word. Eventually, her headache rose in a brief crescendo of unbearable pain before dropping away. She was left with a dry mouth and a dizzy sensation, but her mind was clearer than it had been in days.

Guardian X returned, all serene smiles. Alexa tripped over the vacuum hose and laughed wildly, rolling on her back, hoping the Guardian would believe her performance.

"Let's get you back to your cell." Guardian X helped Alexa untangle herself and retract the hose. "How did everything go?"

"Fantastic," Alexa said, letting the Guardian guide her from the isolation block.

Alexa cast one last look to the Bright One's cell before leaving. Two blue, questioning eyes stared back.

We shall speak again, Alexa.

Chapter 30

Alexa missed music. Her near-constant companion was long gone since she left Earth. The right song could calm the tempest in her mind. When she was angry, she shouted along to Alanis Morrissette. When she wanted a good cry, she played "Fake Plastic Trees" on repeat. She listened to Foo Fighters or Cake when she wanted a jolt of happiness. But now, she had nothing but the electric throb of the lights above her, the steady roar of the ventilation system, and the shuffle of feet in the surrounding cells.

They adjusted her Serenity levels again with her evening gruel. Instead of passing out after her meal, she enjoyed a pleasant buzz similar to the vodka shots on prom night. Prom night. She would never forget how Sid looked at her in the lovely pink dress. Love. Adoration. And sure, a little bit of desire. Standing at the edge of her invisible cell wall, staring at strangers from other worlds, she doubted she would ever see him again.

The Serenity buzz kept her from sinking into sadness. Instead, she felt next to nothing. A dreary blob of flesh and bone. Once the Guardians allowed her back into the general population, could she make friends with a bunch of criminals half out of their minds on drugs? Was sobriety overrated? All she had to do was be honest with the Guardians and let them pump her full of drugs.

Alexa hummed tunelessly until the familiar chorus of Incubus' "I Wish You Were Here" took form. How she loved playing that song on a warm afternoon, driving to Sid's house, or when he took her on a date on a sunny day. What was Sid doing right at that moment? What was her former life like without her there?

"Hey, Earth human."

"What?" Alexa blinked, pulled out of her reverie by Rusty's familiar, rumbly voice. He stood across the hall from her, monitoring the Guardians at each end of the corridor.

"You're not all messed up like you were this morning." Rusty's eyes were in constant motion, first on one Guardian and then the next. "Don't make it obvious. Otherwise, they'll up your dosage again."

"What if I want to be messed up?" Alexa slid down to the floor, resting her head against the wall. "Maybe I don't want to think about everything I've lost."

"That's exactly what they want, for you to sink into oblivion and become a burbling idiot happy to blow spit bubbles without useful thought in your head. Coherence is dangerous. If we were sober, they would never keep us under control."

"I might still get out." Alexa could almost feel the warm touch of Sid's lips on hers. The way his lean, muscular body enveloped hers. No. She didn't want to remember. "They're reviewing my case. They haven't made an official decision yet."

Rusty snorted. "After what you did in the General Populace Room?"

Alexa pouted. "That bad, huh?"

"It's not good."

"How long have you been stuck here?"

"No idea. That's the point. They don't want us to know how long they've let us rot."

"Does it get easier?" She brushed away an unexpected tear. Stop thinking about home.

"There are two choices, Earth human. Either you submit, or you find something else to live for. For more years than I can count, I lost myself to Serenity. After hundreds of lost days, I started to develop more and more drug tolerance. The withdrawals were absolute hell. At least I could think, could feel. So I decided to reclaim sobriety. I started hiding the tablets in my pockets, then crushing and disposing of them in my latrine. By then, I had been here so long that the Guardians no longer paid attention to me. I've become invisible. It's a great gift when you're under constant surveillance."

Rusty stiffened. Alexa followed his gaze toward the Guardian at the end of the hall. Rusty had shifted, cocking his head as if listening to something.

"You want to get home, don't you?" Rusty stepped away from his corner, slithering toward his bed.

Alexa perked up. "Yes?"

"I have an idea. But it's up to you to stay alert for this to work."

She wanted to ask him a dozen more questions, but the tall feminine-presenting Guardian walked past, wary eyes glancing between their two cells. Letting her mouth hang open and her body go slack, Alexa gave the Guardian a sloppy wave.

"How are we feeling, X485?" The Guardian paused beside Alexa, her placid expression unable to hide the scrutiny in her glare.

"Very well, thank you." Alexa drooped against her cell wall. "What a lovely day."

"Glad to hear it," the Guardian—Alexa didn't recognize her—glanced in Rusty's direction. He had slunk to his bed, curled up, and pretended to be absorbed by his tablet. Faint lights flashed across his craggy face. "Have you been speaking to Z128?"

"He promised to play a game with me in the General Populace Room when I felt better."

"How kind." The Guardian's shoulders relaxed. "Once your levels have stabilized, we'll try to reintroduce you to your cohort. We'll take you outside if your attitude and actions are exemplary."

"Outside?" Alexa fought to hide her excitement. How long had it been since she had stared into the moon-scattered heavens above the General Populace Room? Everything had been artificial light and steel walls since she walked through the Instructor's portal.

"Yes, we allow only our most compliant residents to walk in the Common Yard. If you continue your current course, Guardian X will allow you some fresh air."

"That would be nice." Don't be too eager, Alexa reminded herself. She was never good at lying, but she had to try. Pretending to be drugged out may be her only salvation.

The Guardian shot one more look in Rusty's direction and, seeing nothing amiss, glided back to her previous position. Alexa pulled her knees to her chest, pretended to doze, and waited to see if Rusty would tell her more. His talk of escape sent her head spinning. Go home? How could she ever go home?

"Practice."

Alexa casually looked in Rusty's direction, but he hadn't moved or adjusted his previous position. He stared into the flashing screen before him when he said, "Start small. Remove a bolt from the floor. Then you can move on to bigger things."

Start small? Alexa surveyed her cell. At first, she couldn't find anything to move. Every steel sheet, every panel, every bar of light above her appeared seamless and unbreakable. Running her hands along the floor, her fingers tripped against the subtle crannies between the square metal flooring blocks. At the corner of each block was a flat-topped rivet the width of her pinky finger.

Until then, Alexa had only made a few small objects float and glass crack. How was she supposed to move something so small and so specific?

She yawned. Between the overdose of Serenity, her weird exchange with the Bright One, and Rusty filling her head with hope, too many questions tumbled through her thoughts. Una had its story of the Bright Ones, as did the Brume, so what song would the caged bird sing?

That was a question for tomorrow.

Alexa crept into bed and wished to fill the silence with her music. Her days were so quiet, so empty. She missed dissolving into the softer side of her playlists. At that moment, she craved the plucking discord of Jeff Buckley's cover of "Halleluiah." That song used to put her to sleep by the end of his mournful final chorus. Maybe if she covered her ears and dug deep enough, she could still let Buckley's delicate tenor guide her into a dreamless sleep.

Chapter 31

When her rotation started, Alexa didn't know what to expect from the Bright One. She hadn't counted on silence. Even when her Guardian left, the cell block remained as silent as the grave.

They had brought a mobile elevation rig so Alexa could clean places above her head. She wasn't afraid of heights, but the lack of guard rails made her immediately uneasy. The corridor ceiling was roughly twenty feet in height. Did they expect her to get every part of the unit?

She puttered around momentarily, gathering coils of suction hose beside the lift, glancing now and again at the Bright One's cell. When he did not attempt a greeting or a glare through his cell door's window, she went to work.

Like the night before, she dug within and pulled out her inner jukebox. The first song that came to mind was No Doubt's "Just a Girl," which soon led to Alanis Morrissette's "You Oughta Know." A few angry sirens were what she needed to get through another strange day in a strange universe.

As she belted the chorus of Alanis's angry musical diatribe to an ex-lover, the Bright One barked, *Will you never be quiet?*

She ignored him and continued to hum the second verse.

The Bright One banged on his cell door. *By all that is Bright, is that what they call music in your pitiful world? How atrocious.*

"Whatever, you have no sense of taste," Alexa muttered, adjusting the lift height so she could reach the top of a cell door.

Sense of taste? What do you mean by that?

"It's a figure of speech." Alexa flinched when he spoke again. How was his voice so damned loud? And what about the six-inch thick door on his cell? "How can you hear me anyway?"

What did Una tell you about us?

"Not much. Stuff about losing your home and searching for a new one. How the MGA has been killing you off one by one. That's about it."

Poor creature. Good for Una, fighting to live for so long. Most have given up. The rest are dead or imprisoned like me.

"I tried to help it." Alexa swallowed her regret.

Help? No one can help us. You speak of Una as "it". Una must have been a drone. Only the upper castes have the ability to procreate. How a drone made it to your world is ... impressive.

"A drone?" Alexa shifted around on her bottom and dangled her legs over the side of the lift platform. "Caste system? And you're from one of these 'upper castes'?"

The Bright One's face was pressed against his cell's viewing window. His eyes flared in annoyance. *Obviously.*

"So, are you, like, an aristocrat or something?"

I do not know this word. What is an "aristocrat"?

"Like, the top of the hierarchy? Ruling class?"

I am from a very powerful family. Not that any of that matters anymore. Look at me. My bathing unit was bigger than this awful cell.

"How powerful?" Alexa gave up pretending to clean and gathered the hose loops in her lap.

The Bright One let out a long sigh. *The greatest of the Bright Ones.*

"You're not royalty? Are you?"

Deposed royalty. The MGA had dissolved most monarchies by the time they found me, specifically the ones that threatened their supremacy. I expect you are relatively ignorant of the MGA's true brutality. You are not from one of the Class 1 or even 2 planets, are you?

"I don't even know what that means."

Class 1 planets are the original six systems that first formed the Multiverse Governing Association. Class two was the second set to join. I'm originally from a Class 50 planet. A notorious class, for we are the ones who refused to join the MGA when they ... proposed to let us join their association as long as we followed their Ruling Charter.

"Ruling Charter?"

The laws and edicts each member of the MGA is expected to follow. Where did you say you were from again? I have known this from infancy.

"I doubt you've heard of Earth."

Earth? Ah, so I see. Anyway, the Bright Ones were one of the last holdouts in the multiverse. One of the many reasons they chose to exterminate us.

Alexa sighed heavily. "I hate knowing so little about this place. About the MGA and all that. So, were you, like, a king? Do you know what a king is?"

I believe I understand your meaning. That was my mother. My magnificent, fierce, and terrifying mother.

No wonder the Bright One carried such a regal bearing. "So you're a prince?"

My name is Osu, the fifth of my name, rightful heir to the Brilliant Kingdom, and leader of a people who have suffered genocide at the hands of the MGA.

"Osu. It's nice to meet you, Osu." Alexa bowed her head before lowering the lift to the floor. "I've never met royalty before. How long have you been here?"

That is one of my greatest agonies. Those who locked me away have stolen time. I have no idea how long I have been stuck in this cell. I tried to scratch marks on the wall at one point. They somehow removed them while I slept. To this day, I have no idea how they did it.

"Me too. I can't tell when a day ends or begins. I sleep, but I have no idea how long I slept, which meal I'm eating."

And soon, they will wear you down like everyone else. The Bright One paced his cell, nostrils flaring.

Alexa could almost picture the furious unicorn despite her Blinders. "How do you do it? Stay sane, I mean. I've read that social isolation like yours makes someone lose their mind."

My people were born to be resilient. I master my thoughts when I despair. I sleep. I dream. I wait.

"What are you waiting for?"

For them to make a mistake. Because they will someday, and they have already made their first one.

"What's that?"

They have forgotten who I am. And because they forget, they will not remember how many died to put me in this hole. I am confident the MGA believes we have been conquered. Annihilated. Their complacency will be their undoing.

Hadn't Rusty said nearly the same thing, only on a smaller scale? In a hopeless place, she had found those still with hope. Well, more vengeful than hopeful, but she would take what she could get.

The Bright One tapped at his viewing window. *You should return to your cleaning. I may be forgotten, but you are not.*

"Right." Alexa gathered the vacuum, untangled the hose, and rolled the lift along the corridor's arching wall. She caught a glance of the drooling creature within the adjacent cell. Her Blinders showed her an older, thin person, their skin a network of wrinkles and age spots, passed out on their steel slab. "I think they brought me here as a warning."

Here? Please be specific.

"This cell block. They showed me where I could end up if I were not careful. I'm sure of it."

How could you be dangerous? The Bright One chuckled.

"That's what I keep telling them. I'm not." Alexa hit the appropriate buttons, and the platform lifted roughly six feet into the air. "You see, Una wasn't the only one who messed with my head. The Brume did, too. They possessed me for a short time."

Ah, yes. They are known to do that when hunting their prey. It is truly a miracle you are alive. Your brain should be no more than scrambled goo. How strange.

"I don't know what they did to me. I was supposed to forget everything that happened with Una and the Brume, but I didn't. And what they did changed me. I can, uh, move stuff with my mind now. You know, like, telekinesis."

Musical laughter tinkled through Alexa's mind. A laugh that went on for much longer than necessary.

"I'm serious." Alexa thumped her foot on the elevated platform, and the unit shuddered.

You cannot be serious. Osu continued to snigger. Alexa glanced over her shoulder and caught the flash of a flushed face through his cell viewport. *I have not laughed like this in so many years. Perhaps having you around is not all bad.*

Several days had passed since Alexa's unexpected telekinetic moment in the General Populace Room. Did she still have it in her? She pressed a hand to her forehead where her unseen power collected. A spark jiggled. Energy awakened. She gathered the tension, the heated pressure building until it glowed in her mind's eye. Unlike the time in the common room, she could hold and contain the accumulated power for a moment. The bubble of energy begged for release, pounding against her skull.

Alexa released the invisible force toward Osu's cell door. The steel *bonged.* A shudder traveled through the cell block, shaking Alexa where she stood.

"Shit, I shouldn't have done that." Alexa gasped. For a moment, she froze, expecting a furious Guardian X to come bursting through the cell block. The booming sound disappeared as quickly as it arrived, leaving Alexa surrounded by pulsating silence.

Eyes wide, the Bright One pressed his nose against the viewing window. *How did you do that?*

"I told you." Alexa released the breath she held. "Somehow, the combination of Una and the Brume in my head fundamentally screwed me up."

Drones are unable to move objects with their mind. But the Brume could. And what you are now is the result? Fascinating. No one would expect such a result.

"I didn't want this. I just wanted to be normal again."

The Guardians still hadn't appeared. Alexa tugged at the vacuum's hose and recommenced her search for dust. At the very least, she should pretend she hadn't just sent a ball of kinetic energy into yet another door within the Safekeeping Residence. She had to stop being reckless. Try to be a model resident for at least a little while.

You are full of surprises, Alexa.

The entry doors *whooshed* open, revealing a puzzled androgenous Guardian Alexa didn't recognize. "Resident X485, did you hear anything strange while cleaning here?"

"Like what?" Alexa slackened her expression and jiggled the hose in the Guardian's direction. "This lift thingy is kinda loud when I move it. Is that what you mean?"

The Guardian studied Alexa for a moment, lips pursed. "Nevermind. You've done enough cleaning today. Let's get you back into your cell."

"Okie-dokie." Alexa lowered the platform, humming to herself as she gathered the vacuum hose, pretending it was more difficult than necessary. They couldn't know she was stone sober. "Um, can you show me how to put the vacuum back? I kinda forgot."

"We'll need to reexamine your Serenity regimen. *Again*." The Guardian's serene expression broke for a split second, revealing annoyed exhaustion as they took the vacuum from Alexa's hand.

Osu's radiant eyes burned from across the room. He nodded to her once, a silent promise they would speak again tomorrow.

Chapter 32

For the first time since she arrived, Alexa couldn't sleep. Questions buzzed through her brain. She tossed and turned on the firm mattress. The overhead lamps were dimmed to half-strength, indicating that another day had passed. Faint snores echoed through the cell block and, occasionally, a strangled scream. What sort of dreams plagued her fellow prisoners? Did they remember their misdeeds? Did they remember lost loved ones?

Alexa's thoughts bounced between the two new men in her life, Rusty and Osu, and those she had lost. What was Sid doing at that moment? They only had a month left of school when she stepped through the Inspector's door. And what about Mateo? He had watched her walk into that bathroom and disappear. Thank God she had kept everything from him. Her instincts were correct. Knowledge wasn't power. It was a life sentence.

And what about Rusty? She barely knew him, but he had clearly taken an interest in her from the moment she walked into the General Populace Room. Could she trust him? Was he right about attempting to strengthen her powers?

Osu crept in and out of Alexa's spinning thoughts. He reminded her so much of Una, especially his arrogant bravado. Showing off her powers to prove him wrong may have been a mistake. What if he ratted her out to the Guardians? She didn't know him any better than Rusty.

She turned over on her bed, gaze straying to the floor. Dozens of flat-headed fasteners taunted her. How could she possibly focus her unreliable power on something so small? Floating books and plastic unicorns weren't so tough. She simply threw a bubble of current in their direction and beckoned the object toward her. Such a specific movement seemed impossible.

She turned over again, away from the floor. If she wanted to get any sleep that evening, she ought to clear her head and push out all the random thoughts buzzing in a swarm. However, the vision of the flat-headed rivets stuck in her mind. She mentally focused on the rivet's top and how its shaft cut through the metal tile's surface and into the framing below. The rivet wasn't threaded. Some sort of adhesive covered the exterior of the fastener, binding steel to steel. She would have to crack the bond somehow to extract the object.

Her mind's eye scanned several different fasteners, seeking out the one with the weakest adhesive. After searching half the room, she found one and wrapped invisible fingers around the object. For a moment, the bond held, but with one light tug, the whole object came loose. Now it was only a rivet sitting in a socket and one more pull could extract the entire thing. Alexa gave one last tug. The fastener rose from the floor and toppled over with a delicate *clink*.

The *clink* wasn't a figment of her imagination.

"Holy shit, no way." Alexa sat up in bed. Did that actually work? Did she seriously just pull a rivet from the floor by picturing it in her head? At first, everything appeared just as before. She got up and walked the perimeter of her cell.

Nothing.

Every single rivet was in its place, from the latrine to the bed. Alexa swore she heard a sound, and not just in her head. She was about to give up when she spotted a minor blemish in the shadow cast from her bed. Something was catching the light.

Alexa walked over and dropped to her knees. She reached under her bed and wrapped her fingers around a cold, hard object the length and thickness of her ring finger.

One of the flat-headed rivets.

"No way." She turned it over in her hands, triumphant. So, it wasn't so much about staring as hard as she could at an object but picturing every little detail in her mind. The possibilities were endless if that's all she had to do to move something.

"Nice work, Earth human."

In his cell, Rusty sat up in bed, a small smile playing on his lips. She had never seen the man smile. Didn't think it was possible.

"I can't believe I just did that." Alexa waved the rivet then panicked. How would she hide it from the Guardians? She ducked under the bed, fingers searching for an empty hole in the floor. Her pinky brushed over a small gap beneath where she laid her head every night. The bolt slipped back into its socket as if she had never removed it in the first place.

"But you did, Alexa."

"How do you know my name?"

"I know lots of things I'm not supposed to know."

"Do you have a name?"

"I've had lots of names." He sighed, scratching his silver beard. "So many that I don't remember my birth name. I've been here for so long. Z128 is the only name I know."

"Would it be okay if I called you Rusty?"

"Rusty?"

"You remind me of someone I knew a long time ago. His nickname was Rusty."

Again, the faint smile played upon his lips. The expression completely changed his face. "Sure, Earth human, you can call me Rusty."

Feet shuffled. Boots clicked along the cell block hall in their direction. Alexa quickly scrambled into bed, tucked herself into a fetal position, and pretended to sleep. The footfalls clicked toward her cell and stopped. A spotlight burned red through her eyelids before sweeping across the remainder of her cell.

The Guardian's footfalls clicked towards Rusty's cell. Alexa peered through her eyelashes and caught a glimpse of the Guardian who had brough her back from Osu's cell block performing the same ritual in Rusty's cell. When the spotlight dropped onto his face, Rusty pretended to stir in his sleep then rolled onto his side. The Guardian swept their spotlight once more across Alexa's cell, then, with a faint, irritated noise, returned to their post.

As the Guardian clopped away, Rusty whispered loud enough for Alexa to hear. "Tomorrow night, do two more."

Chapter 33

A lexa woke with a spark of optimism and a slight bounce in her step. She even dared to smile a few times while devouring her lightly drugged breakfast. She didn't mind Serenity's warm buzz. The drugs boosted morale when Guardian X came to take her to hours of useless cleaning in the Bright One's cell block.

"You seem different today, X485," Guardian X noted as she opened the door splashed with warning signs.

"I do?" Alexa let her head loll to the side. Pretending to be drugged wasn't so hard under the veil of hope.

"You must be adjusting to your routine." Guardian X's smile reached her eyes for once. "We are all pleased to see it. If this continues, you will be allowed to rejoin the general population shortly. No more work assignments on your own. You will join a crew of other Residents."

"Great." Alexa's smile slipped. She enjoyed her time in the isolated cell block with Osu. She glanced in the direction of his cell, but he wasn't near the viewing window.

Guardian X caught her glance. "Have any of the Residents in this block tried to communicate with you?"

"Ugh..." Alexa fought to play stupid as her heart thundered in her ears. What should she say? "Well, the guy over there sometimes bangs around in his cell, but otherwise, it's really quiet. Everyone just sleeps or drools."

"Has this one tried to speak to you?" Guardian X's smile tightened.

Had they monitored her the whole time? Was this some sort of test?

"Is that possible?" Alexa swallowed, fighting to maintain her blissed-out façade. The weak buzz of the Serenity couldn't keep the rising panic at bay. "The doors look super thick. Especially that one. Do you think he can hear me?"

"Doubtful." Guardian X wandered over to the Bright One's cell, a look of disgust distorting her face as she peered inside.

Alexa shifted to see within Osu's cell, but the Guardian blocked her view.

"Many died before this monster was captured." The Guardian stared into the cell for a minute, jaw flexing. "He has been with us for a long time now. Eating our food. Wasting our resources. Breathing our finely filtered air. We never execute those deemed undesirable by the MGA but—can you keep a secret X485?"

"Sure. Okay?"

"Sometimes we make mistakes." Guardian X's grin transformed into a cold rictus.

Alexa fought the dread twisting her gut. "Oh?"

"Anyway, keep up the good work." Guardian X's serene smile returned. She turned on her heel and headed for the exit. "Let me know if this beast says even a word to you. I'll return in a few hours."

"Yes—uh, okay."

The door *whooshed* closed again, leaving Alexa alone, the cell block draped in an eerie silence. For a moment, she didn't know what to do. What she wouldn't give for a day without someone making a thinly-veiled threat.

Hello, Alexa. The Bright One's intense blue eyes filled the viewing window. *You do not look well. What is wrong?*

"You didn't just hear what the Guardian said?" Alexa shook a frantic hand toward the closed door.

Of course not.

"But you can hear me?"

I cannot enter the mind of a Guardian. Do not be a fool. I can only hear you because you mentally broadcast your words as clearly as you speak them. The walls around me keep out all sound but cannot contain mental communication.

Alexa stuck out her bottom lip. "I want to go home. I hate it here."

You can never go home, Alexa. They will never let you leave. You must learn to live with your lot.

She rubbed her temples, the Serenity withdrawal already faintly making itself known. Her body was adjusting to her current dosage. Soon enough, she might not react at all, only a dull headache. And how long could she pretend to be a drug addict? At some point, she would slip and then what would the Guardians do to her?

"I know you said you're resilient, but holy cow. How can you stand it?"

Habit. The Bright Ones lost our home world long ago when we refused to join the MGA and submit to their hypocritical governing practices. They thought we could be useful if on their side. But when we refused, well, we were weapons to be destroyed. My people have had no choice but to adapt, no matter the circumstances. You would not believe what I have done to stay alive before I ended up here.

"But then they caught you?" Alexa crept closer to his cell, drawn by the melodic voice in her head. Now that she no longer feared him, she realized Osu's voice was quite soothing. His blue eyes radiated their own light, much like his nearly white skin. Despite the Blinders, he was obviously a Bright One.

Yes, they still found me. My kind have long lives. Perhaps this is where everything ends for me. Perhaps not. I thought I would never speak to a living creature again, yet here we are, exchanging words. For some reason, Una found you trustworthy, which is quite shocking, to be honest. We do not trust outsiders.

"You shouldn't trust me." Alexa walked to the vacuum closet. With the fuzz of Serenity nearly out of her system, every raw emotional nerve returned in a sudden rush. Waves of homesickness, despair, loss, and confusion crashed over her as she tugged out the cleaning machine. The elevation rig stood right where she had left it the previous day. Now, she would pretend to clean the quarter of the circle opposite the Bright One's cell.

Why? Because you tried to help Una and could not? There are powers at work so much greater than you, Simple One. You are no more than a speck of cosmic dust riding the celestial currents. Do not blame yourself for being anything other than what you are.

Tears slipped down Alexa's cheeks as she pushed the lift deeper into the cell block. She caught sight of a drooling hulk of a man passed out on the floor of his cell. She envied him and his obliteration as she raised the contraption six or so feet in the air before vertigo once again forced her to her knees.

She switched on the vacuum and scrubbed various nooks and crannies: the top of a cell door, the seams between steel plates, a row of some kind of wiring covered in a thick metal shell. The monotonous movements helped quiet her mind. Where did all the wires go? Were they electrical wires? Communication wires? Like the night before with the rivet, her mind's eye sunk beneath the exterior into twisting wire strands.

But she didn't remain in the cell block. Caught up in the current of power flowing through the cables, she gasped when her mind hurled from one end of the Safekeeping Residence to the other. She flew from one cell block to the next, catching slurred voices and sounds, the bright clip of a Guardian's voice, a hundred monitors in a security center, and then, rounding the corner, racing toward a power station where her focus exploded into a million pieces against the turbines.

"Oh, shit." Somehow, Alexa had ended up at the edge of the lift's platform, head reeling, lost to all sense of direction. She tipped forward and slid off the edge. She managed to land on her feet before crumpling into a bewildered heap.

Gods, did you fall?

"What was that?" Alexa sat up, and the world seemed to fracture for a moment. Half of her mind wanted to return to following the power circuits while the other half fought back waves of dizziness.

Are you well, Alexa? Osu pressed his nose against the viewing window, his breath fogging the glass. If Alexa didn't know better, she swore the Bright One was worried about her.

"Something bizarre just happened." Alexa rolled onto her knees. The cell block blurred momentarily, her conscious mind fighting to stay within her body. "No, stay here. Stay here."

You need to make more sense. Are you not well? The Guardians have an emergency beacon you can send out if you hit the silver button next to the main door.

Alexa fixed her gaze on Osu's face. Perhaps she could return fully to her body if she focused on another living, breathing thing. The urge to rejoin the electric currents faded. Her mind became one again.

Speak, Simple One.

"Please don't call me that." Alexa groaned, probing the throbbing ache blooming once more at her temples.

Speak, Alexa.

Alexa turned her back to the wires, fearing to look at them again. "You know how I can move things with my mind? I think I might be leveling up."

Leveling up? You speak in riddles.

The main doors suddenly *wooshed* open, revealing a confused Guardian X on the other side. She took in Alexa kneeling on the floor, the raised lift, and the still-running vacuum sitting in a heap on the lift's platform.

"What happened here?" Guardian X frowned, her gaze surveying the mess displayed before her.

"Silly me, I tripped on the vacuum hose." Alexa forced out a laugh and dropped her head so the Guardian couldn't see the panic in her eyes. What had brought Guardian X back? Had they been watching her all along, waiting for the right time to catch her doing something stupid or dangerous?

Guardian X approached Alexa and stood over her. "An odd power surge originated from this section, so I was sent to investigate. Anything strange happen here?" She walked straight toward the Bright One's cell and peered inside.

"All I know is I fell." Alexa sat up, spots dancing before her vision.

"Fell?" In the next moment, Guardian X was on her knees in front of Alexa. She gently tipped Alexa's head back, scanning her Resident for possible injury. "Did something happen with the suction device?"

"I don't know. I was on the lift one moment, and the next? Boom!"

"Let's get you back to your cell. Can you stand?" Guardian X put her arm beneath Alexa's shoulders and slowly raised her from the floor. "It's possible your body hasn't yet stabilized in how it reacts to the Serenity. It can take weeks, even months, for some to properly adapt."

"But the mess?"

"I think we'll have someone else take over cleaning this cell block." Guardian X helped Alexa toward the door.

"No, that's okay." Everything came into sharp focus at once. Despite her odd exchanges with Osu, she wasn't ready to say goodbye. She had so many questions she wanted to ask him when the time was right. "I can finish. I like the quiet here."

"Perhaps this wasn't the right assignment for you. We'll have another Guardian put everything away. We'll move you to a cleaning crew, where you can keep both feet on the ground."

Farewell, Alexa.

Alexa glanced back over Guardian X's shoulder the second before the door *whooshed* closed behind her. She didn't even get the chance to say goodbye to the first real connection she had made since leaving Earth.

Would she ever see him again?

Chapter 34

The strange events of the past day left Alexa numb. She just wanted to climb into a blanket-covered hole and disappear. Like she used to do when life was normal, she wanted to create a nest of blankets and pillows, put on her wireless headphones, and listen to her favorite playlist repeatedly until the world beyond faded.

If she let herself go long enough, she could almost hear Gavin Rossdale admitting the chemicals between us or, when she was feeling especially wild, System of a Down screamed in her ears, decrying capitalism and its societal ills.

When the Guardian came for her the following day, Alexa had withdrawn so far within herself—Incubus's "Wish You Were Here" on silent repeat—the Guardian had to shout her name to pull her out of her funk.

"Good day, X485," said the Guardian Alexa didn't immediately recognize. He was slightly taller and thinner than the others, with a broad nose.

Alexa rubbed her face, wishing she could tell her captor to "fuck off," but didn't dare.

"We have excellent news. You will be having your breakfast in the General Populace Room today."

Alexa didn't want to be among the doped-up Residents. She wanted to curl into a ball, doze the day away, and dream of her home, friends, and people who loved her. And, oddly, she wished she could return to Osu's cell block. Their conversations had been strained and sometimes awkward, but at least they were honest.

"X485, are you not well this morning?"

"Which one are you?" Alexa blinked, forcing herself to focus on the present to get through another weird day.

"Guardian F." The tall man who wasn't a man leaned forward, concern shaping his features. "Are you feeling dizzy? Or sluggish? Guardian X reported you had an accident yesterday. Are your internal levels off-course?"

Alexa shrugged. "I guess."

"Well, then I'll send word to the food preparation center. We'll adjust the nutrition components of your meal."

She had no idea what that might mean but dissolving into a serene haze sounded nice after days of oscillating between too much tranquilizer and too little. She unwound her limbs and sat up in bed, a familiar withdrawal pulse reverberating through her skull.

"Come, X485." He deactivated the force field and reached out a long-fingered hand. Hands much like Sid's. A pang of longing added to the dull throb radiating from her skull into her shoulders.

"Cheer up." Guardian F smiled down at her. He was at least a foot taller. "You'll feel much better after some healthy social interaction. The Residents are very excited to have you return to them."

They started down the hall. Alexa didn't pay much attention to where they went. She didn't really care. Her whole being felt like a gaping wound. She was surprised her chest hadn't cleaved open, pouring guts and misery all over the floor.

"X485, you seem almost sad." Guardian F was more attentive than the other Guardians. He paused in the middle of the hall and gently touched her shoulder. "Can you tell me what has brought this on?"

Alexa flinched in his grasp. His hand was cold, almost clammy against her skin. "Bad dreams." She would never forget the monster she had seen when her Blinders glitched: a tentacled beast with clawed hands the size of her head.

"We could help with that." Guardian F gave her such a caring, concerned smile, Alexa's throat tightened. "A few adjustments to your nutrition plan and you will dream of nothing. Would that be suitable?"

Her dreams were all she had left of home. "No. But can I change my mind later?"

"Yes, of course, X485. Our primary objective is to keep our Residents calm, no matter what. It saddens me to see you so distressed, especially when we can ease your discomfort."

"Thanks. I'll let you know."

"Very well, X485. We do not have much further to go."

They walked down several more enormous stainless-steel hallways before arriving at yet another massive door where a Guardian stood guard. He nodded to both Alexa and his co-worker, then pressed several buttons. The door *whooshed* open, revealing the familiar, bustling General Populace Room. Alexa's gaze immediately went to the glass ceiling. The sky was a soft magenta, spotted by puffs of pink cotton-candy clouds. Beyond the clouds, enormous moons covered in dark craters and canyons floated.

"You can see this view daily as long as your moods stay balanced." Guardian F turned his face to the sky and appreciated the view. "However, we cannot have another repeat of the last time you were here. Such a noise! Ah, M365 and D958 look happy to see you. You should join them."

The Residents she had named DeeDee and Murphy wiggled in their seats, excitedly waving Alexa to their table. They were already halfway through their breakfast mush. From their dilated pupils to the goofy grins splitting their faces, one could see that they were stoned out of their minds.

"We're so very happy to see you," Murphy gushed. The round man quivered in his seat. "We weren't sure if we'd see you again."

"Yep, I'm back." Even if it was drug-induced, Alexa couldn't stay down when surrounded by such enthusiasm.

DeeDee blinked her wide, glassy eyes. "The Guardians said they had to regulate your medications before it would be safe to bring you back. This happens all the time with new arrivals. So don't be embarrassed."

On the other side of the table, Curly drooled into the remains of his breakfast. Alexa had to look away. He reminded her of the vacant creatures in the isolation block.

"Here you are, X485." Guardian X set a bowl of Alexa's breakfast before her. "Eat up. I think we've got your levels right where they should be. Please let me know if anything doesn't settle right."

Like before, the oatmeal-like mush barely went down initially but quickly became a satisfying, hearty meal once the drugs kicked in. Alexa had forgotten how she could go from miserable, empty Alexa to a cheerful drug addict in less than five minutes. Her dark mind cleared, the chasm in her chest sealed, and a pleasant buzz emanated from every limb. Maybe this wasn't so bad after all. Maybe she could let go of everything she had lost and become content with her current existence.

Alexa finished her breakfast. DeeDee pulled a deck of plastic card-sized plates from a nearby shelf. Both she and Murphy started teaching her the rules of yet another alien card game called Pairs—which sounded a lot like poker—when Rusty appeared in the empty seat beside Curly. Alexa hadn't seen him when she first came in.

He sagged in his seat and smiled a smile that didn't reach his eyes. Alexa's high was mild enough that her brain still worked, so she recognized that the wizened resident was simply putting on a show for the Guardians.

"Can I join in?" Rusty continued to smile, the edges of his mouth trembling from the effort.

"Yes, of course." DeeDee dealt him in, beaming from ear to ear.

Curly hadn't recovered from breakfast, so Rusty took up the playing cards scattered before him. His pale eyes focused on Alexa briefly before returning to the loose, casual posture he usually maintained. Should she tell him about what happened with the electrical wires? What if, the next time, she couldn't go back into her body? What if she completely split in two, her consciousness running on an unending current until the end of time?

No, she couldn't trust Rusty. Not yet.

Alexa fought to pay attention. She was never very good at cards and thus never very interested in card games. When it was her turn, she laid down a sun and a square card. Murphy burst into laughter.

"I did something wrong?" Alexa glanced between the doped-up faces of her companions.

DeeDee snuffled. "That pair doesn't even make sense The sun and square never go together. Silly, Earth human."

"This was easier last time." Alexa stuck out her bottom lip. Wasn't it supposed to be a bit like poker? She had been so high on Serenity; she could have been playing Eucher or Spades for all she knew.

Alexa tried to giggle with Deedee and Murphy, but an all too familiar tight, empty feeling fluttered at the center of her chest.

"You want to pair celestials and geometrics separately," Rusty explained, his rough voice almost gentle in contrast to DeeDee and Murphy's raucous laughter. "Let's pretend this round never happened. D958, can you reshuffle and begin again?"

"Oh, sure, whatever." Deedee wiped a tear from the corner of her eye and gathered up the cards as the rest of the players tossed them, clinking, into the center of the table.

"Don't get frustrated. You'll get the hang of it," Rusty said. He was attempting to be patient, but he couldn't maintain the front. His desire to speak to her privately hung in every sharp glance in Alexa's direction.

"I have the rest of my life to figure it out, don't I?" Alexa sighed, sagging in her seat. She scanned the room for

Guardian F. He might give her another dose if she requested it.

"You never know," Rusty murmured, barely loud enough to be heard above the cards clacking away. "Yesterday, you lifted a rivet. Perhaps today or tomorrow, something much bigger."

"Sure." Alexa cringed, recalling the wild sensation of becoming part of the prison's electric flow. "Something bigger."

Chapter 35

They played another round of Pairs. This time, Alexa started to see the pattern. The card game was similar to Poker, but they didn't use queens, jacks, or aces. The more complex the "celestial body" on their cards, the higher the value. Same with the complexity of the geometric shapes. Alexa didn't win this round, but she didn't lose either.

When DeeDee gathered the cards to play one last round, Rusty said, "X485, there's a two-person game I wanted to show you. M356, D958, is it okay if I show X485 a new game?"

Murphy shrugged, grinning stupidly. "If X485 promises to play another round of Pairs before the end of breakfast?"

Alexa shot Rusty a questioning look. When he shrugged she said, "You bet." She followed him to one of the large cabinets full of games. Despite being stuck in an advanced civilization, she was surprised that many options looked like board and card games. Or were the Blinders performing such magic?

"Sometimes I wonder what I'm actually seeing." Alexa touched the small Blinder discs near her eyes and ears. The skin was still a bit tender around each device. What she wouldn't give for some lotion. "What do you see?"

"You don't want to know." Rusty frowned and pulled out a black box the size of a large hardback novel. "My Blinders stopped working so long ago. I can't remember when they did."

"What do you see when you look at me?"

"A small, pale biped with eyes that remind me of a frightened youngling." Rusty carried the black box over to an empty nearby table. He smiled and nodded to Guardian F, who had taken a close interest in their activities. "Smile," he told Alexa through his teeth.

Alexa gave her biggest, sloppiest grin to that same Guardian and tossed him an exaggerated wave. The Guardian's hard eyes softened, and he nodded in their direction.

"Good, keep doing that." Rusty removed a square whiteboard covered in a perfectly square grid. "This game is straightforward. You want to create as many uninterrupted rows as possible while the other person tries to create their own uninterrupted rows. Watch."

Rusty pressed a finger in the middle of the center square. When he pulled his finger away, the space had turned blue. "Now, your turn."

Alexa picked a random square. When she lifted her finger, the space had turned red.

Rusty nodded. "Just like that."

They continued for several minutes. Alexa tried to grasp Rusty's strategy as he filled in what seemed like one random cube after another. She began a steady row of squares only to have Rusty interrupt her repeatedly from unexpected directions.

"Pretend you're having fun." Rusty's smile appeared genuine since he was winning the game. "You frown when you're concentrating."

Alexa sighed and did as directed, watching as her rows were decimated over and over again by the older alien. "What did you want to talk about?"

"How we're going to break out of this place." Rusty spoke so casually that Alexa didn't initially realize what he said.

"You're not serious?" Alexa let out a bitter laugh, giving up all sense of strategy and attempting a pathetic defense.

"I have been in this prison so long I know everything about it."

"I don't even know where we are," Alexa lamented, her gaze floating to the ceiling. Actual daylight didn't appear possible in this world where they happened to be. The sky still had the pink, warm tinge of sunrise.

"I didn't either at first. How could I? The drugs were more volatile then. I was in the group they experimented on until they got it right. I'm the only one left now. Everyone else either overdosed or fried their brain... Oh, I win!" Rusty burst from the table and broke into a goofy, exaggerated celebration. Several of the players at other tables broke into applause or cheers.

Rusty waved and bowed, the cold, calculating man disappearing behind a never-ending act. When he sat down again, he whispered, "Eventually, more dangerous and interesting Residents joined us. And eventually, I was no longer of interest. I'm a barely visible ghost who sees and hears all. They only pay attention to me now because you're sitting beside me."

"Okay, so you know your way around. Why didn't you try escaping already?"

"Because I've lacked one important element all this time."

"And what's that?"

"An escape artist."

Alexa blanched. "What are you talking about?"

"Careful." Rusty cleared the glowing board. "You never want to frown in the presence of the Guardians. They'll immediately know your Serenity levels are off."

Alexa lifted the corners of her mouth in a tight grin. "What the hell are you talking about?"

"There's one thing I can't do that you could if you practice hard enough."

"And what's that?"

"Open doors. I know a thousand ways to get out of this prison, but I can't open doors."

"And if I could—which I can't—where would we go?" Alexa turned her gaze up to the beautiful heavens above her. The moons shone yellow in partial daylight. "I know next to nothing about the multiverse."

"I know enough for both of us." Rusty pressed an empty square. "And I know that intergalactic freighters come and go from this place on a regular schedule. It's going to be a long journey, of course. Everything takes much longer when you're not using the multigalactic skyway. We won't be able to pass into another dimension right away, but with a little luck—"

"Intergalactic freighters? Multigalactic skyway? I'm not so sure." Alexa couldn't look away from the heavens. What Rusty proposed seemed impossible. She had no idea how to navigate one universe, let alone multiples.

"Don't you want to go home?" Rusty tapped the back of her hand, pulling Alexa back to earth.

She inhaled sharply. "Is that possible?"

"I've done my share of impossible things." Rusty held her gaze. "The journey will be long and dangerous, but I can get you home."

A delicate spark of hope warmed her chest. A spark so fragile, she was afraid to kindle the fire, terrified he may be getting her hopes up for nothing.

"Here, keep playing. Relax that intense look on your face." Rusty pointed to the game. "How can you practice your skills if they're always watching you? Lay low for a week and keep practicing with your rivets. We'll find new ways for you to practice and improve. And when I feel like you're ready, we'll start messing with doors."

They played the game a while longer, Rusty once more outplaying her move after move. Alexa turned over everything he said as they played. After all she had seen of the Safekeeping Residence, escape seemed impossible. If a Bright One couldn't escape, how could she and a little old man have any chance?

"And we'll need a distraction, of course. I have several ideas, and I haven't settled on one yet. There hasn't been a proper technical mishap in this place for at least twenty years. They won't be prepared."

"And what if we fail?" Alexa whispered. Rusty's words made her head swim and her hands sweat. She pictured the tiny cell in the isolation cell block. If she attempted to escape, that's exactly where they would put her. Then they'd pump her with so many drugs she would become nothing but another drooling pile of flesh. Living but not alive. She shuddered.

Rusty pursed his lips. "That's not an option."

"I've seen what they do to the dangerous ones." Alexa absentmindedly pressed another square, barely paying attention to the game. "They're zombies. Well, except for Osu, of course."

"Osu?" Rusty smiled as he cut off yet another one of her rows.

"Yeah, the Bright One they're keeping in the isolation cell block."

"Its name is Osu?" Rusty's calm visage broke for a split second. "How do you know that?"

Alexa shrugged. "He told me."

"What?" Rusty's fingers slipped over the white game board, causing him to hit several squares at once. The game board made a small beep then cleared.

"Residents!" A strong, clear voice spoke from the front of the room. "Common time is over. Time for a nap before you head out to your work assignments."

All the Residents rose at once, stumbling or tripping out of their seats. Alexa lurched to her feet as well. Her conversations with the Bright One felt like a secret she wasn't meant to share. Rusty tossed Alexa a few undecipherable looks as they waited for their Guardians to usher them back to their cells.

"Did you have a nice time with Z128?" Guardian X appeared at Alexa's side.

"Yes, he taught me a new game." Alexa plastered on a sloppy grin, waving to the clear gameboard. "Beat me twice. Well, maybe more than twice."

"Z128, can you put your game away while you wait for Guardian Z? They are running a little behind today."

Rusty did as he was told but with slow, sloppy movements, flicking Alexa one more cold, hard look before she headed off with her Guardian. Had she told him too much? Why was she so worried? The old man wanted to break out of prison and trusted her with such information. She ought to trust him too.

"Did you have a nice time with the other Residents?" Guardian X glanced over her shoulder as she led Alexa toward her cell block.

"I did." Alexa beamed. "Thank you."

"Seems you are making new friends. M356 and D958 have been some of our best Residents. They would make excellent companions. Did you know that Z128 is one of our oldest Residents? He also has an impeccable record."

"He's nice," Alexa said. Her heart accelerated. Could one of the Guardians have heard their conversation?

They continued to walk with the rest of the Residents in silence. Residents returned to their cells one by one, quietly tipping into their beds.

"Here you are." Guardian X paused outside of Alexa's cell. "A helpful reminder: you aren't like any of the

Residents. They were once the worst of the worst. So far, our rehabilitation has worked wonders for them all. But never forget, they're all killers."

"But everyone is so nice." Alexa looked over Guardian's X's shoulder just as Rusty staggered into his cell and flopped onto his bed.

"Indeed, they are. Nonetheless, never turn your back on any of them. And know I am here for you no matter what."

Was this another thinly veiled threat, or did Guardian X truly care about her welfare? Alexa walked over to her bed and sat.

"You look sleepy. A nice nap will help you recharge." Guardian X hit the button to activate Alexa's cell's force field. "This afternoon, we'll introduce you to your new work crew. I think you'll enjoy your new assignment. It'll be your first time outside."

She perked up. "Outside? Really?"

"Yes, now get some rest."

Alexa curled into the fetal position, grateful when the Guardians turned down the overhead lights. So many things had happened in one day that her brain could barely process it all. She wished to examine every question and concern buzzing through her brain, but exhaustion quickly descended. She fell into a troubled sleep.

Chapter 36

E *arth human?*
    Did someone speak? Alexa blinked, rubbing heavy eyelids. The sounds of gentle snoring greeted her.

Can you hear me, Alexa?

She sat up. Was that Rusty? No, he was lying on his bed, taking the slow, deep breaths of someone lost in slumber.

I knew this would not work. I am foolish to think it would. She is nothing more than a low, simple-minded—

"Osu?" Alexa whispered. She slipped out of bed. How did he get free? A single Guardian stood on the far end of the cell block, studying a small tablet and fighting back a yawn.

Ah, so you can *hear me.*

Alexa swept her gaze across her tiny cell. "How is this possible?"

I have been looking for you for the last twenty-four hours. I was about to give up, but I sent my voice to the farthest reaches of this damned place, and there you are.

"Are you still in your cell?"

Of course, I am still in my cell. Where else would I be?

"But, how—"

My people were skilled in projecting their voices across vast distances when we were at our greatest strength. Only the ruling class had such an ability, of course. This projection saved us many, many times. I was not sure if you would be receptive,

244

and once again, you have proved to be an exception to your species. To most, in fact.

"I'm surprised you bothered trying." Alexa couldn't help smiling. He reminded her so much of Una. "I thought I was too low to be worthy of your attention."

You are. At least, you should be. However, speaking to another living, breathing creature is much better than losing my mind. I have not had a conversation in years before you came to my cell. And I have no wish to be so isolated again if it can be helped.

"I guess I'm better than nothing, huh?"

If I am stuck in this horrible room for the rest of my life, I'd rather not suffer alone. And you are not afraid of me, which is quite strange. Most gape at me in horror once they realize what I am.

"You're not so bad."

The overhead lights brightened. Throughout the cell block, creatures stirred, grunting and yawning as they woke up.

"They're turning up the lights here." Alexa turned her back so she could hold onto her conversation for a couple of seconds longer. "I'm not cleaning in your cell block anymore. They're sending me somewhere else."

I guessed as much when they took the lift away. Why did they have you clean the Supreme Security Unit anyway? The place was already spotless.

"I was right, it was just a threat," Alexa whispered into the wall. "Be good, or else you'll end up here too."

You are dangerous too, you know. They must be frightened of your telekinetic power. It is a rare ability, even across this vast multiverse. Whatever you do, never show them just how powerful you are.

"Good advice." Alexa turned over at the clip of Guardian footfalls near her cell. "We'll talk later."

Guardian X appeared outside her cell, a serene smile in place. "Are you ready for your new assignment, X485?"

Alexa sat up and faked a yawn. "Sure."

Never had Alexa felt so small as when she stood on the roof of the Safekeeping Residence and peered into the vast purple heavens of an alien world. Residence Darkstar stood at the top of a great mountain in the middle of a mountain range that easily rivaled the Himalayas. Craggy, blue rocks pierced the sky as far as the eye could see. No other signs of civilization were anywhere in sight.

Above her, a violet sky displayed several golden moons, each bigger than the next. The celestial bodies nearly obliterated the heavens. Stars winked in the distance, and once, some sort of satellite or rocket sped across the sky.

Alexa hadn't been able to tell from within the Residence, but the building was nearly the size of a football stadium and protected by an enormous, transparent dome that was almost invisible, except when she angled her gaze just right. That was why the temperature was perfect despite being on the top of a mountain range. She and a dozen other Residents scoured the rooftop while a couple of Guardians looked on.

Guardian X touched her shoulder "X485, you need to keep working."

"Sorry, it's just so beautiful." Alexa adjusted the pack strapped to her back and vacuumed the accumulated dust. At least this time, she wasn't pretending to work.

"You've earned the view." Guardian X peered across the vast landscape, a genuine smile tugging at her lips as she absentmindedly tossed a three-foot steel rod end-over-end before catching it. The Guardians were armed while overseeing the Residents. This tossing action was as menacing as it was playful. "It's so peaceful here, so far away from all the troubles of the multiverse. I never tire of this view."

Alexa hummed, reminding herself not to be too aware or too present. Further across their section of the rooftop, Deedee and Murphy bounced along, attacking each other with their vacuums when the other Guardian wasn't watching. Alexa's tuneless hum soon altered into a recent favorite from her updated playlist. What she wouldn't give to listen to Weezer again. To listen to any music again.

Guardian X turned from the mountains. "What's that sound you're making?"

"You mean my humming?"

"Is that what you call it?" Alexa's Guardian appeared genuinely interested. "I did not know your species made music."

"We live for music." Alexa shrugged.

"If you continue to be a good Resident, perhaps I can get special permission to let you listen to some of our libraries. We have music from all members of the MGA. Even some non-members, I believe. At least three thousand worlds. Would you like that, X485?"

Alexa couldn't hide her excitement. "That would be awesome."

"Very well." Guardian X clasped her hands behind her back and beamed. "Give me seven more days of good behavior, and I'll see what I can do."

Alexa didn't have to pretend to smile after Guardian X's offer. What sort of music did other worlds enjoy? Would it be so weird it hurt her ears, or would she hear the echoes of the universe?

"Guardians! I need immediate assistance!"

Halfway across the roof, a burly Resident the size of a small mountain was screaming. He wrenched his vacuum from his back and threw it full force at the nearest Resident, Deedee. The skinny woman cried out as the device knocked her off her feet. At the same time, all three Guardians surrounded the enormous man, arms spread wide. Electricity snapped and buzzed at the end of each steel rod.

The large man howled and charged through a gap between the Guardians. Despite his size, he moved fast, knocking over another Resident who got in his way. He zigged and zagged, arms waving wildly, his screams growing from a roar to a screech. Guardian X managed to send a quick zap between his shoulders, but the madman easily smacked her away. Guardian X's attack redirected the wild Resident, sending him barreling toward Alexa.

She caught the red gleam in his eyes. Saliva streamed from his bellowing mouth as he raised his arms as if intending to pummel her into the roof. She collapsed into a tiny ball, extending a useless hand to protect herself.

"Stop!" she cried out, preparing for impact.

The collision never happened.

Alexa looked up in time to see the insane Resident floating several feet off the ground. He writhed and bellowed, pie-plate-sized hands reaching for her.

"No," she whispered and mentally pushed him several more feet into the air.

While the Residents gaped, the Guardians electrocuted the madman until he lost consciousness. The moment the man stopped moving, Alexa let him go. All she had to do was withdraw her focus from him, and he slammed like an enormous bag of meat onto the rooftop.

Everyone on the roof, in various states of surprise, confusion, and delight, stared at Alexa. As the two other Guardians sorted out the Residents, Guardian X was the only one lucid enough to approach the unconscious man and stick him with a needle.

Alexa froze. She had just exposed her ability in front of three Guardians. They would probably throw her into one of the isolation cells and pump her full of drugs. Then she would slowly lose her mind while Osu told her she was a stupid, silly Earthling who got what she deserved.

"Well, I guess we underestimated your skills." Guardian X gave the colossal man a nudge with the toe of her shoe. "Looks like we'll need to give you another evaluation. Immediately."

Chapter 37

The Guardians sorted out the mess on the roof with practiced efficiency. Several more Guardians joined them. The injured Residents were gathered and led to the infirmary. The remaining residents were taken back to their cells. The Resident who went rogue was strapped securely to a floating gurney and carried off.

Guardian X ushered Alexa away from everyone else down a narrow corridor. Alexa didn't bother pretending she was drugged anymore since the jig was up. Her terror mounted, but her vision remained clear, and her feet steady. She had already lost everything. All that was left was her life.

Or her sanity.

Guardian X didn't say a word as they wound through an endless series of narrow corridors. Lights popped awake with a loud *woom* as they passed through the hall, startling Alexa repeatedly. She gnawed the inside of her cheek and laced her trembling fingers before her. *Be brave*, she silently told herself. *Be brave.*

They finally came to a door. Guardian X hit an unseen switch, and the steel slab opened to reveal a large meeting room with a circular steel table at its center. Each side of the square space held a similar door.

"Please take a seat." Guardian X pointed to one of the many stools surrounding the table.

Alexa did as she was told. The stool was cold and hard, like most of the furniture in the Safekeeping Residence. She tried to find a comfortable position while she laced and unlaced her sweaty fingers in her lap.

Guardian X drifted to the opposite side of the table and stood behind one of the many stools. She pulled a tablet from her pocket and vigorously typed various bits of information into the device. Her face was neither serene nor upset and utterly devoid of emotion.

"What's happening?" Alexa croaked, her voice tiny in the large room.

"I'm not sure yet." Guardian X continued to type, scroll, and press buttons on her tablet. "Please stay calm. I don't want to drug you."

"Okay, sure." Alexa squirmed and rubbed a hand over the stubble covering her scalp.

Two Guardians stepped through opposite doors when they opened, greeting Guardian X with a nod before shifting their pale eyes toward Alexa. Each did the same as Guardian X, pulling out tablets before taking one of the dozens of seats. Soon, several more Guardians arrived, enough to fill the entire alphabet, A to Z. Alexa didn't recognize most of them and wondered if perhaps the alphabet they used had more than twenty-six letters.

Guardian X surveyed her co-workers and gave them all a quick nod. Anyone who still stood took a seat. Only Alexa's Guardian remained standing.

"You have all been made aware of what happened on the roof not long ago," Guardian X began, her expression remaining neutral. "We find ourselves in a rare position. Our protocols would have us put X485 into a permanent isolation chamber. She has proven to be a threat to the continued quietude of our Safekeeping Residence. Serenity does not weaken her unique power, which makes her unpredictable."

Blood drained from Alexa's face. She should have let the mad Resident pummel her.

"I recommend we sedate her and put her into an isolation cell block immediately," a sharp voice chirped from the other side of the room.

Alexa turned toward a skinny, tall man who reminded her of an angry stork as he glared at her. She had never seen him before, but he had obviously already formed a strong opinion about her.

"I think we should attempt to re-adjust her Serenity levels first." A soft-bodied Guardian lifted her chin and gave Alexa a pitying look. "She's just a tiny Earth human. We've never had one before, and we should give her more opportunity to adjust to her foreign surroundings."

The Guardians started speaking at once, agreeing with the first or the second recommendation of Alexa's fate. Half of the group wanted to lock her in a cell and never let her out, while the others took pity upon her.

"She's so tiny. She can't cause that much harm," a high-cheekboned Guardian declared beside her.

The portly Guardian to Alexa's left disagreed. "Sometimes the simplest creatures can be the most dangerous. She doesn't have the intelligence levels required of the MGA's accepted worlds. She's a primitive."

"And yet this so-called primitive can do what few can." Guardian X raised her voice above the others. "You've all read my proposal. What say you?"

The Guardians' collected voices rose again, louder than before. Some sounded appalled by what Guardian X had suggested, while others worried about the precedent such a policy change might set.

"What if she becomes uncontrollable?" Guardian M said. "We must have safeguards in place."

"Of course. We'll simply install a kill switch." Guardian X waved a dismissive hand. "This was included in my proposal."

"We've never done anything like this before," Guardian M continued. "It's against all protocol. This place is meant to keep Residents safe and happy and thus keep the rest of the multiverse safe from the Residents. What you're asking does not fit within our prime directive."

"But imagine if she could work for *us*," Guardian X said. "Imagine no longer putting our lives in danger when dealing with Residents who have a poor reaction to their Serenity. Think about the Residents who aren't even affected by Serenity. And what about recent acquisitions? Every new Resident has their own reaction to the medication. What if we never have an incident like V269's happen again?"

The Guardians murmured among themselves. Alexa noticed a shift in tone. More Guardians agreed with X than dissented. Less accusatory glances turned her way, and one Guardian even gave her an honest smile.

"Um, what's going on?" Alexa's small voice managed to break through the noise.

The room fell silent, each Guardian turning their gaze toward Guardian X who surveyed her cohort, having clear command of the room.

"Shall we take a vote? Those who agree with my proposal, please raise your hand?"

Three-quarters of the Guardians immediately raised their hands, leaving an awkward few to shift in their seats, including the stork-like Guardian who initially wanted to put Alexa into an isolation cell. One of the dissenters unable to stand the pressure, also raised their hand.

"We have a clear majority." Guardian X nodded, tossing a smug grin to the fuming angry-stork Guardian. "Thank you, everyone. You can return to your business. My plans for X485 will immediately commence."

The Guardians rose from their seats, exchanged a few pleasantries, and headed out. Several Guardians paused to speak to Guardian X before they exited, apparent excitement in their quiet discussions.

Alexa still had no idea what was going on. The moment the last Guardian left she bounced up from her seat. "What happened? Please, I can't take it anymore."

"Something that should please you." Guardian X sauntered around the table's curve. "I think we've taken the wrong approach to your situation. After what I saw on the roof, I felt there must be a better way than to use Serenity to weaken your abilities. And I know you've been lying to me."

Alexa inhaled sharply and dropped back into her seat. What did the Guardian mean? She hadn't lied but had kept some dangerous information close to her chest.

"I know you were pretending." Guardian X leaned against the table, standing over Alexa. "I figured it out this morning. Your eyes were the clearest I've seen them since you arrived. Why didn't you tell me Serenity wasn't working on you?"

"I, uh ..." Alexa dropped her gaze, rubbing her sweaty palms against her pants. What could she say that wouldn't upset the Guardian?

"There's no wrong answer."

That's what her teachers sometimes liked to say. However, Alexa could always tell when an answer was not good enough. "I wanted to feel like myself again."

"Having memorized your file, I don't believe you've felt like yourself since you found the Bright One, Una."

Alexa's throat tightened. She had gravely underestimated her captor. "You're right."

"Well, good or bad, meeting one of the most dangerous beasts in the multiverse eventually led you to me. Your new life with us is a matter of circumstances beyond your control. You have no history of murder, violence, or societal upheaval—unlike most Residents here—so I feel we should treat you differently."

Alexa swallowed the knot in her throat. "Differently?"

"How would you like to work for us, X485?"

Alexa nearly choked on the words. "*Work* for you?"

"Our Safekeeping Residence cares for some of the most dangerous and deadly creatures in the multiverse. We're always looking for new ways to maintain the safest facility possible. Until today, we have had three hundred and forty days without a violent incident. We at the Darkstar

Residence take safety personally. What happened on the roof today should never happen. Before Serenity, those were dark days I never wished to return. But it's not a hundred percent reliable. And that's where you come in."

"I do?"

"As you may have noticed with the Bright One in the isolation cell block, some Residents don't react to Serenity. Or their bodies burn it up too quickly to administer in safe doses. And there is always that tricky time when a Resident first arrives. We're never quite sure about dosage or reactions. All Guardians have agreed to avoid carrying lethal weapons. Not after—well, that's a story for another day.

"This brings me to the proposal I set before the other Guardians. We want you to work for us. Be there for us as a non-lethal, Serenity-free, restraint option when things go wrong. Just like you did with B191."

"You mean, you want me to use my telekinesis to help you?"

"Precisely. Sometimes, we have to move the more volatile Residents around, which is incredibly dangerous. It takes considerable preparation to move the Bright One from its cell every ninety-day-cycle to wash it thoroughly."

Alexa tried to picture herself mentally dangling furious residents in the air. "But, my ability is still all over the place. I don't have a lot of control."

"I have a plan for that. Over the next couple of days, we'll put together a sort of 'exercise room' for you to practice and stretch your abilities."

"What if I never get control?"

Guardian X locked her pale eyes on Alexa. "Then we'll have no choice but to put you into an isolation cell."

Float or drown, and nothing in between. "I won't disappoint you."

Guardian X laid a heavy hand on Alexa's shoulder. "I'm counting on it."

Chapter 38

Guardian X returned Alexa to her cell after her new assignment. It was nap time, and Residents big and small slept away the stupor that had arrived after a Serenity-laden lunch. Alexa's meal waited on a steel tray on her bed, and she was momentarily confused when she saw a sandwich on a white platter.

"I've been researching your planet." Guardian X nodded proudly to the sandwich. "It seems that Earth-humans like these things called subs, sandwiches, or grinders. Essentially, two slabs of carbs with protein and vegetables between. Does that sound right?"

Alexa's jaw dropped. "Yeah, it does. You did this for me?"

"It's easy for us who have grown up in the MGA to forget what this might be like for one such as you. Even with the Blinders giving you a sense of normalcy, this is all beyond strange. So I wanted to give you a small piece of home. Consider it a thank you and a final farewell to what you once knew."

Alexa walked over to her bed, placing the tray with the sandwich on her lap. "What do you mean, farewell?"

"If you are to work with us, you must assimilate. You must completely forget your home. We will provide you with lessons so you can better understand the multiverse.

Ignorance is fine for a Resident but unacceptable if you are to be a member of our team."

"Assimilate." Alexa gathered the sandwich between her fingers. The bread was spongy, like angel food cake. She parted the slices to find two grey slabs of a manufactured protein.

"We will gradually wean you off Serenity, so it no longer clouds your mind. We need you at full mental capacity if we're going to succeed in this new endeavor. And one more thing."

"Yeah?" Alexa dropped the sandwich, trepidation writhing in her gut.

"We will also have to install another bit of hardware into your system."

"Okay?" Her fingers brushed the Blinder's small discs above her ears and temples. Whatever else they planned to do to her was still better than being trapped forever in a cell the size of a closet.

"It's for our protection if this doesn't work out as planned." Guardian X laced her fingers together. "Call it a 'kill switch' of sorts. If you dare ever raise a hand against us, the kill switch will do exactly that. I trust you to do the right thing, but I also knew the other Guardians would never accept my proposal without it. Trust can't always be earned, but it can be manufactured."

Alexa didn't know what to say, so she stuffed half of the sandwich into her mouth. The spongy bread dissolved like cotton candy, leaving the tough, chewy protein slices behind.

"What do you think?" Guardian X nodded toward the sandwich.

Alexa gulped down the salty blob. "Tastes great."

"Wonderful. Well, I have a great amount of information to input. Enjoy your meal, and I will see you tomorrow." Guardian X hurried away with a bounce in her step Alexa had never seen before.

Alexa set aside the remaining part of the sandwich and collapsed on her bed. So, she was about to become Guardian X's pet project, and if everything went well, her life might change for the better. And if it went badly, she might end up dead after all.

The chorus of snoring was louder than usual. Had the Guardians added a little extra Serenity to everyone's midday meal after what happened on the roof? Even Rusty was gone from the world, laid out on his bed, his chest rising and falling in the steady throes of sleep. Alexa's eyes became heavier despite her mostly empty stomach. She stuffed down another disgusting bite, picturing a double-decker club from one of her favorite cafes in downtown Riverview as she chewed.

She closed her eyes, trying to picture the sun glistening on the St. Croix River: the gulls squawking, powerboats rumbling, and waves lapping the hull of her dad's bowrider. She could almost feel the sun beating on her face, making her warm and sticky. Music would drift from other boats, and from beach bar-and-grills near the river. There would also be the laughter of teenagers racing around a small island, joyful, free, and likely a little drunk.

Alexa curled her body into a tighter and tighter ball as she counted all the moments she had lost. Could she ever go back? Could her life ever be what it once had been?

Osu's voice broke her reverie. *Are you back in your cell, Earth human? I could not find you for a while.*

A hollow laugh escaped her. No, her life would never be normal again. She turned to face the wall and murmured, "I was on my new work crew assignment."

Was it better than your assignment with me?

"We were cleaning the roof. I got to see the mountains, so it wasn't so bad."

I have never seen the sky here. I felt we were in a high place, far from everything. If I listen hard enough, sometimes I can hear the wind whistling against this gods-forsaken place.

"I've never seen mountains like those. The sky is purple, even in the middle of the day. And there are giant moons in the sky. The sun isn't bright here. Maybe that's a normal thing in the multiverse? I've never been to a different planet before."

My home planet had blue skies. Sapphire heavens. Or so the stories claimed.

"We have blue skies on Earth," Alexa said, pulling her knees up to her chest. "I was just thinking about home before you called. I have this feeling I'm never going to see it again."

Imagine never having a home. Imagine trying over and over again to find one, to make one, only to have the multiverse's most incredible power tell you that you do not deserve to have a home, that you are monsters for being different. That your way of life is wrong.

"I can imagine that easier than you think. The Brume told me that Bright Ones overtook planets and destroyed them."

That is what the MGA has led everyone to believe. The truth is, we were too powerful, and we refused to join their so-called alliance and, thus, we were a threat. The MGA's annihilation of the Bright Ones has proven them as the decisive power once and for all.

"They sound like an evil empire. And all this is happening while little ol' Earth spins around and around. Lots of us think we're the only ones in the universe. Like we're something special. Did you know some people on Earth think the Earth is flat?"

I am never surprised by ignorance. Not anymore. Not after what I have seen in my lifetime.

Alexa let out a long, sad sigh. "I was happier when I thought we were all alone."

As a child, I had a smaller life. There was a time—I was just a little one—and we were so happy, my family and I. We had a beautiful home. I did not know we were in hiding. Not until they came for us. When I feel the most alone, I think back to that time.

"I miss my family too."

I am sorry. There is no need to talk about maudlin things. Did you enjoy your time cleaning the roof? I cannot imagine your fellow Residents are much for stimulating conversation.

"No, we're not supposed to talk to one another when working." If Alexa didn't know better, she would suspect Osu missed having her around. "I can't exactly communicate with them the way I can with you."

No, of course not. I imagine they are a bunch of stupid, simple, violent beasts high on drugs.

"I got to see what happens when a Resident has a bad trip."

What is a bad trip? Did they fall off the roof?

"No, it was like the opposite of what Serenity is supposed to do to you. This huge, terrifying guy came right at me. I thought I was going to—"

Did the Guardians stop him?

"No, um, I did."

Silence hung between them for several seconds before Osu said, *They saw you? The Guardians? You showed them what you can do?*

"Yes."

I do not understand. How are you still in your old cell? How are you not drugged into oblivion?

"The Guardians and I have a sort of arrangement." Alexa bit her bottom lip. She hadn't thought this out. She shouldn't have mentioned what happened on the roof. "They want me to work for them."

Again, a tense moment of silence emerged between them. Crossing the many halls, slipping through the six-inch thick steel, Alexa pictured Osu in his cell, his little closet, blue eyes blazing. His lovely, Blinder-manufactured face tensed, his lips tight. The face in her mind spoke. *Get out of my cell, Alexa.*

"I'm sorry." Alexa sensed her mind was being drawn back across the distance and re-entering her body.

How is this possible? How can you work with the ones who keep us caged?

Alexa let out a hollow laugh. "I didn't really have a choice."

There is always a choice. Always. I see what you truly are. A creature who convinces another they can be trusted right before they turn them over to their enemies. I have met many like you. You use others to your advantage. And you lie.

"No." Alexa's voice cracked as she pictured Una's death repeatedly in her mind. Was she a traitor? A liar? Someone who did whatever it took to survive, even if it meant the death of a friend?

Never speak to me again.

"Osu, please, wait," she whispered, but she knew he had already left.

Chapter 39

The Guardians put together her "Practice Room" in less than twenty-four hours. Guardian X had never looked more pleased with herself than when she opened the door to Alexa's new playpen. At first glance, the room reminded Alexa of a cross-fit gym or, at least, that's what the Blinders showed her.

Unlike the stone or steel floors she usually tread, the floor bounced beneath her feet. Mirrored spheres of various sizes sat in a heavy row along one wall. Boulders cut from the surrounding mountains sat on the opposite wall. Steel frames of multiple shapes hung along another wall.

"You will be monitored at all times." Guardian X pointed to several black glass squares at each corner of the room. "We expect there may be some accidents while you explore your abilities, so the Guardians have deemed it best to remain outside the room."

"Cool." Alexa approached a black plastic bin filled with ropes and palm-sized steel rings. She picked up one of the rings and weighed it in her hand.

Guardian X frowned. "Are you cold?"

"No, it's just Earth slang." For a moment, Alexa fell into her memory of Una asking the same thing. Una would never have believed where she had ended up, locked in the same place the Bright One had refused to go. She shoved her unsettling thoughts beneath the steel ring, focusing on the shape and heft of the object. The object easily lifted into the air, spinning end over end.

"Excellent." Guardian X's gaze followed the ring's path as Alexa spun it round and round above her outstretched palm. "Well, continue your exercises. I will return to take you to lunch with the other Residents. You must not tell them where you go during the day. They may wonder why you didn't join them on the roof."

Alexa let the ring rest in her hand. "What should I tell them?" Rusty would have a thousand questions. Would he freak out like Osu if she told him the truth? They had kept her in her cell yesterday while everyone went to their evening meal and recreation time. She avoided Rusty by pretending to sleep, but she couldn't do that forever.

"If they ask, tell them we decided to give you a different assignment." Guardian X shrugged. "That should be enough. Serenity can affect the short-term memory in some Residents. It's quite possible they won't remember anything from yesterday. They may feel a sense of worry surrounding you but won't know why."

Alexa walked over to the first of the six mirror balls and took in her distorted reflection. She hadn't seen herself in so long she had nearly forgotten her once-shaved head. She ran a hand over the short, soft hair that covered smooth skin. Would they let her grow it back?

"There's another thing I wanted to mention," Guardian X said as Alexa lifted an orb the size of a grapefruit. "The kill switch has been approved. We're moving forward with its placement soon."

"Okay." Alexa half-listened to the Guardian, focusing on the orb in her palms, cold and smooth against her skin. If she could focus on the object's shape, size, and weight while picturing the sphere rising, maybe she could—

"Mostly, we use it to knock out the subject when necessary, but it could kill you."

"What?" The orb darted from Alexa's palms and shot toward the ceiling. It banged against a supporting truss, sending a loud *bong* through the room—reminiscent of Alexa's first day in the common room—before ricocheting into a group of steel rods hanging in a far corner. Three rods fell, clanging against each other before thudding onto the mat-covered floor.

Guardian X sighed. "And this is why I will watch your exercises outside the room. It seems extreme emotion creates an extreme burst of telekinesis."

"Is that necessary?" Alexa shouted over the chaos as more bars fell and the orb rolled across the floor. She gestured to the mess. "I mean ..."

"Trust has to be earned before given." Guardian X frowned when the ball settled at Alexa's feet. "Your abilities are treated with great caution by the MGA. This facility accepted my proposal, but many of the details must be worked through in the remainder of the bureaucratic process. So, in the meantime, think of it like a safety device next to your brainstem."

Alexa ran a hand over her fuzzy scalp. "Will it hurt?"

"Oh, no. Nothing more than a poke." Guardian X waved her hand. "Just a simple implant. A light pulse of electricity will knock you out. A larger pulse will kill you on the spot."

"Superb." After all the insane things that had happened to Alexa, this was hardly a surprise. She picked up the mirrored ball and winced at the dent in its once-perfect shape. She focused on the orb's fresh mark and telekinetically lifted the object. All she had to do was decide where to move the ball next. "I suppose I can't refuse?"

"Unfortunately, that is correct." Guardian X's eyes never left the ball as Alexa orbited it around her and the Guardian.

The orb returned to Alexa's fingers with a satisfying *smack*. "Just another day, then."

"Well, enjoy your practice time. I see you're already making strides." Guardian X headed toward the door, never turning her back to Alexa.

"I will." Alexa easily tossed the orb between her hands as if the object were as light as a baseball.

The Guardian left, and Alexa tossed the ball even higher before it gently returned to her hand. She smiled, staring back at her pale-faced reflection. She didn't feel like a weak, helpless girl for the first time since the Brume had possessed her for a moment beside Crater Lake. And she no longer had to hide her unique, frightening new ability.

She turned to the row of mirrored balls.

Time for something much, much bigger.

Telekinetic object manipulation, just like the muscles in Alexa's body, could reach the point of exhaustion. She had outdone herself, raising the second largest of the mirrored orbs a whole foot off the ground before it *thunked* back to the floor and lazily rolled across the room.

A wave of fatigue buckled Alexa's knees, forcing her to sit down when blood rushed into her ears. Her head seemed heavy, drooping forward as she heaved in deep gulps of air. She wasn't much of a physical fitness type back on Earth and couldn't remember the last time she had drained herself physically and mentally. Not since Una died.

She dropped back, facing the open ceiling full of exposed steel trusses. The room was warm enough, and she was tired enough that napping wasn't such a bad idea. She closed her eyes and pictured herself lying on her bed in her bedroom back in Riverview. She could remember every inch of her former sanctuary, every poster on her wall, every book stacked on her bedside table, every figurine on her chest of drawers. She was reading *A Tree Grows in Brooklyn* because they hadn't read it in AP Lit, and she wanted to be a well-read woman before heading off to Boston.

A city she would likely never see.

Alexa opened her eyes to her impossible present and let out a long sigh.

The room's door opened, revealing Guardian X. She paused at the threshold, taking in the three-foot-diameter ball sitting in the middle. "I hear you've done some great work today. Did you primarily focus on the spheres?"

"Yeah. It was the first time I'd ever really pushed myself." Alexa rolled onto her side then slowly curled into a sitting position. Stars danced before her eyes. "I need to be more careful next time."

"Guardian F sent me a recording of some of your exercises," Guardian X said. "The sphere right there weighs twice as much as the Resident you suspended yesterday. I'm very impressed. You must be famished."

Alexa's stomach gurgled in response. "Yeah, I might need a moment to recover first."

"I'm so pleased." Guardian X beamed. "It'll take at least four of us to move that sphere back into place. And more good news: the Regional Safekeeping Governance has approved my proposal. Now on to Multiverse Cluster Level C."

"Great." Alexa shifted to hands and knees to see what would happen. Her vision swam for a moment but recovered quicker than before. "How many more have to approve it?"

"Oh, you'll learn all about it after your midday meal. Several other Guardians have assembled a vid for you to watch after your nap. It will help you understand the governance system all Guardians follow."

Alexa forced a smile. "Sounds like going right back to high school."

"High school?"

"I was finishing my secondary education before you decided to incarcerate me." Alexa took a chance and stood, keeping her hands braced on her knees before straightening her back. This time, everything stayed in focus. She turned to find Guardian X's mouth twisted into a skeptical frown.

"X485, you were sent here for the good of the multiverse. For nearly a decade, we've had peace, and anything that might topple that peace must be dealt with decisively. Imagine the chaos you could have caused in your home world. Your people are much too primitive to understand your gifts. When others found out the truth—because they would—how did you expect they would react?"

"I don't know," Alexa said, surprised by Guardian X's candor.

"From my knowledge of primitive worlds, they would have likely destroyed you. You should be glad to be here. You are safe here with us. You are a creature with no place, no home, and nowhere to belong. I hope you see I am doing everything possible to create a place for you."

"I have a home." Alexa crossed her arms and stuck out her chin. "My mother hasn't forgotten me. She's probably completely freaked out. And my friends. I have lots of people who love me."

"And what would they do if they knew you could crack their skull with a single thought?"

"But I wouldn't—"

"From my reports, you broke glass back on earth, which means you could easily break Earthling bone. Your skull is astonishingly delicate."

"There's no—"

"I'm not saying you would do it on purpose. Your abilities aren't under control. Would you take that chance?"

Alexa didn't know what to say. Until that point, she viewed the Safekeeping Residence as an elaborate cage and not a place for her to belong. But there was truth in her Guardian's words. Her time with Una and the Brume had changed her irrevocably.

"Can you walk? You'll feel better after a proper meal." Guardian X headed to the door and waited for Alexa to catch up.

Alexa took some experimental steps and followed her Guardian out of the practice room.

Chapter 40

Several days passed. Then days became weeks. Alexa continued moving heavier and more complicated objects while avoiding conversations with Rusty. He was persistent and noticed her increased absences. Alexa wasn't sure how long she could hold him off with her half-hearted lies before he lost patience.

The Guardians began her education about Safekeeping policy and procedure, but the translations proved so poorly phrased that Alexa couldn't understand anything. As a formerly excellent student, her new inability to comprehend or retain information frustrated her to the point of throwing her tablet across her cell. When she told the Guardians her troubles as they frowned over the tablet's cracked screen, they promised to attempt another translation.

The only useful part of her day was her morning exercises. As Alexa's telekinetic muscles strengthened, daily sessions left her more and more drained. Despite the exhaustion, her sleep patterns grew increasingly irregular. Dreams of home were achingly vivid. The empty hole in her chest where those she had loved and lost cratered deeper and deeper.

How long could she maintain her sanity? What she needed more than anything was a friend, a sympathetic ear, but Osu continued his prolonged radio silence. She attempted several times to reach him, but a mental wall stood between them. He didn't know the Guardians were planning to relocate him and that they might ask Alexa to help with the process.

During post-lunch rest time, Alexa tossed and turned on her bed, wishing for a blanket to toss over her head or press to her chest. As the snores and grunts grew in depth and volume, soft footsteps approached her cell.

Alexa turned over to find the constantly smiling Guardian X, who then deactivated the invisible wall and gestured for Alexa to join her. They walked out of the cell block into one of the many enormous corridors.

"Great news. A fresh disabling device finally arrived today." Guardian X paused at a door that seemed to appear out of nowhere.

"You mean the kill switch?" Alexa touched the base of her skull.

"Yes." Guardian X appeared to almost quiver with delight. "And more good news. My proposition for your modified position in the Residence has already moved to the next phase. Many of those in higher authority are interested in my plans."

They walked down an exceedingly narrow, poorly lit hallway. Alexa wondered how a creature who was in reality much larger than Guardian X managed to navigate such a space. She would never forget the monster she beheld the last time her Blinders glitched.

The door opened, revealing a space-age operating theatre. A table big enough to fit a draft horse sat at the center of the octagonal room. A dozen high-wattage lamps blazed above the table. Their arrangement reminded Alexa of bulging insect eyes made of thousands of lenses. Near the top of the room's walls lay a windowed gallery filled with Guardians.

"Please, sit here." Guardian X directed Alexa to the enormous table. Beside it stood a single cart bearing a massive syringe. "As mentioned, we will place the device near your brain stem."

"You're sticking that in me?" The needle was at least a foot long with the girth of her pinky.

"It will only hurt for a second." X patted the table.

"Can't I get something to numb the pain?"

"Your reactions to our medications are extremely unpredictable, so we would prefer not to use an anesthetic. What if we give you too large of a dose, and you never wake up? I've been assured that this a brief and relatively painless procedure."

"I've heard that before." Fighting a wave of dread, Alexa heaved herself onto the table and turned away from the needle.

The anticipation of pain was sometimes worse than pain itself. Alexa had never watched when nurses stuck needles in her arm, and she wasn't about to watch X shove a needle into her spine. Above her, the Guardians stirred, leaning closer to the observation window. Some smiled, some stared with fascination, while others appeared anxious to get it over with.

Guardian X said, "Hold perfectly still."

Alexa inhaled, praying the pain wasn't anything like the horrors she had experienced with the Inspectors. This time, the agony was more localized, as if someone took a scorching hot poker and thrust it against her flesh. Her cry of pain echoed through the chamber, the wail increasing in strength as a building fire ignited the back of her head.

Unspeakable agony seeped further, spreading along the base of her skull, down her spine, up and around the rest of her head, and blurred her vision. She grasped at consciousness for a moment, but her brain cleaved in two. A thick black curtain descended, and the world went dark.

Sunlight flickered against her eyelids.

"Wake up, sleepyhead," a familiar, warm voice whispered against her cheek.

Alexa didn't have to open her eyes to recognize who had spoken. "Hey, Sid. What time is it?"

The pressure of a soft kiss on her mouth pulled her from her sleep. Sid hovered over her, his sultry smile spreading across his perfect face. Alexa brushed back his hair from his forehead. She tried to pull him closer, but he leaped to his feet.

"Did you see that?" Something had drawn his gaze. He raised a hand above his brows, peering off into the distance.

"What?" Alexa propped herself on her elbow, scanning the perfect mirror of Crater Lake. Wizard Island loomed in the distance, a shining emerald against sapphire water. A white figure bounded along the perimeter of the island.

The steep shoreline threatened to dump Alexa right into the cool mirror. Even on such a warm day, the water would be ice cold. "How did we get down here?"

"Una." Sid pointed to the bouncing diamond, running impossibly fast among the scrubby trees dotting the island. He frowned as the unicorn splashed along the water, its panicked call trumpeting across the still lake. "No, that's not Una. Una's gone. You didn't save the Bright One. You let it die."

Clouds gathered on the eastern horizon. Tears welled in Alexa's eyes as the unicorn cried out over and over again. "I tried. I wasn't strong enough."

"Help Osu, then." Sid shrugged as if he didn't ask the impossible.

"How?" Pressure built at the base of Alexa's skull. "I'm just as trapped as he is."

The pain in Alexa's head built into a steady throb, each pulse rising with the beating of her heart. The tension gathered into a fist, slamming against the back of her head repeatedly.

"Alexa?" Osu appeared in Sid's place in the body her Blinder gave him. "What's happening to you?"

"It hurts." She clutched the back of her head, her vision swimming. Clouds obliterated the sky, creeping in fat, dark fingers toward where they stood.

"I heard you scream." Osu ran gentle hands along her skull. "What did they do to you?"

"My head." Alexa whimpered as the black ceiling of clouds crashed down upon them.

Everything went black again. She blinked, and the dark curtain wavered. Voices murmured in hushed concern. Someone turned Alexa's head and forced open her eyelid. Light pierced, and the throb in her head dulled. Alexa flinched away, throwing an arm over her eyes.

"What the hell happened?" Alexa croaked.

"You had an unexpected reaction to your implant." Guardian X appeared beside her. Several other Guardians drifted around the operating theater, having intense but hushed discussions. "Which seems to be happening much too often with you, X485. Our technology just isn't suited for Earthlings."

Alexa reached to the back of her head, her fingers touching tender, puckered flesh. A sharp bite of discomfort made her whisper, "Ouch."

"Don't touch it!" Guardian X barked. Her voice was so loud and sharp that Alexa flinched. "Gods, how is your species not extinct? We just cleaned your wound and must do it again."

The Guardian beside Guardian X rolled her eyes and pulled over a rattling tray full of bandages and ointments.

Alexa, are you well? Osu's voice was so loud in Alexa's head that she looked behind her to see if he somehow stood in the room with them.

"X485, can you please stop moving," the Guardian, with a fresh handful of gauze, said in an annoyed tone.

"Yeah, sorry." Alexa wasn't used to seeing the façade of calm break away from her captors. She didn't move or breathe as the Guardian gently cleaned her wound.

Something stung against her neck. Alexa sucked in a whimper between her teeth.

Alexa? Osu repeated.

She wished she could speak to him but didn't dare when surrounded by Guardians. Hopefully, he would understand.

Guardian X said, "Good news is, despite losing consciousness for ten minutes and having a bizarre rash all over the back of your neck, the procedure was successful. The implant is active and ready to go."

"You mean ready to fry my brain?" Between the burn at the top of her neck, the itching sensation crawling down her back, and the dull vibration behind her eyes, Alexa was pissed.

"Yes and no," Guardian X said. "This, in theory, could kill you. But we're not savages here. This little device will simply knock you out if, for any reason, you lose control of your powers and must be subdued."

"Cool," Alexa grumbled.

The Guardian tending Alexa's head wound peeked over her shoulder. "Are you cold? Do you need a blanket? Can you feel all your fingers?"

"It's Earth slang," Alexa grumbled. "Can I go lay down after this? Everything today has been too much. Ugh, I wish you had chocolate."

"Yes, Guardian AA should be finished in a moment, and we'll take you back to your cell. We'll skip your MGA lessons for today. You look a little pale. Should I bring your dinner to your cell too?"

I heard you screaming, Alexa. What are they doing to you? I thought you were in league with the Guardians. Why would they harm you?

"I'm fine," Alexa barked.

Guardian X and AA stepped back, surprised.

"Sorry. I'm like, really, really tired." Alexa cradled her head in her hands.

"She can go." Guardian AA nodded. "I'll need to re-dress her bandages after exercises tomorrow."

"Let's get you back to your cell." Guardian X helped Alexa off the table. "I'm sorry this procedure was painful, but I can't help my excitement, X485. I have a feeling you'll be a wonderful new addition to our Guardians. We'll add a minimal dose of discomfort inhibitors to your evening meal to accelerate your healing process."

I will speak to you later, Alexa. Something is wrong, and I may need your help.

"I'm here to help." Alexa forced a pained smile.

Chapter 41

The cell block was empty except for the one Guardian on duty. Alexa immediately put herself to bed, tucking her hands between her knees so she didn't prod the itchy wound and bandage at the back of her neck. She had survived yet another alien procedure, but what about the next one?

Exhaustion—sweet and simple—soon overwhelmed her spinning mind. Her body relaxed, the irritation in her neck faded, and she was just about to fall asleep when—

Alexa Baxter, are you in a place to receive me? Osu's voice held something sharp, almost panicked.

"I am. What's wrong?" She kept her voice as small as possible, testing the strength of their mental bond.

Thank the gods you are alive. What happened to you?

"Just another alien surgery that didn't go as planned."

I see. Something unexpected happened today. I have seen this done before. However, I never expected it would ever happen to me. The audacity. If they dare, I shall rip this place apart. His words held an electric bite that sizzled in her mind.

"Tell me."

Once, another creature almost as dangerous as me was in my cell block. We used to glare back and forth from our cells. I liked the beast; she was powerful and violent. Like me.

Alexa snorted. "Of course."

Then, one day, a group of Guardians entered the isolation block. Of course, the Guardians are much too stupid to realize I can hear everything they say. With them came more Guardians, but from a different Safekeeping Residence. I heard their plans to move the other dangerous beast to the visitors' Residence where she would be more adequately "contained."

I could not warn her. We did not speak the same language. Gods, how she screamed. They nearly killed her before moving her. Their plans to give her a near-lethal dose of Serenity did not work, so they electrocuted her until she passed out—poor creature. I never saw her again. I think of her every day.

Alexa squirmed. She had a feeling she knew what was coming next.

A similar conversation happened before my cell today. Several groups of Guardians came, claiming they had a new procedure they planned to use in a month or two to move me as well. I cost too much to contain. The new facility can better hold a monster like me.

"Maybe the new facility will be something different? Maybe this is a good thing? Aren't you sick of being stuck in that little cell?"

There is more. They also want to question me again, much like when the MGA took me into custody. They nearly killed me, hoping to find other Bright Ones, but I said nothing. The MGA has brought down a decree after your incident with Una and a few unsubstantiated rumors of other Bright Ones hiding on the edges of the multiverse. Allegedly, the new facility has more convincing interrogation devices.

"That sounds awful." Alexa would never forget how the Brume had slipped into her brain and tried to coerce her into giving up Una. They had managed to trick her in the end.

She let out a long, slow breath. Osu's information corroborated what Rusty had said. The Guardians believed they had finally found what they needed to move one of the most dangerous creatures in the multiverse: her. Their confidence in her was as troubling as it was unexpected.

If Alexa told him she was their "new procedure," would he disappear again? Would he try to kill her when the Guardians forced her to help move him? She owed it to Una to help Osu. The stain of her betrayal might fade if she could somehow save and help him.

"What if I told you I knew something about their new procedure?"

I would be disappointed and surprised. When you said you were working with the Guardians, I knew they would manipulate you, and feed you their lies.

"If they're feeding me lies, they're doing a piss-poor job of it." Alexa pulled her knees to her chest, the itch at the base of her skull rising.

Unfortunately, I do not have anyone else who can help me. There are things I know, Alexa. I will die before I betray my people. Yet, I worry they might find a way. I have been here many years, and the MGA is as brutal as they are inventive. What do you know?

"I'm not positive, but I think they plan to use my telekinetic abilities as part of this new procedure."

Are they mentally deficient? I have seen what you can do, and I am hardly impressed. There has always been a current of over-confidence with these Guardians, but this is pure foolishness.

"Osu, I can do much more than suspend a crazy Resident in the air." Images of the six mirrored orbs floated through her brain. The largest had weighed at least a ton. "The Guardians set up a space for me to practice. To push myself. It's not hard for me to grow stronger when I'm not hiding my ability."

Osu went silent. Soon, the silence drew out to the point of discomfort. What had she done the last time they spoke, and she had slipped into his cell? She had closed her eyes, pictured the Bright One, and somehow ended up there. She did the same again, her mind's eye carrying her through the steel walls, the doors, the wiring, and the structure holding the Safekeeping Facility together.

Osu paced his cell, but this time, Alexa saw him for what he truly was. A Bright One, blazing like a captured star in his cramped cell. He was bigger than Una, closer to the size of a small horse. Muscles rippled beneath his pure white coat as he walked in tight circles, his horn slashing the air.

He paused, turning his sapphire eyes in Alexa's direction. *You are here again. How do you do this?*

"My abilities, they're more than just moving heavy things around," Alexa said, simultaneously in her cell and Osu's. A body and mind divided. "You know how I fell off the lift while cleaning outside your cell?"

Of course. Osu blasted a snort through his pink nostrils.

"I wasn't sure what happened, but I think I know now. Somehow, I can separate my mind from my body. I can move, like your voice moves to me. And when I was cleaning around a set of wires, my mind got caught in the electric current. I literally flew from one side of the residence to the other."

What you are saying is impossible. Not a single creature in the multiverse can do something so remarkable. Are you sure you are remembering this right?

"Osu, you see me, don't you?" Alexa waved a hand in the unicorn's face.

Osu shied, backing into the corner of his cell. *Yes, you are here, and yet you are not. I was so angry the last time we spoke that I did not consider what I saw or heard. I believed it was my doing. It appears I have underestimated you again, Earth human.*

"Story of my life. What should we do?"

Everything you can to become as powerful as possible before they do to you what they have done to me. And never show them just how powerful you are. If they knew what I now know, they would destroy you. To be different is dangerous.

Alexa's fingers strayed to her bandaged head. "Obviously."

I have an idea, but I need time to think it over. Meanwhile, you must stretch your limits. Go as far as you can go. Become the perfect weapon.

"Okay. I'll try."

There is no trying. Not anymore, Alexa Baxter. There is only success or death.

Chapter 42

Only success or death. She had been there once before. Her old friends—anxiety and withdrawal—attempted to make a reappearance as she rose to greet another sunless morning. Rusty glowered at her from his cell, pacing the length of his invisible wall. What did he know, and what did she dare tell him?

Her breakfast arrived, but Alexa didn't have an appetite. How could she eat when her life dangled in the balance once again? She fingered the bandage at the base of her skull as homesickness came in waves. She missed her family, Sid, and, most of all, she missed Mateo. When everything else failed back in Riverview, she always had Mateo to get her through. She never would have survived Una and the Brume without him. She pictured him throwing his hands in the air and crying, "This is insane!"

Yes, truly insane.

Guardian X returned once the other Residents were taken off to breakfast. Something about the twinkle in her eye put Alexa on edge. The Guardian's smile only appeared genuine when something crazy was about to happen.

"I have a surprise for you this morning." Guardian X practically bounced in place. "We'll be working in the outdoor recreation area today."

Alexa sat up straighter. "Outside?"

"Yes, we want to try something new. Let's go."

They took another one of what Alexa liked to call the "secret tunnels" through the building. One moment, they strode through a dim hall; the next, she stood within the rose-hued glow of Resident Darkstar's mountainous planet. The sky was free of clouds, giving the moons more room to overwhelm the heavens. An open plane of dirt and scrubby grass, roughly the size of a football field, spread before them. A towering concrete fence topped with thick, twisting wire surrounded the area. The wires hummed, buzzing with electricity, and beyond the yard, the mountain range spread as far as she could see.

"Right there is today's exercise." Guardian X pointed toward the center of the field.

A strange contraption roughly the size of her Honda Civic—even Alexa's Blinders couldn't make it normal—stood in the middle of the field, surrounded by a half-dozen Guardians. The stack of metal cylinders, wires, and steel hummed even louder than the surrounding fence which quivered with unseen power.

"What's that?" Alexa hesitated to move any closer to the droning metal beast.

"One of the many fusion storage cells that help power this amazing facility. It's recently begun the process of breakdown, which happens after several decades. Usually, we discharge the gathering energy into another cell before meltdown. However, this time, we thought it would present a perfect opportunity to test your progress."

Alexa's empty stomach clenched. "What do you want me to do?"

The storage cell bounced and thrummed. Electric arcs snapped and curled around the device, causing each of the Guardians to leap back several feet.

"We want you to contain the cell when it goes into meltdown." Guardian X beamed.

Thank God she hadn't eaten anything. "Seriously?"

"Yes, of course. You've done such a wonderful job moving heavy objects. Let's see how well you do at containment. When this cell discharges, it will emit a small explosion. Your goal is to keep it from doing any real damage. We are outside its blast perimeter."

"But this is completely different." Alexa's heart raced. In high school, failure only meant a lousy grade or maybe even going to a lesser college. Such stakes were ridiculous compared to an actual bomb going off.

Guardian X shrugged. "Instead of lifting, try containing. If it doesn't work, we've learned something new. There's no harm in trying."

The cell bucked in place—a beautiful but terrifying stream of arcs radiating like miniaturized light clusters. The hair on Alexa's arms and neck stood on end.

"You've got to be fucking kidding me," she gasped.

"Don't worry." Guardian X placed her hand on Alexa's shoulder. "None of us will die. However, some minor burning is possible. Oh, look. It's entering its final phase. Get ready, X485!"

"Minor burning?" Alexa squeaked.

White-hot sparks burst from the guts of the cell. Alexa let go of the physical, ignoring her panic and galloping heart and reached outward with her intention. She focused on each detail of the juddering fusion unit, reaching out unseen hands to press back the curling electric arcs before they could whip out far from the cell. Her invisible hands became a dozen arms. Now she spread them wide, embracing each shock, each current.

"Despite all my rage," Alexa whispered, pulling deeper within. Focus could only go so far. She had to get a little angry to subdue a raging lump of power.

The cell fought back, bolting against her invisible arms. Where one arc subdued, another snapped outward. Alexa spread her arms wider, stretching her invisible limbs into walls. Her head throbbed from the effort. A faint, green haze encompassed the quivering beast.

"You're doing great, X485," Guardian X shouted as a roar rose from the storage cell's guts.

"Still just a rat in a cage." Alexa fought to maintain her invisible wall around the contraption. When one part of her wall stabilized, another started to crumble. She didn't have it in her.

Then it happened. All the storage cells' bluster came out in a blossoming fireball. Alexa's lower walls held tight, but the ceiling immediately shattered. A flaming column shot up toward the sky, but only up and not out at the surrounding Guardians. The column blazed for a moment, then disappeared, leaving a lump of smoking wreckage behind.

Alexa bent forward, relieved, then slumped to the ground. Her face smashed into the dusty earth. She inhaled the mineral scent of the dirt, turned her head, and let out a pathetic sneeze when her muscles slackened. It was as if every bit of strength had been sapped from her body. A dark halo ringed her vision. The world tipped as the Guardians hurried to her side, each wearing a huge grin.

"That was wonderful!" Guardian X dropped onto her knees beside Alexa. "You did as well as I expected."

Alexa coughed, kicking up a cloud of dust. "I can't move. Can you roll me onto my back?"

"Of course." Guardian X gently lifted Alexa's head from the ground and turned her over. "Wasn't that magnificent?"

She cleared her throat to get their attention. "Just so you're aware. I can't move."

The Guardians, all of their heads bobbing, hovered above Alexa, each one congratulating Guardian X as if she had done all the work. Alexa ought to be annoyed, but another wave of exhaustion blurred her vision. She didn't want to pass out. Not again. Passing out was becoming much too much of a habit.

Guardian X bent over. "I'm sorry, I barely heard you."

"I can't move." Even filling her lungs and moving her lips took effort.

"Oh, so sorry. Everyone, let's get her to the infirmary and give her fluids. I don't want her near the general population until she returns to normal. Amazing work, X485. I can't wait to try again."

Chapter 43

This time, after grappling with the fusion storage cells, the Guardians returned Alexa to her cell instead of the infirmary. Guardian X fed her something new—a series of crumbly pellets called "acid tabs," which reminded her of the protein powder Sid used to put in his post-workout shakes. The flavor was fruity, like strawberry, except with a chalky aftertaste. At least Guardian X hadn't rewarded her with another "sandwich."

Sid. Lightyears away. Along with everyone else she loved. Alexa pressed her fists against the hollow pulse in her chest. Their absence left a hole she would never fill. How could she survive the multiverse without Sid or Mateo by her side?

Maybe it was time to finalize her new alliances. She ought to tell Rusty everything. He wanted to get out of this place as much as she did. What about Osu? The deposed royal needed to be a part of the plan, whatever it may be. Perhaps the three of them could figure out how to escape their prison.

Osu usually contacted her first. Why couldn't the reverse be possible? The last time they spoke, Alexa had simply followed the invisible communication path between them until his cell appeared. She closed her eyes and let her mind stretch out beyond her body. Between the walls, the electrical currents, the whispers of Residents, and the occasional Guardian, she searched for Osu's glittering aura.

"Osu?" she whispered with her mind.

For several minutes, she crept forward, seeking Osu's blistering hot spark of life among the physical, mental, and emotional cacophony of Residence Darkstar.

Are you looking for me, Alexa Baxter?

A burst of light appeared behind her, a beacon in the dark. Once she had a course to follow, she quickly found Osu. The Bright One stood in his true form—the radiant, shimmering unicorn.

"I thought I'd try to find you myself," Alexa said. "And it worked. I can't stay long. They made me subdue four fusion storage cells today."

Fusion storage cells?

"Guardian X's newest 'exercise' is to have me contain the meltdowns on their old fuel cells. Of course, she doesn't know that I know exactly why she's making me do this."

Your Guardian is quite resourceful. I wondered how they would prepare you to subdue me. I am not one to speak well of those who cage us, but I am somewhat impressed. How did you do?

"Nearly died twice."

Nearly dead is still very much alive. The Guardians returned to my cellblock yesterday. From what I can tell, they hope to send me off within the next few weeks, though they are planning for a contingency if you aren't deemed ready.

"You said you had an idea last time we talked?"

Naturally, when you pretend to help move me to the transport vehicle, I will destroy every Guardian present and anyone who gets in our way to the cargo dock.

Alexa gasped. "You mean, kill them?"

Of course, Alexa Baxter, how else would we get off this wretched planet?

"Is that ... necessary?"

It's them or us, Earth human.

"There's gotta be another—do you even know how to fly a spaceship?"

Well, no, not really. I am still figuring out what to do once we are on the vessel. We need a pilot. Perhaps we'll just use the one already on board. I'm sure between the two of us, we could convince them.

"Sure, *convince* them." For a moment, Alexa felt as if she had fallen onto the set of a space opera. Did Rusty know how to pilot transport freighters? "So, there's this other Resident, I call him Rusty. You could call him a friend, I guess. He wants to get out of here too, and we've discussed escaping the Safekeeping facility."

Why did you not mention this before? Osu's eyes flared. He switched his tail, smacking it against the surrounding wall. *What have you told him? Does he know about me?*

"He only knows you exist and that I will be helping move you when the time comes."

You're full of secrets, Alexa Baxter. The Bright One stomped his hoof. *What sort of creature is this Rusty? This place is filled with liars, killers, and thieves. You cannot trust a single one of their lot.*

"Can I trust you?"

I would ask you the same. The last Bright One whom you attempted to help ended up dead.

Alexa sensed herself withdrawing. "I didn't mean for that to happen. The Brume got in my head. They made me believe things that weren't true."

Before we go further, you must decide where your loyalties lie. From my point of view, you have no idea who you are or what you want—nor whom to trust.

Her mental self slipped through the facility, returning to her prone form. Exhaustion from that afternoon's undertaking had extracted a toll.

Her eyes grew heavy. "I just want to be Alexa Baxter again."

You stopped being that, Earth human, when you met a Bright One. Osu's voice faded, to a small, whisper. *Who are you now? Are you the lackey of the Guardians? An escapee putting your trust in one of the other killers? Or are you the one who will help me get away from the MGA? You are not the weak, simple creature you pretend to be. Find your strength, Alexa Baxter. Show me who you are.*

"But they installed a kill switch in me. The Guardians could kill me at any moment."

They would be foolish to kill you. You have become their greatest asset.

"I'm scared, Osu. I'm scared of everyone and everything in this awful place."

Including me?

"Honestly?" Alexa rubbed the bandage at the base of her skull. "No. For some reason, you don't scare me."

I would not hurt you, not on purpose. He paused, and Alexa pictured him pacing in his cell.

As powerful as we may be, we cannot fly out of here without help. Tell this Rusty only as much as is necessary. Do not let him know we can communicate with each other. No one can know. Accept his proposal. When the time comes, he will have no choice but to help both of us.

"What if he refuses?"

If he is desperate enough to attempt escape, he will do whatever it takes. But watch your back, Alexa. Desperate creatures will do the most desperate things to survive.

"I'll tell him I'm in. I'm not sure where he's getting his information, but I have a feeling he'll know when your transport day arrives before either of us."

Very well. Keep me updated. We either escape with our lives or die trying. After being trapped in this cell for so long, I am willing to take that chance. Are you?

Alexa had faced such dangers before. At least this time, she wasn't a weak girl at the mercy of much more powerful forces. She, too, was becoming something powerful. The time had come to embrace it.

"Yes. I'll do whatever it takes to get us out of here in one piece."

Good. Now, get some rest. You have much to do until our day arrives.

Chapter 44

"Okay, okay, okay. Say we get on a ship, then what?" Alexa said after swallowing her last bite of alien gruel.

After two days of recovery, she was allowed to have lunch with the rest of the carbon-based population. Rusty had plopped beside her when she shoved her first spoonful of gruel between her lips then waited for her to finish lunch.

"I reach out to my old contacts." He grinned at her change of tune.

DeeDee and Murphy were on the opposite side of the table, making silly shapes with a series of multi-colored discs.

"Someone's still out there." Rusty also toyed with the discs and made a flower resembling a daisy. Or was that the Blinders working their magic? "I was a well-known figure in the multiverse thirty years ago."

"But what if they're all ..."

"All what?"

Alexa dropped her voice. "Dead?"

Rusty shrugged. "I have considered the possibility. We're only allowed access to heavily censored current events. But I have faith. Unlike me, my old friends were good at getting out of a tight bind. And good at causing lots of trouble. We caused the most wonderful trouble."

"Like what?"

"Like leading a major rebellion in one of the most MGA-friendly quadrants in the known multiverse. That was my first of five."

"You've led *five* rebellions?"

"They caught me attempting the sixth." Rusty twisted his mouth into a goofy grin when one of the Guardians casually strode past their table. Rusty's shrewd eyes followed the Guardian for a moment before he spoke again. "They're keeping a close eye on you lately. Eventually, you'll have to clue me into what's happening. And don't tell me it's nothing. I've never seen the Guardians so giddy and on edge simultaneously."

Alexa attempted to make her own disc art, but her hands hadn't stopped trembling over the last two days.

"The Guardians have me working on a special project." Alexa's trembling fingers dropped a disc. "I'm not allowed to talk about it."

Another Guardian passed their table. Rusty bellowed out a false, ridiculous laugh and swept away his flower picture, causing the discs to scatter across the table and ruin DeeDee and Murphy's composition. Murphy and DeeDee broke into a cacophony of giggles and did the same.

Once the laughing had settled and another Guardian passed, Rusty whispered to Alexa, "It has to do with your, uh, abilities?"

"How do you—?"

"And for some reason, they decided to use you instead of throwing you into a hole."

"Maybe?" Alexa braced for his reaction.

"Thought so." Rusty rubbed one of his bushy eyebrows and glanced around the room at each of the six Guardians keeping watch during their midday meal. "So, they think you can contain a Bright One?" He turned to Alexa, studied her for a moment, and broke into laughter. Not the fake, goofy kind he used in front of the Guardians, but an honest, cruel laugh. The sort of mocking chuckle Alexa had once faced from her peers back in Riverview High.

"What's so funny?" She grumbled, tossing a blood-red disc at him.

"That's perfect." Rusty wiped his eyes and gathered a handful of the scattered discs. "There's no possible way you could contain a Bright One. They must be desperate or out of their minds to rely on you."

Alexa withered in her sea, although no one knew she and the Bright One were becoming acquainted.

"This presents a whole new range of possibilities." Rusty organized his handful of discs by color. "Unless you've decided to become the Guardians' pet? From that incision at the back of your skull, looks like you already have. Did they insert a subduing device?"

"Maybe." Alexa ran a hand through her short hair, pausing just above the mostly healed scab. "I mean, I don't—I don't know."

"You're just a tool to them. They'll use you, and when you break, they'll toss you out. Or throw you in one of those isolation cells to rot the rest of your short life. You don't want that, do you?"

Alexa shook her head.

"Whatever you do, if you want to get out of this place, you need to convince those Guardians that you can do what they tell you. Even something as ridiculous as attempting to contain one of the most volatile creatures in the multiverse."

After a few days of rest, Guardian X brought Alexa to yet another about-to-explode fuel cell. Instead of fear, resignation filled her. She turned her face to the purple sky, appreciating the pale-yellow cast of the moons.

"X485, are you paying attention?"

Guardian X's unexpectedly shrill voice brought Alexa back to earth. Each of the four surrounding Guardians held a faint trace of terror in their eyes. Instead of the previous four, six cylinders bucked and spat out a shower of sparks.

"Maybe X485 isn't ready?" An especially pale-faced Guardian backed further and further away from the rattling cells.

"Nonsense." Guardian X turned to Alexa. "You can do this. I have seen you do impossible things before. You can do it again."

A faint, green glow circled the storage cells. The last time that happened, the cell exploded seconds afterward. Alexa started building her invisible walls to contain the inevitable explosion.

What if that was the problem last time? Maybe holding up the walls for an extended period drained her further?

"Guardian X, were the calculations—"

"Yes, my explosion radius calculations are correct. Let X485, concentrate."

Stretching out her telekinetic arms for over a minute and pushing against each spark or flare had exhausted her, then when the final explosion came, she had just enough left to shove it upward. What if she waited until the very last moment?

"Something is wrong with her. We need to get out of here!" A Guardian backpedaled from the coming onslaught.

Guardian X's cheeks reddened. "You are all overreacting, even if—"

The cell ruptured. Alexa had anticipated the ball of fire, which she immediately surrounded with a giant bubble of intention. She pushed her full strength into the bubble. The growing explosion shoved outward with a force that knocked her off her feet. The hot flames kissed her face and threatened to scorch the flesh from her bones, but her bubble stretched to accommodate the blast.

The blaze flickered for a moment then subsided. The fuel cell's structure took the full brunt of the outburst, leaving nothing but compressed, blackened metal behind.

Alexa stared up at the enormous yellow moons. Her arms refused to move when she attempted to scratch an itch on her nose. An object streaked across the sky far above them. Its speed and trajectory reminded her of the tiny pinpoint satellites she sometimes saw when staring at the sky on a dark Riverview night.

"What did you do differently this time?" Guardian X sat up a few feet from where Alexa lay. Her lightly scorched face expressed both anger and relief.

"I didn't expend energy until I absolutely had to." Alexa attempted to wiggle her fingers. They worked. She reached for her throbbing nose and fingered a bit of tender, burnt flesh. "Ouch."

Guardian X let out a long sigh and slumped forward. The woman who wasn't a woman let down her walls, and for a moment, Alexa saw her as another living, breathing being with worries and losses just like her.

"Next time, have a better evacuation plan in place, Guardian X." A lightly blackened Guardian sat up and dusted their uniform.

The other Guardians sat up, too, each appearing mildly singed but mostly unharmed. One frowned at the scorch marks on their once flawless uniform, attempting to rub black streaks from their pants.

Guardian X nodded. "I agree."

"Don't let your ambitions get in the way of safety." The blackened Guardian shook an angry finger before hopping to their feet. "X485 is just a simple Earth citizen—no more, no less. Now, I need to lie down somewhere."

The other Guardians nodded and followed their lead.

"Please don't scare me like that," Guardian X murmured to Alexa as her cohort limped away.

"Then let *me* decide when I'm ready for the next challenge." Alexa grunted, attempting to sit up. The world spun, so she flopped back onto the dry turf. Even though she knew the answer, she said, "Why are you making me do this? Containing explosions is nothing like moving around heavy chunks of metal."

"You'll find out soon enough." Guardian X surveyed the melted metal lump. "We've got a whole room full of these expiring storage cells. When you're ready, we'll try eight."

Chapter 45

Alexa had spent too much time scared, allowing everyone from the Guardians to Rusty to Osu, to intimidate her. The time had come for her to step up and show the multiverse she wasn't just a weak Earth girl.

After resting in her cell for the remainder of the day, Alexa woke the next morning feeling better than ever. Guardian X checked in before everyone else headed to breakfast, almost chipper. She handed Alexa a plate with the usual gruel and two more acid tablets.

"You have performed beyond expectations." Guardian X buzzed with pleasure. "My proposal has passed through yet another round of oversight. We should have full support in the next few days, which is perfect timing. Supply Day is in another ten days, bringing with it a Resident transfer. I can't wait to have you on our transition team."

"I can't wait either." Alexa forced a smile and choked down one of the dry acid tablets.

"About that Resident transfer. They're not incoming, but outgoing." Guardian X sat at the edge of Alexa's mattress.

"You mean leaving this place?" Alexa fought the urge to lean forward. She had to pretend she knew nothing and had no idea what Guardian X would say next.

"And if my proposal goes through, we'll have an extra exciting job for you."

Alexa swallowed. "What?"

"You remember the Bright One you saw in the isolation block?"

Her heartbeat took off in her chest. "Sure."

"There's a new Safekeeping facility, Firestar Safekeeping Residence, opening on the other side of our system. A place for the most dangerous Residents in the MGA. Do you know why our fuel cells melt down all the time? Because of the Bright One. He requires an enormous amount of power to keep contained."

Alexa donned her biggest, most innocent expression. "What does that have to do with me?"

"The last time we moved this particular Bright One, we lost several Guardians." A hint of sadness clouded Guardian X's gaze. "We've spent the past few months preparing to move the Bright One with the help of those from the Firestar Safekeeping Facility. We have contingency measures in place, but nothing is foolproof. Especially with *this* Bright One."

"Is this one different from Una?"

Guardian X nodded, her expression somber. "He's nothing like the one who crossed your path. You see, he's the most powerful Bright One still in existence. The last one with similar power destroyed a whole city rather than be taken alive. I'll bring the Bright One file to you before the end of the day. You need to know as much as possible to prepare yourself."

Would this be the same truth the Brume fed her? This time around, she would make Osu defend each and every one of the accusations against him.

"And you think I can help?" Alexa didn't hide her anxiety. "What if I'm not strong enough?"

"Of course you are. Have you seen how quickly you've improved? Like nothing I've ever seen. If you can help us, this could change the course of your Residency."

"How?"

"First thing, we'd give you a private residence." Guardian X gestured toward Alexa's sterile cell. "Somewhere quiet, near the Guardian's lodging center. You would no longer be a Resident. You would be a Guardian of sorts." Guardian X brushed the discs at Alexa's temples. "Someday, we'll wean you off the Blinders, but perhaps it's best to see the world as you wish. If the day comes that you want to see what's really in front of you, we'll help you in your transition."

A world filled with monsters or a world that resembled home? Who could tell what would happen in ten days? Perhaps Osu would lose his temper and destroy himself and everything around him. Alexa shivered.

"First, we have to transfer the Bright One. I'll sleep better when that wretched beast is far away from here. Do you feel up to working today, or would you like to rest?"

Alexa yawned. The acid tabs were unexpectedly filling. "Rest would be good."

"When I return, I will bring the Bright One's file. Best to know one's enemy as much as possible before facing them." The Guardian breezed out of her room with a hint of a smile.

Alexa curled into a tight comma. What deceptions would the Guardians feed her? And how would Osu respond?

Sleep first. Questions later.

What lies does it say about me?

Instead of reading Osu's file alone, Alexa had called across the distance and asked him to join her. Una had claimed never to lie, but it didn't speak the whole truth either. Same as the Brume, lies, deceptions, and mistruths, one on top of the other. Osu's honesty would be his salvation or his downfall.

"Born on, uh, I can't read that word. Oh, and I don't understand. Is this supposed to be the year or the month? Do you have months in the multiverse?"

If you live according to the MGA's calendar, what you would call a year is separated into fourteen parts. Common time is based on the calendar followed at MGA's capitol, The Center. It is considered the "center of the multiverse." Months are numbered because too many ancient societies named times of the year after their gods. The MGA has decreed an entirely atheistic state.

"Wow." Alexa ran her hand over the fuzzy image of Osu on a distant planet, surrounded by enormous trees with leaves the size of his head. Her Blinders didn't work so well on digitized documents. At one moment, she would see Osu in his proper form, and in the next second, she saw a young boy grinning from beneath an oak tree. "I was born in September. I think it's named after a Roman number, not a god."

Who are your gods on Earth?

"We have lots of different ones." Déjà vu hit Alexa in a wave. Wasn't that one of the first things Una asked Alexa after she pulled the poor unicorn out of the handicap-accessible stall? "Una never spoke about gods. Do Bright Ones have a religion?"

Yes. An ancient one. The MGA decreed it illegal right before they started rounding us up. I will tell you about it someday. We need to focus on what lies they want you to know about me.

"Um, not a lot of crazy stuff so far." The current translation was a considerable improvement over the last, but several sentences tripped her up. "Mostly condemning your caste system, the primitive and dangerous nature of monarchies ... oh."

What? Tell me.

"What happened in a place called the Blue Gem?" Alexa rubbed her forehead and checked for the hundredth time if the nearest Guardian was still at the far end of the hallway. According to her tablet, Osu had murdered a whole family, taken over their home with the help of several servants, and hid there for over a year. The MGA officers had found their rotting corpses long after Osu moved on to a different hiding place.

My ship had broken down while I and my remaining family were moving to a new safehouse after our first one was discovered. We came across a beautiful home filled with several generations of family. They were frightened of us, but we came to trust each other. We stayed for as long as we felt safe. It was a happy time while it lasted. Why, what are you reading?

"You don't want to know." Alexa set aside the tablet. "How did they eventually catch you? What I'm seeing here doesn't make sense."

Betrayed—well, that is not quite right. Someone I loved was captured and tortured into disclosing my family's hiding place. Anu could not help it. Even the strongest eventually succumb to torture. They brought an army to capture me, but I fought well.

They cannot harm me here, but this other place they want to take me is different. I heard them conversing about how they may trick my mind, dig into my memories, and pull out dangerous things. I know too much.

"What do you know?"

For your safety, Earth human, I shall not tell you. If they found out the two of us were friends, they would torture you too. And, no offense, you are built of softer stuff than my kind.

"I'm your friend?" She felt a slight quiver in her heart when he said the words.

You have promised to help me, even at the risk of your own life. Thus, you are a friend.

"So, say I convince Rusty to help us, where do we go next? I mean, he's got his own agenda too. Who is to say that he'll take us where you want to go?"

If this Rusty has a tiny bit of wisdom, he will not refuse me. After all, I am one of the most dangerous creatures in existence.

Rusty didn't seem like the type to take orders.

"This could go really well or really bad."

We must risk everything to escape this place, even our lives. I am ready, are you Alexa?

"I guess." Alexa pulled her knees to her chest, fighting the panic dancing just beneath the surface of her skin. Her fingers traced the healing mark at the base of her skull. "What about the kill switch? At some point, they will realize I'm not on their side."

If you can disable a fuel cell, can you not disable a little speck in your head?

Alexa had never considered such a simple solution. She closed her eyes, focused within, and searched the foreign objects around her skull. The Blinders were easy to pinpoint, including the slight surges of energy pulsing behind her eyes and ears. She moved her focus back, creeping along her skull toward her neck.

"Ouch!" A burst of light flashed behind her closed eyes, and a sharp bite of pain smacked the back of her head. She crumpled forward, grasping her throbbing skull.

What happened?

"There's some sort of protection around the implant." Alexa opened her eyes. Pinpricks of light danced before her vision. "I can't disable it."

Then we will have to adjust our performance. We have to pretend the whole time that you are my enemy, and you are scared of me. I may have to throw a few attacks your way to convince the Guardians we are not on the same side.

"I'm a terrible liar." Alexa rubbed her eyes. The stars began to clear. There were too many variables to juggle. Too many things that could go wrong. But they had no other option but to try and find Osu a way out.

There is a high probability of failure, to be sure. I will do whatever it takes. Even if I die trying.

Chapter 46

Alexa decided to go full-in, eyes open toward what could be even more terrifying than her night on Crater Lake. She was the girl who survived a Brume, hypothermia, invaders from other worlds, and now, she was going to try to break out of prison and defy the authorities. No more slinking around the corners, drifting into rooms, and hoping to remain unnoticed.

Guardian X woke her early that morning to tango with a single storage cell. Only one other Guardian joined them. Alexa recognized him immediately. He was the one who wanted her put away forever. He looked at her with the same sour pinch of condemnation as the first time they met. Why did Guardian X have such a miserable person join them? And why only a single cell when she had last danced with eight?

Guardian X gestured to the bouncing, spitting fuel cell. "You've done so well before. I thought we'd work on finesse this morning."

This time, the explosion came without the tell-tale green warning halo. Alexa threw her invisible arms out and around the blast, shielding the Guardians just in time. Her unseen wall expanded into a full dome between heartbeats. The explosion's heat flared against her cheeks, but her force field held and absorbed the heightened energy change. Startled by the unexpected pulse, she sent her shield hurtling into the yellow-mooned heavens before Guardian X noticed the difference.

Did the explosion feed her shield with additional power? That was new.

The two Guardians stood gasping behind her. She tingled from head to toe. Electricity danced along her fingers before snapping out of existence. She exhaled, and a faint fog lifted from her open mouth. Neither Guardian must have realized what happened. Guardian X beamed while her detractor's shoulders slumped an inch.

"See, I told you she could be everything and more, Guardian AA." Guardian X rested a hand on Alexa's shoulder and squeezed. "Imagine the possibilities."

"Yes, she's a wonderful tool." Guardian AA crossed his arms over his chest, frowning at the fuel cell's smoldering mass. "Perhaps I underestimated the Earth citizen's value. Very well, you've made your point."

"We sure have." Guardian X's smile and affection for Alexa had never been more apparent. "How are you feeling?" She surveyed Alexa from top to bottom. "Any weakness?"

Alexa flexed her hands. "I think I'm okay."

"Can you walk?"

She took some test steps, hiding the energy surging through every part of her being. Why, she could run a marathon if needed. This new detail needed to stay under wraps until she better understood her constantly changing powers.

Guardian X's face lit with pleasure. "Let's get you some food."

As usual, most Residents were in their regular state of drugged-out ecstasy. Alexa walked into the Common Room like she owned the place. She plopped beside the always bubbly DeeDee and Murphy and nodded to Curly, who blinked once and dropped backward onto the floor. Deedee, braying donkey-like, hurried over to his side and helped him back onto his seat. The moment Curly settled on the narrow seat, he dropped forward, arms splayed, scattering everyone's midday meal.

"I won't miss this." Alexa wiped a glob of goop from her cheek.

Rusty settled into the space beside her with a bowl full of gruel. "You'll miss the schedule. The food. A relatively soft bed and a roof over your head at all times. You'll miss the quiet. You'll miss a sound night's sleep."

"I haven't slept soundly since I got here." Alexa set aside the remnants of her lunch.

"So, you've spoken to your, uh, friend?" Rusty's gaze swept the room.

"I have. You'll be ready to go in the loading area?" Alexa turned in her seat, nodding and smiling to the Guardians when they tipped their heads in her direction. In a week, they would feel quite the opposite.

"Yep. I've been helping with Supply Day for years. They'll likely clear the area for your friend's arrival. I get the feeling everyone will be so distracted that an old Resident like me hiding in a corner won't catch anyone's attention.

Anyway, I'm good at disappearing in plain sight. Old skill of mine from my warring days."

Alexa's fists tightened. "When we get closer to the loading dock, we'll make our move. I pretend to lose control of him and let his species do what they do best. It'll be up to you to fly us out of there, and then, well, I guess we'll decide what's next once we're out of danger."

"We'll be running for the rest of our lives." Rusty shrugged. "But I'll take that over being stuck in a cell any day. I have a place in mind. And you, what will you do, Earth human?"

She and Osu hadn't discussed what would happen once free, but she saw only one path forward. "I'll go with Osu for as long as I must. And then I'll try to find a way home."

"Good luck with that." Rusty's crooked smile split his tired face. "Can I give you one more piece of advice, X485?"

"Sure."

"You've tangled with a Bright One before, so you know this already. Never put your trust in creatures more powerful than you. Especially the Bright Ones. Maybe their reputation is all a big lie, but the best lies are built on a foundation of truth. You can never truly be friends with a beast that can level a city on a bad day."

Alexa raised her chin, defiant. "Maybe I'm a little dangerous too."

"You could be." Rusty's smile disappeared. "If I could give you a safe place to land, I'd take you with me in an instant. My rebels could use your help, but our battles are not yours. You've got a better chance of survival with your personal supernova. But don't let them change you. I see your compassion among all of us monsters. Don't let your friend change that. And don't let yourself change it either, even if you surpass us all someday."

Alexa snorted. "Surpass? I highly doubt it."

"An Earth human that survives a Brume and makes friends with Bright Ones? You're well on your way to becoming extraordinary." Rusty nudged her gruel-spattered plate. "Eat up. Eat everything you can. There will be days when you don't eat at all."

Alexa shoved a cold spoon of mush into her mouth and, for once, enjoyed the commotion that came after everyone ate their meal.

Could Alexa ever become dangerous? With her powers constantly changing and augmenting, she had no idea what she could do.

The following week passed in a blur. While Alexa battled several more exploding fuel cells with increasing ease, Osu and Rusty laid out their action plan. Alexa had little confidence in what they were about to do, but what other choice did she have?

Her relationship with Guardian X grew closer despite Alexa's attempts to keep her captor at arm's length. She often rested her hand on Alexa's shoulder after each successful fuel cell containment, giving several reassuring squeezes. Once, Alexa was sure Guardian X was about to pull her into a hug, then thought better of it. Whatever happened, Alexa would do her best to keep Guardian X from being harmed.

The evening before the big day, frenetic energy buzzed among the Guardians while their Residents ate another drug-laced dinner.

Even Rusty—stoic, cold Rusty—could barely eat his gruel. He carefully spooned mouthful after mouthful between his lips, fighting to swallow each bite. Alexa wasn't in much better shape. She had choked down her acid tablets, but the gruel was particularly gluey that day.

"Whatever happens," Rusty said, giving up and shoving away his plate, "you keep moving forward. Ignore the chaos, ignore the noise, just take one step after another toward your goal."

"Okay," Alexa murmured. She, too, gave up on her dinner and stared out across the Common room. The plan was to move Osu tomorrow before breakfast, so, in theory, this was her last meal with DeeDee and Murphy.

Rusty shifted his gaze skyward where nighttime had fallen. Giant blue-and-yellow moons hovered above them against a purple-blue-black sky dotted with stars. Alexa turned toward the ceiling, too, wondering what other worlds and skies existed beyond this one. And was she ready to face them?

Alexa said, "What's your real name?"

Rusty grabbed her hand and buried it between two calloused palms. "If you ever get lost and need to find me, say you're looking for Clyre the Red."

Deedee and Murphy's usual babbling grew to a fever pitch, rising above already loud voices. The Guardians, too busy talking among themselves, ignored them. Alexa leaned closer to Rusty. They seemed to sit in the eye of a building storm.

Out of nowhere, Murphy launched his pudgy body onto their table and started wailing, "The Gods will destroy all of us on Supply Day!"

Murphy's screams instantly grabbed the Guardians' attention. The six of them spread out, going from table to table, speaking quietly to calm their agitated Residents. One directed Murphy to take several more Serenity pills, and the weeping man gladly crunched them down. Other Guardians handed out several more pills to those who appeared especially agitated.

Guardian X strolled over to Alexa and grinned. "At least someone in here has a clear head."

Rusty had dropped his gaze and picked his nose the moment Guardian X approached.

The Guardian's face twisted in disgust, and she directed her attention to Alexa. "Try to get some rest. I'd offer you a dose of Serenity, but I need you ready to go in the morning."

"I'll be ready." Gnawing her bottom lip, Alexa bobbed her head.

"Of course you will." Guardian X smiled. She cleared her voice and shouted across the room. "Residents, let's get you back to your quarters."

"Listen to your Guardian for once," Rusty murmured before entering his cell. "Could be the last night in a bed for a long, long time."

"We'll see." Alexa fought back a yawn. She dropped onto her mattress and tucked her knees to her chest. The familiar sounds of the other Residents relieving themselves, yawning as their Serenity transitioned from giddiness to exhaustion, and some already snoring, had become routine.

Was this truly her last night surrounded by the thick steel walls? One more restless sleep among a chorus of snores and wheezes, one more night waking to the steady cadence of a Guardian walking past their cells with heavy boots.

Are you still awake?

Osu's voice startled Alexa out of a light doze.

"Yep."

You should rest. I will leave you.

"I don't think that's going to happen. I haven't slept through the night since I learned to wrangle exploding fuel cells."

I am sorry to hear this. We need you rested for tomorrow. There is no room for error, Earth human.

"If I'm too anxious to sleep, then I'm too anxious to sleep," Alexa whispered between clenched teeth. Earth people couldn't be the only ones with difficulty sleeping. She turned over to check on Rusty. A thick, guttural snore drifted from his cell.

When I was young, my caregiver would often sing me to sleep.

"You mean your mother?"

No, my mother died soon after I came into existence. She gave me to the caregiver for safekeeping. The caregiver was a creature much like you, Alexa. Humanoid. I never knew where she was from, but she kept me hidden for a long time until I was strong enough to travel without assistance. At night, she would sing to me. I never understood the language, but I still remember the tune. Would you like me to sing it to you?

"You mean a lullaby? You want to sing me to sleep?"

Indeed, if you find that suitable.

"Sure. Might be nice." The little bits of alien music Alexa had been exposed to over the last few months were nothing like her 90s playlists.

The song began so light and delicately that it didn't sound like it came from a living being, more like the whistle of a star streaking through a vast night sky. Alexa closed her eyes, tugging herself into a tight fetal position. She imagined herself home, earbuds in, blankets piled on top of her, disappearing into the warmth and security of her childhood bedroom.

Osu's song continued, curling through her brain, taking her on a gentle journey far away from her cell. If Alexa were to dig into her well of SAT words, she would call Osu's song "crystalline" or "incandescent." Her body lifted, carrying along the soft melody, soaring far across a plain of stars.

She wouldn't be sure if the song ever ended, for she had fallen into a deep sleep.

Chapter 47

"**H**ere we go," Alexa whispered, brushing the sweat from her brow. "Whew, did you adjust the climate control?" Her skin was flushed and clammy at the same time. She rubbed damp palms against her prison garb and attempted several shaky, calming breaths.

"You ready to do this?" Guardian X touched Alexa's shoulder. "Looks like all of us are a bit nervous."

"We sure are."

The dozen Guardians from Residence Darkstar and Firestar stood outside the large doors to the isolation cell block. Each appeared to be in varying degrees of agitation. A few straightened their backs, grim determination written across twitching features. Some were as flush and sweaty as Alexa, while others clenched their long electro-shock rods for dear life. One of them carried a weapon Alexa had never seen before. Her Blinders translated the gun-shaped weapon into something like an AR rifle.

"The process is simple," Guardian X announced. "The containment unit is already in place to receive the departing Resident. If he refuses to comply, it will take all of us to get him into the unit. Your batons will do little to subdue him." She gestured to the cattle prods. "So don't rely on them. Same with the Stunner." She pointed to the rifle. "There simply isn't mobile weaponry powerful enough, and too often, we end up harming each other.

"Moving him from his cell to the containment unit is the most dangerous point of this operation. You know your positions. You know your assignment. X485 must have a clear view of the Resident at all times. She is our last hope if this does not go as planned."

The Guardians from the other prison cast wary frowns at Alexa. They treated her like a time bomb, keeping their distance and an eye on her most of the time. They were wise to be cautious.

Guardian X raised her arm, displaying a watch-like device on her wrist. "And if X485 is put in a compromised position for any reason, she is outfitted with a kill switch and will be knocked out."

The visiting Guardians nodded, clutching their cattle prods tight.

"Don't worry, it's only to reassure them." Guardian X leaned toward Alex. "I have absolute confidence in you. We'll have much to talk about when this transfer is successful."

"Yes, *when*." Alexa swallowed the tight lump in her throat and gave her Guardian a quavering smile.

This is our moment, Alexa Baxter. Osu's silent voice cut through the shuffling feet, whispered exchanges, and shifting postures in the hall. *Do not be afraid. We shall protect each other and escape this cage.*

Alexa swiped away another drop of sweat from her brow. She may never forgive herself for abandoning Una, but helping Osu would hopefully dim the guilt she carried across the multiverse.

The large doors *whooshed* open to reveal an Osu-sized glass cube reinforced with a thick steel frame. The containment unit had a single open door made of solid steel. Within his cell, Osu paced. His explosive presence caused the air to vibrate. The hairs stood on Alexa's neck, and a noticeable shudder moved through the Guardians.

Guardian X squared her shoulders and approached. She pressed one of the many buttons on the console beside Osu's cell. "Greetings, Bright One. You have undoubtedly noticed the containment unit outside your cell, along with the visitors that have come and gone over the past month. There's a new Safekeeping facility in a nearby system that can care for you better than we can. You'll have more room to move—a window with a view. Better meals. A better living situation if you simply come with us peacefully."

May the Gods damn you all to the deepest depths of the Pit. Osu pressed his nose to the viewing window, eyes blazing.

Alexa shivered. Good thing she was the only one who could hear him.

Guardian X raised her chin. "They will be able to communicate with you, unlike us. They have someone on staff who specializes in telepathic communication. Wouldn't that be better? Having a Guardian who knows what you want?"

Osu's nostrils flared. *A Guardian who can penetrate my thoughts, manipulate my senses, and dig into my memories? I think not.*

"If you come voluntarily, then this will be so much easier for all of us. We have planned for this transfer for a long time now, much longer than you know. You may have murdered several Guardians during your last transfer, but you nearly died too. Remember?"

Osu stepped back, bowing his head.

"Of course, you remember." Guardian X nodded to the Guardian next to her, who hit a switch, opening the door to the containment unit. "We want you to have a more comfortable, fulfilling life, Bright One. All you have to do is be compliant. Can you be compliant?"

Sweat poured down Alexa's flushed face. She could do this. She had to be strong if she ever wanted to go home again.

Osu gave Guardian X a single nod.

"Now, move slowly. Once properly secure, we'll leave this block and take you to the docks. There, you will be put on a freighter and, two days later, you'll be in a new, better facility. However, all of this is up to you. You decide how this will go."

Osu nodded again and stepped back from the door. Each of the Guardians went on high alert, pointing their electric prods in the Bright One's direction. Alexa flexed her fingers, tried to quiet her mind, and focused on Osu.

Guardian X pressed her palm to a screen on the cell door, and it *whooshed* up faster than a blink of an eye. A delicate surge of energy struck Alexa and touched each of the other Guardians. Someone gasped, and another cursed. Osu's radiant eyes surveyed the crowd before him. Alexa's

Blinders couldn't hide his true form anymore. The unicorn, twice Una's size, lashed his tail and stamped a hoof.

"I can close this door again." Guardian X's voice cracked when she spoke. "The offer will be rescinded immediately. I've read how your kind lives for nearly a millennium. You've already spent ten years in our facility. Do you want to spend hundreds?"

Osu laid his ears back against his skull. *Are you ready, Alexa?*

Alexa held her breath as Osu took one then two steps toward the containment unit's entrance. Even though he lowered his head, ears relaxed forward, Alexa sensed the itching vibrations cascading from his white hide. He turned his elegant face in her direction, connecting eye to eye for only a moment before surveying the rest of his captors.

The Guardians stared at Osu, wide-eyed with terror and admiration for such a powerful creature. Even Guardian X lost herself momentarily, gaping in awe before she returned to the present reality. She signaled to one Guardian positioned at Osu's cell door as Osu put his front hooves into the containment unit.

At that exact moment, Alexa sensed the shift in air pressure. Osu—for lack of a better word—exploded.

Alexa gasped and threw up her unseen walls around the Bright One to contain the explosion's pressure. Osu was supposed to have signaled her before he unleashed his incredible power. The containment unit's door burst from its hinges and landed on the other end of the cell block. Alexa easily held back the bubbling orb of electricity and, once again, the force of the blast absorbed into her shield. And into Alexa's flesh.

Everyone was knocked from their feet. Some were thrown into walls or sent halfway across the main hall. Alexa tingled from head to toe. She felt amazing, indestructible, nothing like the skinny little teenager from Wisconsin. Having subdued the blast, she was supposed to attempt to shove Osu into the containment unit and fail miserably. She raised her hands, approaching the Bright One, who gave her a grin and a wink.

Guardian X cried out, crumpled into the far corner of Osu's cell, "Alexa, wait, don't—"

Just like she did with the energy cells, Alexa created a wall where one didn't exist. She built an invisible door over what was left of the containment unit's broken entry. Osu wasn't supposed to blast the door off the unit entirely, so it would be up to Alexa to play her part. Osu lashed his tail and sent a light pulse to test Alexa's telekinetic barrier. The Bright One's pulse ricocheted off Alexa's wall, and it was Osu's turn to be knocked off his feet.

That was unexpected. Osu quickly rolled back onto his hooves, pinning his ears and playing the enraged unicorn. *All the better.*

Alexa breathed hard, not from the effort of holding the barrier in place but because she knew this was only the beginning. Now, Osu would attempt to knock her back a second time. Not too hard, though, just enough to scare the pants off all the Guardians.

"Hold him back, Alexa!" Guardian X cried out.

Osu flared his pink nostrils and, rearing, threw out a much stronger pulse than before. Too strong. Alexa threw up her unseen walls just in time. However, the force of Osu's electric burst sent Alexa airborne for a second before she fell against two Guardians struggling to their feet. Spots bloomed before her vision. The world spun, and the air smelt of something burning. Guardians screamed and shouted. This wasn't at all what they had planned to do.

"Goddamn it, Osu." Alexa fought to regain equilibrium. When she tried to get up, to pretend that she had the strength to put her unseen wall back in place, a hand rested against her chest.

"It's okay, X485," Guardian X gasped, stumbling out of Osu's cell. "Look."

Alexa raised herself to her elbows. "Holy shit."

Osu lay in a heap within the containment unit. Alexa reached out to him with her unseen senses, panicked. His heart still beat a steady rhythm, and his lungs gently rose and fell.

"He's passed out." A Guardian laughed, eyes glazed over from what he and everyone else had just experienced. "Thank the gods, I thought I was going to die."

At a loss for words, Alexa let Guardian X help her to her feet. She and the Bright One had each underestimated each other. He had pushed too hard, too fast.

Guardian X said, "Let's get that door back on while we can. Who knows how long the Bright One will stay unconscious."

"Fuck." Spots continued to float before Alexa's eyes. She sagged in the Guardians' arms. "Oh, fuck, fuck, fuck."

Everything they planned had gone wrong.

Chapter 48

Nothing was going according to plan.

The Guardians quickly repaired the containment unit door while Osu lay unconscious within. Alexa couldn't stop staring at Osu's crumpled form, all tangled legs and shimmering coat. She silently and repeatedly screamed in his mind to "wake up!" Osu's only response was the steady rise and fall of his ribs. Why did he have to show off? Couldn't he have let go of his ego for one moment?

"Absolutely astounding." Guardian X shook her head. "Practicing with all those power cells did the job. Thanks to X485's quick thinking, the Bright One knocked himself out with his own power. If we're lucky, we'll get this beast loaded up and off planet before he revives. Wonderful job, X485. This could change everything for you. Perhaps you could even become a Guardian. Once the higher-ups hear about this—"

Please wake up, Osu!

The Bright One didn't even twitch.

"We're ready to head out." A smiling black-clad Firestar Guardian gave the repaired door a final tug. "I'm confident our new Resident will be easy to extract once we reach Firestar. Our facility was designed to deal with beings like this."

"Excellent. Shall we continue?" Guardian X opened the cell block door.

The Guardians gave a little cheer. The atmosphere had completely changed the moment Osu lost consciousness. All the fear and tension lifted, giving Alexa the same vibe as when school let out for the summer. The containment unit, surrounded by Guardians on all sides, rolled out and began steady progress down one of the main corridors. Alexa drifted toward the back, her thoughts a wild tangle of panic and dread.

Rusty would be disappointed, of course. Perhaps he could still find a way to sneak onto a ship while everyone focused on Osu at the landing dock. Alexa wouldn't be going with him. The Guardians' attention bounced constantly between herself and Osu. She could hear the muttering among the visiting Guardian team, considering all the ways Alexa's powers would be useful to them too.

Alexa slowly wilted. She had wanted to be a rebel. Instead she was quickly becoming a tool of oppression.

The journey from Osu's cell to the loading dock was a long one. The Darkstar Peacekeeping Facility, from the little Alexa was able to read, was designed to keep the most dangerous Residents as far from everyone else as possible.

The distance gave Alexa a trickle of hope. "Wake up, Osu, please wake up."

But the farther they walked, as doors opened to corridors Alexa had never seen, the more her hopes faltered. Rows of Guardians had come out to watch the procession, their faces as relieved as those who guarded the unconscious Bright One. Several Guardians asked to get a closer look.

Like teenagers with their smartphones, they captured images of themselves standing beside the unconscious Osu. The sight turned Alexa's stomach.

Soon, every Guardian in the facility appeared to follow the procession. An almost festive spirit moved among them. They laughed openly, practically bouncing down the hall. Several gave Alexa words of congratulations. She dragged herself along behind them all, wearing a false smile.

"I'm sorry, Una," Alexa murmured when the last door opened, revealing a vast warehouse the size of a football stadium.

Palettes of supplies filled the enormous space, along with additional fuel cells, various types of equipment, and several large vehicles that reminded Alexa of giant school buses, only taller and made entirely of stainless steel. Several large doors and hatches lead to other parts of the facility. Natural light poured through the three gigantic doors at the far end of the warehouse. The loading dock.

Dozens of voices echoed through the chamber. The loading dock was abuzz with activity. Both Residents and machines unloaded palettes from the freighters beyond. Alexa craned her neck to get a better look at the spaceships, a thrill running up her spine at the very idea of space flight.

All movement at the loading dock ceased when their entourage crossed the threshold as if the whole warehouse held their breath for what must happen next.

"Resident B909 ready for loading!" Guardian X shouted across the distance, her clear voice echoing through the cavernous space.

Everyone moved at once. A dozen black-clad Guardians headed in their direction, holding the same electric prods as everyone on the Bright One transfer team. Their caution turned to immediate relief when they realized Osu wasn't awake and storming around his containment unit.

Alexa searched among her fellow Residents' gray uniforms, but Rusty was nowhere in sight. There were too many people doing too many things. The moment they entered the warehouse, Alexa was meant to pretend to lose control of Osu, and he was supposed to raise hell. Desperate, she shouted to him one last time. The Bright One's blue tongue lolled out of his mouth, a puddle of drool gathering beneath his muzzle.

She paused, taking it all in. How had her life become such an insane space drama, and how had she, once again, repeated history? Forces beyond her own had toyed and manipulated her so many times. But she wasn't the scared little girl standing on the edge of Crater Lake watching a Bright One being torn to pieces. She was powerful too. She didn't have to accept this fate.

With invisible fingers, Alexa picked at the previously broken door on the containment unit. The metal had weakened in several places, and the additional bolts used to re-secure the door weren't as tight as they should be. She tested each weak spot, the surrounding Guardians oblivious to her tampering as the door shifted on its frame.

"X485?"

Alexa froze.

Guardian X waved her hand above the crowd. "Come here. I want you to meet the warden of Firestar. They want to meet the remarkable Resident who has done so much to keep our facility safe."

No, she couldn't let anyone distract her from the insane thing she was about to do. She jiggled the door once again, testing for the weakest spot. There it was, just above the top hinge. All she had to do was—

"X485?" Guardian X slipped beside the transport guard, a tall Guardian wearing various medals and badges following in her wake. "Are you okay? You look—"

With a hard yank, the door flew across the warehouse, smacking into a stack of crates. A chorus of panicked voices rose above the door's clang and the snapping of breaking wood. The impact from the door knocked several containers loose. Boxes blew open. Yellow spheres scattered across the floor.

Amid the chaos, Alexa ran into the containment unit. She dropped to her knees in front of Osu and screamed his name. Even then, the unicorn didn't stir. At some point, the Bright One pulled his tongue back into his mouth, and she swore his nostrils twitched.

"Osu, you have to wake up. I can't let them take you. You have to help me!"

"X485, what are you doing in there?" Guardian X shrieked, electric prod in hand. "Have you lost your faculties? The Bright One will kill you."

Alexa wrapped her arms around the unicorn's neck. "Please, please, you have to get up. You must, you must!"

A hand tugged at Alexa's shoe. "X485, get out of there right now, or you will regret it."

"I'm not X485." Alexa raised her head. Guardian X's finger hovered just above the kill switch strapped to her wrist. In her panic, Alexa had utterly forgotten that, at any second, her Guardian could knock her out or even kill her.

Earth human? Alexa, what has happened?

Alexa laughed, tears of relief cascading down her cheeks. She scrambled to her feet, facing her captor. "I'm Alexa Baxter, and I don't belong here."

Guardian X's face twisted as if in pain, her finger pressing the switch. "Then I have no choice but to do this."

Alexa, get down, I'm about to—

Every muscle in Alexa's body slackened, and everything went dark.

Chapter 49

The sky blazed, hot and bright above her, the sun spotlighting her face. Crater Lake stretched below, the water so still it became a mirror displaying each tuft of cloud lazily meandering across the electric heavens. Alexa yawned, her head strangely heavy. Her feet dangled inches from the gravel below as she sat on the hood of her old Honda Civic.

"God, that sun is something else," Alexa groaned, leaning against Sid, who sat to her right.

"We should put on some sunscreen. It's easier to sunburn at high elevations." Sid ran a warm hand down her back.

"My head feels like it's a thousand pounds." She dropped her face into her hands.

"I guess that happens when someone hits your kill switch." Mateo leaned back on the hood, soaking up the sun's rays.

"How did we get here?" Alexa said.

"We're not really here." Sid gently touched her brow. "This is your brain trying to sort out all the crazy things that happened."

Alexa sat up. "Shit. Am I dead?"

"I know I'm not," Mateo said. "Can you believe that you're so far away from us? We must miss you."

"Somehow, if I live through all this, I need to get back to you." Alexa grabbed Sid's warm hand, clutching it tight.

"I don't want to be with aliens, monsters, and Bright Ones anymore. I want to be in Riverview. I want to graduate from high school. Start the next part of my life."

Sid whispered, "Maybe. Someday. But you have to stay alive. Don't give up."

The sun seemed to expand, overtaking everything. Alexa winced and tried to bury her head in Sid's chest, but he drew back.

Sid pointed to the sky. "Look up, Alexa. Time to go back."

"I don't want to go back."

"You must." He tipped her chin toward the burning atmosphere. "And you must fight. Fight to come home to us someday."

The sky incinerated, blinding Alexa. Sid and Mateo disappeared into the radiance, sad smiles on their faces. The surface of the Honda's hood flattened and cooled, becoming a hard, damp floor.

Good. I was hoping you were still alive.

Alexa opened her crusty eyelids and peered into the face of the Bright One. Osu. A strange, diffused light glinted off his horn.

Careful. The floor is slick.

Alexa pressed herself upright, her hand landing on something warm and wet. She blinked, took one look at her surroundings, and screamed.

I killed most of them. They left me no choice.

She raised her hand and found it covered in blood. Her Blinders glitched briefly, showing her what existed beyond her false visions. The blood was blue, not red. The pristine, steel cavern was more like a cave. The black, textured structure arched above her like the ribs of a giant beast. And the Guardians were the tentacled creatures she first beheld upon arriving at the Safekeeping Facility.

Osu shone like a beacon among the wreckage. He flicked his lion-like tail, sapphire eyes glowing in the dim, ruined cavern. *We must go before reinforcements arrive.*

Alexa's Blinders glitched again, but the view wasn't much better. The bodies of Guardians covered the floor, some lying in frightful positions. Twisted and broken arms. Lifeless eyes staring at the ceiling. No one moved. No one breathed.

"What have you done?" Alexa brushed her sticky hand against her blood-spattered pants.

They left me no choice. I had to defend myself and you. Do you know what they would have done to us? Come, we must go. Hopefully, I can figure out how to pilot one of the freighters.

Alexa searched the faces of the Guardians for one face in particular but she didn't have to look far. Guardian X lay to Alexa's left. Her slackened face still held a faint, horrified expression.

"Oh no." Alexa dropped beside her dead Guardian. Her chest ached as she closed the woman's eyes. "I'm sorry."

Alexa Baxter, we have run out—

"She was only doing what she thought was right. She was kind to me."

This is not the time for sentiment. Osu turned and headed toward the loading dock, avoiding pools of blood and pieces of Guardian. *The MGA will not be kind when they see what I have done.*

"Did you need to kill them all?" Alexa stared out across the carnage and swallowed a sob. Tears blurred her vision as the rancid yet sickly sweet scent of all that death filled her nose. Her stomach lurched. Luckily, she had no appetite for breakfast and only spat out bile.

Come, Alexa. We will need each other if we are to get back to what is left of my people. You are much more powerful than I realized. We could use someone like you.

"I thought you were going to help me get home." Alexa stumbled to her feet, avoiding the twisted, outstretched hand of a Guardian who no longer had a face. Osu was already halfway across the warehouse, but Alexa found walking difficult. She staggered into a scorched stack of palettes, blinking away the dark spots swimming before her eyes.

Silly Earth human. Did you think that was possible? Perhaps if our plans had gone right, but this carnage was … somewhat unexpected. Osu trotted to the nearest freighter, its cargo door open wide. He kicked aside a Resident's body that lay slumped on the gangplank. The off-loaded supplies lay scattered across the dock. Beyond, the enormous yellow moons hung in the rose-tinted heavens, serene despite the butchery beneath them.

Alexa paused, realizing what he had said. "What do you mean that's not possible?"

Osu pointed his horn toward the wreckage. *When they finally realize what has happened, when they cannot find your body among the dead, they will come to know you left with me. Perhaps they will assume I took you hostage. Perhaps not.*

However, they will come looking for you, and where do you think they may go first?

Alexa wanted to curl into a ball, find a dark, quiet corner, and never emerge. The reality of her new situation crushed the tiny flicker of hope she had held tight since walking through the door into another world. Guardian X was right. Osu was a brutal, dangerous beast, and Alexa had helped him. What did that make her?

Alexa Baxter, the time has come for you to cast aside your empathy. To be free and survive, you must become more like me. Self-preservation above all. Now, Osu tossed his head and stamped an impatient hoof. *I have no more time for your tears. Let us go.*

In a daze, Alexa regained her footing, dodging bodies and blood until she, too, walked up the gangplank into the freighter's bowels. The Blinders showed her a vessel much like a cargo plane. Half of the cargo bay was still half-full, holding a fresh batch of softly humming fusion cells. Beyond the cargo hold stood a series of doors leading to different rooms. Osu had opened one. Perhaps he had found the cockpit.

She could hear Osu stomping about in another section of the vessel, but she didn't follow him. Burying her face in her hands, she wished to slip back into her dreams, feel the warm sun next to Crater Lake, and the warm brush of Sid's hand down her back. Would the MGA hurt him or her family as they searched for her? Did they dare?

A sharp, frustrated whinny echoed deep within the ship. A string of curses banged through Alexa's mind. She let out a hollow laugh. "Maybe you shouldn't have killed everyone after all. Now we're stuck here."

"I can help."

Alexa lifted her tear-stained face. "Rusty?"

"That's me." The older man emerged from a nook behind a stack of metal containers. He glanced in the direction Osu had gone, understandably worried about the monster within.

Alexa fought the urge to launch herself into his arms. "You're alive?"

"I ran the moment I saw you go down." Rusty remained partially tucked inside his hiding place, fear glimmering in his eyes. "I know the beginnings of a massacre when I see one. I did what I always do: run through chaos until I found a safe hiding place." Another bang came from the front of the freighter, and Rusty flinched. "I'll fly the ship as long as your friend promises not to hurt me."

"He won't. We need you." Alexa hoped what she said was true. She couldn't handle any more death that day. The image of Guardians X's vacant eyes haunted her. "Follow me. But keep your distance, just in case."

Alexa wiped away her tears with the back of her hand, avoiding the drying blood that covered her palms. She headed toward Osu's curses through the one open door, fighting back the knot of fear in her gut which threatened to start another round of dry heaving. They passed what looked like small common room and a small supply closet until they reached a half-ajar door. Alexa immediately sensed a tickle of electricity race across the delicate hairs on her arm.

Rusty hung back, clinging to shadows.

"Osu?" Alexa peered around the door and fell back. Osu's irritation filled the whole cockpit, a hot ball of rage as he glared at a series of levers, wheels, and knobs that made not a lick of sense to Alexa. The window beyond displayed the ragged mountain range. The window ended near her feet, showing the cavernous, bottomless drop below. One wrong button and they would plummet to their death.

Osu stamped a cloven hoof. *I have no idea how to run this thing.*

"You should have been more careful." Alexa swallowed the bile sticking in her throat.

I could not control it. Osu snorted defiantly, but the bright glow from his hide softened. *I thought they had killed you.*

Alexa inhaled a sharp breath. "You did that because of me?"

You have been my only companion since I was taken here—the only one to show me kindness. You are the reason I had hope. You know how I told you that I did not kill that village of people? I lied. The enemy killed someone I loved, and so I burned it all to the ground.

Alexa swayed on her feet and dropped into a wide steel chair. "Well, you didn't kill everyone."

Osu's ear pricked forward. *I did not?*

"Do you remember my friend Rusty? The one who was supposed to help us?"

Rusty broke through the shadows beyond the open door. He nodded to Osu.

"He can pilot this plane, but you have to promise never to harm him. No matter what. He was a prisoner, just like us. And we can't get out of this place without him."

A dangerous gleam flickered in Osu's eyes. *Very well. I will not harm him.*

"You have to promise me. If you hurt him, you hurt me. And you don't want to hurt me, do you?"

No, I would never harm you. I owe you a life debt. Osu's tail smacked against a control panel.

"Promise."

I swear on my family, both living and dead, that I will do nothing to harm your friend. I would rather harm myself than harm the Earth human who saved my life.

"Rusty?"

"Praise the Elders." Rusty rushed into the cockpit and immediately started flipping switches and pressing buttons. "Someone managed to send out a distress signal. Regional Protection units could get here any second. We must move fast before they enable the secondary defense shield covering this place."

The ship sprang to life. Rusty's fingers danced over the dials, his focus bouncing from one display to the next. A screen appeared on the glass before them, showing something Alexa didn't understand.

"Yep, they've nearly reached our system," Rusty said in a rush. Alexa and Osu stepped back to give the man some room. "Hang on, this could get a little crazy. Next stop, as far away from here as possible!"

Epilogue

As they moved through the glittering darkness of space, images of blood and carnage plagued Alexa every time she closed her weary eyes. She ached for sleep, to run away from what she had witnessed, but the vision of Guardian X's vacant stare wouldn't leave her. This was her fault. She chose death, self-preservation, and one of the most dangerous creatures in the multiverse over those who believed they were maintaining order.

However, each time tears and despair threatened to overtake her, a cold certainty settled deeper into her bones. Though Osu was far from the perfect ally, he was also the only one who might save her from a life trapped in a glass box.

You should rest, Alexa Baxter. Osu lay on the floor beside her, blue tongue lolling from his mouth as he yawned. *When on the run, it is important to rest as much as possible when you have the opportunity.*

Ever since Alexa woke in the middle of the warehouse floor, the Blinders had stopped working on Osu. The magnificent, deadly creature had calmed since they escaped off-world. Except for the occasional stray blood drop marring his otherwise perfect white coat, no one would suspect he had just murdered dozens of people that morning.

Rusty had fallen asleep in the seat beside her, his guttural snores filling the cockpit. Alexa promised to wake him if anything "started making funny noises" while he took a quick nap. She was surprised he could drop into sleep after what had happened at Residence Darkstar.

They had spent a long, tense day together: the unicorn, the girl, and the former revolutionary. Rusty had vaulted their freighter into the hazy rose sky in a matter of minutes, apologizing for a few moments of intense turbulence as they cut through the atmosphere and hit space. A few brief warning calls announced the arrival of MGA security teams. Without blinking, Rusty brought the ship toward the nearest moon, then hid behind the planet's shadow until he determined they had clearance to continue. His steady demeanor never faltered. He had, "seen and survived worse."

Alexa kept an eye on Osu at all times. After Osu admitted to her what he had done when he thought he had lost her, she no longer feared him —but she didn't trust him either. She had the nagging feeling that Osu would be happy to kill Rusty once he was no longer useful. She would never let that happen.

She toed the thick glass cockpit window that protected them from the vast emptiness of space beyond. After punching in a long series of coordinates, Rusty aimed them into deep space and warned Alexa and Osu it would take a week before they would again reach any sort of civilization and a month before achieving their destination.

"You'll get used to it," Rusty had assured her. "Give it time. Eventually, their visages blur."

"I don't want to get used to it. I see—I see awful things when I close my eyes." Alexa had folded deeper into her seat, pulled a stiff blanket to her chin, and stared at the stars until they blurred.

Osu pressed his muzzle to her foot. *I am sorry for what you have lost. Unfortunately, I know the feeling all too well. Perhaps I was wrong before. Perhaps you, too, can go home*

"I don't want to think about that right now." Alexa rubbed a hand across her face, her chest aching the way it did when she desperately wished to be back in Riverview, surrounded by her parents and sister while chatting away about their mundane lives. "When we go to where Rusty is taking us, what next?"

We are going to the nearest safe house. If they have proper communications equipment, I will send a message out to my network. We shall go to whoever responds. And we must be careful. I have undoubtedly become the most wanted beast in the multiverse. And you with me, unless...

"Unless?"

I could claim you as my hostage.

"No, I don't want that. I'm no one's prisoner. Not anymore. And someone needs to stick around so you don't pull shit like that ever again. No more killing, Osu."

Osu tapped the seat of her chair with his horn. *Unless necessary, of course.*

Alexa hesitated before she said, "Unless it's us or them. Wow. If my mom could see me now. In the company of killers on a frickin' spaceship."

Be careful, Earth human. You also have a power whose limit you do not know. Do not be surprised if, someday, you also lose control. What you did, reflecting my powers back at me, no one in the multiverse has ever done that before.

"Never?"

Not even another Bright One could do that. You have come far from the girl I met cleaning the spotless isolation cell block. You single-handedly incapacitated one of the most powerful beings in the multiverse.

"By accident." Alexa shrugged, unable to wrap her head around the changes happening within her. "You're right. I have no idea how far this power in me could go. But I'm tired of being a victim. And, no matter what, I'll never stop trying to get home."

When they realize what has happened, they will do everything in their power to destroy us. This is only the beginning. And, there is something else I must try to do. It may not work, but I cannot go out into the multiverse looking like this.

Alexa frowned at the unicorn. "What are you talking about?"

You will not believe me until I try it. We have enough of the fusion cells to give me the power required. After my rest, I shall try to do something nearly impossible.

"Nearly impossible. Sounds like another day in the multiverse." Alexa gazed without seeing into the darkness before her. A chorus played repeatedly in her head. She hummed the tune, hoping the familiar song would chase away her gory memories and lull her into a dreamless sleep.

Do you know how often you do that?

"What?"

Sing a song without words. You did it constantly while cleaning outside my cell.

Alexa smirked. "I doubt you've heard of Radiohead?"

No more than you have heard of the Mountain Whistlers of Black Cliffs? Sing me a song, Alexa Baxter.

Alexa rolled her eyes. "Fine. But I'm warning you, I have no sense of pitch." She took a deep breath and sang the first few lyrics of Radiohead's *Bulletproof* as they soared through space's black, star-studded emptiness.

Also by T. J. Fier

The Bright Series
The Bright One
Ever Bright

Watch for more at https://linktr.ee/tjfier.

About the Author

Theatre professor by day and writer by night, T.J. Fier's other works include the short stories "Kelpie" in *Nothing Short of Horror*, "EVP Session #454" in the September issue of Brilliant Flash Fiction, "The Hunt" in *Tales From the Frozen North: A Winter Anthology*, "Reindeer Games" in *The Colour Out of Deathlehem*, "Hoarfrost" in *Seasons in the Dark* and *Welcome to Effham Falls* which includes her short story, "Heart's Desire." You can also find her @iamfierless on Twitter, and Facebook, and @tjfier_author on Instagram and Threads.

Read more at https://linktr.ee/tjfier.

Milton Keynes UK
Ingram Content Group UK Ltd.
UKHW041221021124
450589UK00005B/532

9 798227 940766